FAMILIES and FELONS

A Brenna Wickham Haunted Mystery

by

Kathleen J. Easley

Copyright 2024 by Kathleen J. Easley

Published by Ames Lake Press

ISBN-13: 979-8-88488-710-7

Cover art by Dar Albert, Wicked Smart Designs

Also by Kathleen J. Easley

SIBLINGS and SECRETS

Book One in the Brenna Wickham Haunted
Mystery series

Coming Soon

UNDER the APPLE TREE

A paranormal tale of love and suspense

Praise for Siblings and Secrets:

A slow-burning contemporary mystery using red herrings, psychological insights and clever twists. The intricate plot, nuanced relationships, and well-hewn characterization are among the book's major strengths. The dialogue is adept and the catchy title is fitting as it provides an emotional hook and a hint of what readers should expect. The book ably delivers much more than it promises. Siblings and Secrets conveys satisfying appeal and a text sure to entertain readers at the turn of each page.

—Pacific Book Review

Kept me guessing!
The book kept me turning pages to find out what happens next. A classic "whodunit" shifts from one potential perpetrator to another in a gripping climax.

—Richard G. Hunter, author of *Lamplight Declassified*

Fantastic Read!
The characters are very real, and the story is so touching. This is a great first-in-series, and I'm looking forward to book 2! Don't miss this lovely book.

—Regina Duke, USA Today Bestselling Author

Excellent plot with twists I never saw coming!
The book flows from page to page. Once you start you won't want to put it down.

—Amazon Reviewer

Readers will be amazed and shocked while following the twists and turns. This story is about reconciliation, love lost yet found again, misunderstandings, and revealing the truth. If you want a great book to curl up with, look no further than Siblings and Secrets.

—Readers' Favorite

Dedication

This book is dedicated to my wonderful husband, Ken, an abundant source of great ideas, helpful critiques, and really delicious concoctions in the kitchen. You know I couldn't do this without you.

Chapter One

Forty-eight dollars for cat food? I tossed the receipt into the box with the rest to be sorted later. So many random receipts, so many magazines, ads, solicitations, and unopened envelopes. I'd been sitting here for over an hour sifting through piles of mail and barely made a dent in the stacks of paper that covered every horizontal surface of the house.

My nose tickled as years' worth of dust was stirred up. I grabbed for my box of tissues, fearing an imminent sneeze. How could anyone live this way?

"Ms. Wickham? Would you like some tea?" The soft, reedy voice interrupted my musing.

"Thank you, Mrs. Hansen," I said, smiling up at my eighty-six-year-old hostess, "that sounds wonderful. And please call me Brenna."

"Yes, of course, dear, that's a lovely name—and you must call me Norma. Would you like anything in your tea?"

Slightly stooped and wrinkled as a dried apple, Norma Hansen was bright-eyed and cheery. She wore a pink cotton dress with a loose-fitting blue cardigan and scuffed orthopedic shoes that clomped when she walked. Her home was plain and comfortable, with aging furniture and a dull green carpet. I was using the living room couch and coffee table as a temporary work space while I struggled to wrest order from the chaos.

"A little sugar would be nice," I said. "By the way, I found a receipt for cat food. Do you have a cat? I haven't seen one."

She shook her head, barely disturbing her tight thatch of white curls. "I used to—a lovely tabby named Muffin—but I'm afraid she died years ago. At my age I didn't think I should get another."

I frowned. "Then why are you buying cat food?" *Please don't tell me you're eating it.*

Six weeks ago, I started a new job as legal assistant to Ross Cavendish, Attorney at Law. At his subtle urging, I volunteered to take on this guardianship. Maybe it was a moment of weakness, wanting to curry favor with my new boss, or maybe it was fond memories of my grandmother, but I allowed him to draw up the necessary papers to proceed. In due course an order was entered in Superior Court appointing me as Mrs. Hansen's guardian, and my oath was filed with the county clerk.

It all started when Mrs. Hansen's nephew, her

nearest relative, came out from Denver for a visit and found his octogenarian aunt in dire need of help. Judging by the mountains of paper engulfing her house, she hadn't bothered to open her mail in years; bills hadn't been paid, stock dividends hadn't been deposited, her checking account hadn't been balanced, and enough junk mail had accumulated to fuel a week-long bonfire. The nephew went to his aunt's bank in desperation, stymied by the clutter and the state of her affairs. The bank manager recommended a guardian and referred him to Mr. Cavendish, a local attorney with a reputation for altruism.

Mrs. Hansen had been only too happy to let someone else deal with the mess, so the case was uncontested and I received my Certificate of Qualification. Now it was my responsibility to look after the elderly widow's well-being, to make sure she was safe and healthy, and see that her finances were put in order. It would be a huge job, but Mr. Cavendish assured me he would help if I ran into problems.

"Oh, it's for the raccoons." The old woman's face crinkled as she tittered.

"Raccoons?"

"Yes, I put food out for them every day by the back door. They're so cute, I love to watch them squabble."

My first reaction was to utter a stern reproof, but instead I said, "Oh, my gosh, Mrs. Hansen—Norma—that is so risky. They're wild animals, unpredictable. They have sharp teeth and claws. What if they were to bite you? You could get a terrible infection, and they probably carry all sorts of diseases."

A city girl, I was no expert on raccoons, but my instincts told me this was a very bad idea.

She waved a knobby hand, a road map of blue veins discernible through crepey skin. "Don't worry, I'm very careful. Besides, they're practically tame. I put the food out in the afternoon and they don't come around till evening. They're nocturnal, you know."

"Trouble is, you're encouraging them to hang around. Next thing you know you'll have them living under the house, or worse, in your attic. They can cause all kinds of problems." I could just imagine the dark, cavernous space beneath the pitched roof of this 1950's era home. It would provide an ideal den for a pack of marauding raccoons.

She pursed her narrow lips and turned her eyes to the ceiling. "That must be the noises I hear in the attic sometimes. I think they may have a nest up there. But I don't mind," she added. "They really don't bother me, and they have to live somewhere—especially now that it's getting colder outside."

I rose from my place on the couch and faced her. The lady was an animal lover and she saw these raccoons as pets of a sort. She wouldn't allow them to be injured or killed.

"I'm sorry," I said, "but we can't have raccoons living in your attic. They can cause all sorts of damage up there, plus it's a health hazard. Think of their droppings, the mold and bacteria, and the flies, not to mention the odor. And what about your neighbors? They probably don't want raccoons living nearby, either. Wild animals don't get along well with kids and dogs. Wouldn't you feel terrible if some child was bitten or someone's pet was injured—or for that matter, one of the raccoons was attacked by somebody's big dog?"

She nodded thoughtfully. "So, what do we do? I won't have them harmed." Her voice was soft but determined.

"Well, the very first thing you've got to do is quit feeding them. Then I'll call a pest control company to come out and assess the situation. They'll know how to get rid of them without hurting them."

She chewed her lip, looked at the floor, then finally agreed. I pulled out my cell phone and began to search for exterminators specializing in humane removal of raccoon infestations. After a few calls, I was able to secure an appointment for the following week.

That settled, I took my place again on the couch and began going through another pile of papers, separating junk mail from legitimate correspondence. I'd keep at it for another hour and then head back to the office for the rest of the afternoon.

The old woman tottered off to the kitchen, and after a few minutes returned with a steaming mug on a tray. "Brenda? Here's that cup of tea I promised." Her smile was sweet and ingenuous.

I started to correct her, then decided it wasn't worth it. I smiled as I reached for the mug. "Thank you, Norma."

The law offices of Randall, Cavendish, and Torres were located in a large refurbished house, yellow with dark brown shutters, set on a hill overlooking Puget Sound in the town of Edmonds, Washington. It was just a few minutes north of Shoreline where I lived with my cousin Connie Kestler.

I said hello to Shannon at the receptionist's desk, then made my way up to Mr. Cavendish's office at the top of the stairs. My office was in the next room down the hall which I shared with Rhonda Barnes, Mr. Torres's assistant. I had plenty of work waiting on my desk, so I intended to merely stick my head in to let him know I had arrived. Instead, he motioned me to enter.

"How'd it go with Mrs. Hansen?" Ross Cavendish, a stalwart man of sixty, looked distinguished as always in a navy suit and tie. Glasses framed piercing blue eyes set deeply in a rugged face topped by a full head of graying flaxen hair. He generally wore a sober expression, but his mouth often alluded to a well developed sense of humor. After six weeks as his assistant, I found him to be not only hard working, but gifted with a keen intellect and quick wit.

I gave a short laugh. "Well, she definitely needs help, that's for sure. I wouldn't call her a hoarder exactly, she just doesn't seem interested in dealing with her mail. She's let it stack up all over the house for who knows how long."

"Not going to be too much for you, is it?"

I shook my head. "For now I'm just sorting everything, separating it all into boxes. A lot of it will be shredded or recycled. I thought I might take some home to work on in the evenings."

Because I have nothing else to do with Thanksgiving next week and my whole family coming from Phoenix, and the craft fair I'm helping organize the week after that.

"Be sure to keep track of your time," he said.

"I will," I said, then added, "Oh, and I have to go back there on Monday to supervise the removal of a family of raccoons from her attic."

Rolling his eyes, he uttered a sharp guffaw.

As I turned to leave, there came a tap on the door, followed immediately by the entrance of Troy Cavendish, the boss's son. A hot, younger version of his father, Troy's appearance never failed to kick my pulse into high gear.

We met two months earlier while I was helping out at my cousin's flower and gift shop. The lawyer I'd worked nine years for had just retired and I was between jobs, trying to sell my Seattle condo and get my life back on track two years after the death of my husband.

By sheer chance, Troy, a downtown defense attorney, came into the store to purchase flowers for his office. We hit it off from the start, and he helped me get this job when his father's previous assistant quit to stay home with her new baby.

"Hey, Brenna." He gave me a bold smile. He had the same vivid blue eyes as his father, same blond hair, narrow face, and strong chin.

Stylish tortoiseshell glasses gave him a classy, intellectual look.

"What brings you clear out here?" I said, giving my mass of brown hair a quick finger-brushing.

"Well, besides hoping I might take you to lunch, I wanted to swing by and say hello to a friend of mine who's coming here this afternoon. She just lost her father and I wanted to give her my condolences." He narrowed his eyes. "In fact, I think you may know her too."

"Oh? Who is it?" I didn't think Troy and I had any friends in common—we hadn't known each other that long—and I hadn't heard of anyone losing their father.

"When you worked at the flower shop, didn't you go next door sometimes for coffee?"

"Sure," I said. "Everyone in town goes there. They make the best cinnamon rolls anywhere."

The Good Stuff, a small bakery and coffee shop next to Connie's Pretty Petals, had been my go-to place to sit and recharge during breaks. The owners had been gregarious and accommodating, happy to make a coffee delivery if things got busy and I couldn't leave my post. I swear they had saved my life on more than one occasion.

"The owners are James and Kayla Donnelly—"

"Kayla—yes, of course I remember! She's about my age. Really friendly and funny. Was it her father who died?"

Troy nodded. "It was in the paper and all over the local news, an accident. He was out fishing when apparently he fell out of his canoe and drowned."

"Oh, that's awful." *Fishing? In the middle of November? Brrr. Who does that?*

The elder Cavendish broke in. "He was a client of ours: Ed Glassner, co-owner of GreenGro Nursery & Garden Supply in Lynnwood. Ms. Donnelly is coming in this afternoon to go over her father's will and get the paperwork started for probate."

"I'm familiar with the nursery," I said. "They sometimes supply potted houseplants for my cousin's store. You said 'co-owner' so I assume he had partners. Did they have a Cross-Purchase Agreement in place?" Basically, this is a legal contract stipulating that the deceased partner's share in the business be sold back to the remaining partners. This is usually done so the surviving partners don't become saddled with a bunch of clueless heirs who have no expertise or interest in the business.

"There's one partner," he said, "and they just had an informal fifty-fifty arrangement, which means that Ms. Donnelly will inherit her father's half of the business."

"What time is her appointment?" Troy asked. "Do we have time to run out for a sandwich?"

His father scratched his chin and shuffled a few papers on his desk. "Yeah, go ahead," he said. "She'll be here at one thirty."

———

"Clever how you timed your visit to coincide with lunch," I said as we settled with sandwiches and soft drinks at a small table in a nearby deli.

"Just lucky." He gave me a cagey smile. "Dad told me Kayla would be in his office this afternoon, and I wanted to see her just to say hello and tell her how sorry I was to hear about her father."

"I get the feeling you know her as more than just a barista."

"Good guess. Yeah, Kayla and I go way back. We went to the same schools growing up. She's a year younger than me, but we went out for awhile in high school. I was on the football team and she was a cheerleader."

My mind immediately conjured an image of Troy's tall, lean body in a football uniform. *I'll bet he was the captain.* I cleared my throat and rearranged a piece of lettuce on my tuna sandwich. "So, what happened?"

He shrugged. "Nothing. We just went in separate directions. Different interests. She met her husband James at a concert and now they own their own business, and have a little girl too."

"Living the dream," I said. "Too bad about her father. I can't believe he was out fishing in the middle of November. Is that a *thing?* Sounds miserable."

"Yeah, she told me once that he had a canoe he liked to take out on Sunday mornings. He'd been doing it ever since Kayla's mother died twelve years ago. She says he liked the solitude—gave him time to think and feel closer to his dead wife. I guess some of the smaller lakes around here are stocked with rainbow trout year round."

"Does she have any siblings?"

He shook his head. "Huh-uh. She's an only child."

"So she'll probably be named executrix."

He glanced at the time on his phone and wiped his mouth with a paper napkin. "Speaking of which, we should get back to the office."

Kayla Donnelly was just as I remembered: a slender young woman with dark brown hair and a pretty heart-shaped face. At the bakery she had always been lively, laughing and telling jokes with customers, and her colorful clothes had matched her perky, outgoing personality.

But today she wore a plain gray coat accessorized simply with a blue and white scarf. She shuffled as she walked, shoulders hunched, eyes downcast. Her face appeared splotchy, like she'd been crying. The sudden loss of her father must have been devastating. My heart went out to her. I remembered that crushing grief only too well.

Troy greeted her warmly when she entered the office, giving her a hug and offering words of sympathy. Then he stepped aside and waved a hand in my direction. "This is Brenna Wickham, my dad's new legal assistant. Brenna used to buy gallons of your coffee when she worked next door to you at the flower shop."

I took a step forward. "I'm so sorry for your loss." I was just one of hundreds of customers so I didn't really expect Kayla to remember me, but to my amazement she greeted me like an old friend.

"Yes, of course. *Brenna*—from Pretty Petals. Tall double-shot mocha with whipped cream and sprinkles, right?" She sniffed and wiped daintily at her nose with a tissue.

"That's right," I said with a laugh of surprise. "You've got a great memory."

"And now you work *here?*" She gazed around, taking in the solemn features of the mahogany-paneled office with its dark leather furniture, shelves of legal tomes, and imposing oaken desk.

I nodded. "I was just working temporarily for my cousin while I waited for this job to come along." I toyed with the ring on my left hand. "It's a long story."

Mr. Cavendish, sitting at the desk with his hands folded, gave a subtle cough. "Shall we get started?"

"I guess that's my cue to take off," Troy said. "Brenna, I'll talk to you later. Kayla, it was nice seeing you again. Wish it had been under better circumstances."

She thanked him and he strode from the room, closing the door as he left. Kayla took a seat in one of the leather chairs across the desk from Mr. Cavendish; I grabbed a steno pad and sat beside her, ready to take notes.

"You'll inherit your father's share of the business," the attorney said. "Have you given any thought to what you want to do with it?"

Kayla shrugged. "Dad's partner, Ward Thurmond, has already approached me about buying my half. I hate to sell it, but what do I know about running a nursery? That was my father's thing. He always had a passion for horticulture. He could grow anything." Her voice broke and she sighed, staring down at her hands. "All I ever manage to grow is weeds."

"You could keep your share, and let Mr. Thurmond run the business," Mr. Cavendish said.

"Like a silent partner?"

"It's one option. But remember, that would also make you liable for half the operating expense: maintenance, insurance, taxes, as well as inventory and wages for hired workers."

Kayla's face fell. "Whoa...I don't have that kind of money. I think the nursery did okay, but I got the impression it was more a labor of love than anything else. My dad never made a lot of money."

Mr. Cavendish nodded, his stern face remaining neutral. "Well, if you do decide to sell, you'll want to get an independent appraisal to find out what the business is worth. Now, let's talk about the rest of your father's estate: his house, his car, bank accounts, investments. Did he have a safety deposit box? What about life insurance?"

I recognized the confusion on Kayla's face. I had felt the same way after Jason's death. So much to do, to sort, to organize. Where to start?

The attorney droned on with details of what to expect in the coming months, what was required for the estate taxes, the disposal of assets, and steps that would need to be taken. After an hour, I could see Kayla's eyes starting to glaze over.

Chapter Two

When I got home that evening, I was greeted as usual by Buster, my cousin's stout little black and tan beagle. He bounced around my feet, vocalizing in his characteristic houndish *wooo*. I tried not to step on him as I reeled past, balancing the heaping box of papers I'd brought home from Mrs. Hansen's to work on.

Buster had a nose for mischief, but it was his nose that had helped me discover what had happened to Hannah Moreland, the little girl next door, who had disappeared twenty-five years ago without a trace. Only a very small handful of people knew that I had also been aided by Hannah herself—that is, by her *ghost*. It was not a fact I tended to broadcast.

Connie emerged from the kitchen then, wiping

her hands on a towel. She was a plumpish woman of thirty-six, two years my senior, with a pleasingly round face and short ash-blond hair. Peering through wire-rimmed glasses, she noted the box I had dumped on the couch.

"Homework?" she asked.

I peeled off my coat. "'Fraid so. I told you about that elderly lady I'm guardian for now. Well, it's going to take more than just a few days to sort out the mass of papers she's got stacked up all over her house. Plus, it turns out she's got raccoons living in her attic. I've got a pest control company coming on Monday."

She aimed a smile at the little beagle who stood nearby gazing up at her with big liquid eyes. "You should take Buster over there," she said. "He'd love to get rid of those raccoons for you, wouldn't you, boy?" His whiplike tail wagged vigorously in response. The little hound lived under the assumption that he was the center of the universe. In this house, he wasn't wrong.

"I don't know," I said, eyeing the pudgy canine. "I think a pack of raccoons could take him."

Connie snorted. "Go get your clothes changed. The meatloaf's almost done, and I want to talk to you about plans for Thanksgiving."

I rolled my shoulders wearily. It had been a long day. All I wanted to do was hole up in my room, unwind and listen to music while going through the heap of bills and random papers I'd brought home.

"What's to talk about?" I said. "My family arrives on Wednesday; I'll leave work early and pick them up at the airport. Then I'll take my parents to the motel, and my brothers will come here and sleep on the floor in the living room."

We had already discussed this and decided on the arrangements. I would have loved to invite my parents to stay with us, but there was no way we could all cram into this small three-bedroom bungalow. Connie had converted the smallest room to an office, stuffing it with bookshelves, a desk, a filing cabinet, secondhand armchair, and a potted fern on a small end table. One could barely turn around in there. It would require a lot of rearranging to turn it into a guest room. My mother knew the limitations of this small house as well as anyone, and had insisted that she and my dad get a motel room nearby.

"You're in charge of the menu," I continued. "Just tell me what you need me to do and I'll do it." My cousin's cooking skills were for me a source of constant amazement. I had seen her master more than one culinary triumph with no more than half a pound of hamburger and a few random vegetables. I could make a salad and chop veggies, set the table and fold napkins, but I had never roasted a turkey in my life, and at this point had no real desire to do so.

Connie nodded and flicked her hand at me impatiently. "Go change. There's something else I want to talk to you about."

I cocked an eyebrow curiously, but did as I was told and hurried to my room to get out of my work clothes. Fifteen minutes later I was piling mashed potatoes on my plate next to a slab of Connie's fabulous meatloaf.

"Okay," I said, "so what's on your mind?"

Connie's eyes lit up as she leaned forward eagerly. "What would you think about inviting Bill Prescott for Thanksgiving dinner."

I drew back in surprise. I stared at her and tried to digest her words and all their ramifications. Two months earlier, I had learned that the neighbor, Bill Prescott, was my real father. Since all my life I'd been told that my father was dead, finding out he was alive and living just two doors down had been a huge shock. When I had confronted my mother, she'd apologized awkwardly and fumbled for an explanation, but had finally just blurted that they'd been foolish, careless teenagers. Not the tragic romantic love story I had imagined.

I put my fork down and rubbed a hand over my mouth as I considered having my recently-discovered biological father sit at the same table as the stepfather who had raised me since I was ten years old. I cleared my throat. "Might be a bit awkward, don't you think?"

"Maybe a little," Connie said, undeterred. "But the cat's out of the bag now—everybody knows Bill's your father. That makes him family, doesn't it? And Dennis is a great guy. I really don't think he'd mind, do you?"

Indeed, my stepfather had taken the news about Bill in stride and been exceedingly gracious about the whole thing, but somehow setting them up to meet for the first time over Thanksgiving dinner seemed a bit much to ask.

I gave Connie a sideways glance. I suspected an

ulterior motive. "Tell me the truth. Why do you *really* want to invite him?"

She smiled sheepishly. "I was just thinking... he's got that whole house and we're so crowded. Maybe he'd let Paul and Michael sleep over there. He's got lots of room."

"No way," I said adamantly. "We've just started getting to know each other. I don't want to start imposing on him. Besides, I have a feeling my mom wouldn't like it."

She gave a little shrug. "I thought it was worth a try. I'm sure he wouldn't mind."

I took a deep breath and blew it out again. "I'll phone Mom after dinner and see what she says. I know she called Bill after I told her I'd found out, but this visit will be the first time they've seen each other face-to-face in years. It could get weird."

Long before Connie inherited this house, it had been our grandparents' home and the place where both our mothers were raised, Aunt Peggy being the elder. As an eighteen-year-old fresh out of high school, my mother had fallen for the older neighbor boy. Devilishly handsome, with long hair and tattoos, riding a smokin' Harley, he had been described as cool and rebellious. In time, my mom had found herself pregnant. Attitudes toward pregnant unwed teenagers had been less tolerant thirty-five years ago, so my mother and grandparents had invented a husband who had conveniently joined the army and been killed overseas before I was born.

As a child growing up, I had been acutely aware of my lack of a father, but by the time I was ten years old, my mother had married Dennis Danfield and my life had changed. We moved to Phoenix and before long my mom had presented me with two little brothers. I thought of those days fondly; I loved my stepfather, and we had been a happy family.

"You don't think Dennis is jealous, do you?" Connie said.

I poked at the potatoes on my plate. "Not exactly—at least not of Bill and my mom. More like jealous of my affections, if that makes sense. I mean, Dennis is the only dad I've ever known. I don't want him to feel bad, like he's being replaced."

"Look," she said, "you can't control how Dennis feels, but you *can* show him how *you* feel. Just treat him like you always have, like he's your *dad.*"

I stared at my cousin. "When did you get to be so smart?"

She smirked and bounced her shoulders, hazel eyes twinkling behind her glasses. "I just think of men like dogs; it doesn't take much to make them happy—a few strokes, some extra food, and a bit of love and attention."

"*Huh.* If you think I'm going to scratch Dennis behind the ears, you can forget it." I sucked my lower lip. "But actually, it would be nice to invite Bill over for Thanksgiving. He shouldn't have to be all alone." With a sly smile I added, "Too bad your parents aren't coming too. We could make it a family reunion."

She laughed out loud. "Oh, yeah, that'd be *really* exciting. My mom's still pissed that she wasn't in on the secret."

Once the dinner dishes were cleared away, I went to my room to call my mother. As expected, she responded with a resounding *no* to Connie's suggestion that we ask Bill to put the boys up at his house over the weekend.

"Brenna," she said in that disapproving tone I remembered from childhood. "I know you want a relationship with Bill. That's understandable. But regardless of what transpired thirty-five years ago, he's still practically a stranger—and hardly the kind of man I want schmoozing with your brothers."

I bristled at her reference to my conception and birth as something that had *transpired,* like some unfortunate event in history that was best forgotten.

"Paul and Michael aren't children anymore," I said. "They're grown men. Give them some credit. Paul's graduating from college in a few months. They're perfectly capable of thinking for themselves. And besides, Bill Prescott isn't the same man you knew thirty-five years ago. He's been through a lot and he's changed. He's mellowed. He builds birdhouses in his garage, for pete's sake."

For a moment she didn't speak and I expected her to retort, but finally I heard her expel a breath. "Fine, invite him for dinner if you want, but that's all. I'll talk to Dad about it and let him know what to expect."

I wasn't surprised by my mom's reaction. I had the feeling she and Bill hadn't parted on very good terms, and she still thought of him as a low-life. The very fact that my mom had ousted him from my life all those years ago spoke volumes. All she would tell me now was that she had once thought herself madly in love, but that she had been foolish and Bill had been irresponsible, happy to give up his parental rights and shirk his duty. I knew he'd changed, but my mother was less forgiving.

She hung up and I set my phone on the nightstand before sprawling backward on the bed. As I did, I glanced over at the framed photo of Jason smiling at me. Unconsciously, I fingered my wedding ring—a nervous habit I'd picked up lately. "I miss you," I whispered.

When I told Connie about my mom's response to her great idea she just shrugged. "Oh well, not too surprising, I guess—and your brothers would probably ask a lot of awkward questions. We don't have to invite him for dinner either if you don't want to. It was just an idea."

"No, I've thought about it, and I *do* want to. Regardless of everything, he *is* my father, and he's been through a lot. I want him to feel included. I'll go over there on Saturday and ask him."

––––––––––

Mr. Cavendish wasn't in the office the next morning. He'd gone to the courthouse to file Ed Glassner's will and get the order signed by the Court Commissioner authorizing probate and the appointment of Kayla Donnelly as executrix.

At eleven, Kayla called. "Brenna? I'm so sorry

to bother you. I know you're busy, but I'm going crazy. I was wondering if there's any chance I might talk you into coming to my father's house for a few minutes, maybe on your lunch hour? I'll make us something to eat. It's in Edmonds, not too far from your office."

"Whoa, Kayla, hold on," I said. "Are you there now? What's wrong?"

"Nothing's wrong." She gave a quick laugh. "I'm sorry—just a little panic attack, I guess. I'm at Dad's house and I just don't know where to start. Mr. Cavendish gave me a whole list of instructions and my mind's gone blank. I don't know what I'm doing."

"Okay, one thing at a time," I said. "Is there a desk somewhere or a filing cabinet? Where would he have kept his important papers?"

"Oh, right. There's an office in the basement. It's always been off limits. I was never allowed to go in there, never had a reason to."

"Well, you do now. You need to look for life insurance policies, investment accounts, and bank statements. Check for a key to a safety deposit box too. Just put everything aside for now and I'll help you with them later. Our office will send a Notice to Creditors to the paper so you don't need to worry about that." I leaned back and ran a hand through my hair. "At some point, you'll need to make an inventory, but for now why don't you just start thinking about which personal items of your dad's you want to keep."

Kayla exhaled in a breathy whoosh. "Who knew death could be so complicated?"

"I know, but you'll get through it. Hang in there." I tried to sound encouraging and sympathetic at the same. "Tell you what—I'll come over there at noon just to help you get started, okay? You don't have to fix lunch. I brought a sandwich this morning and I'll bring it with me."

"That's perfect," she said. "Thank you, Brenna. I really appreciate it."

The neighborhood consisted of typical 1970's split-level houses with fake brick façades and flat green lawns. Kayla must have been watching for me because when I approached the front door, she threw it open and greeted me with enthusiasm.

"Brenna, I'm so glad you could come. I've been going through Dad's office. It's kind of a mess, but at least his files are pretty well organized."

I followed her up the steps to the living room: a schlumpy man-space with tired furniture and threadbare shag carpet. A worn Naugahyde recliner faced a flat-screen TV, while a coffee table stood nearby covered in gardening magazines, old newspapers, and beer can stains. The whole place reeked of stale cigarette smoke.

Glancing around, I noticed a dark stain on the ceiling above the fireplace. I turned to Kayla. "Looks like there might be a leak in the roof. You'll probably need to get that fixed before you sell the house."

She grimaced and rolled her eyes, heaving a big sigh. "Yeah, another thing I have to deal with.

Dad had the roof replaced this summer but they did a lousy job, and now it leaks every time we get a heavy rain. Dad told me he called the company to come back and fix it, but the owner's been dragging his feet, making excuses. I told Dad he should leave a negative comment on one of those online review sites, but he didn't want to. He probably thought it would just make matters worse. Now I'm going to have to deal with it."

I thought for a moment. One of the perks of working for a lawyer was the availability of legal stationery. "If you get me a copy of the contract or an invoice or something, I'll be happy to write a letter. Nothing lights a fire under a deadbeat like a letter from an attorney's office. There's no excuse for the company not coming back and fixing their mistake."

Kayla laughed. "That'd be great, thanks. I'm sure the paperwork's somewhere downstairs in Dad's office. But first, let's go eat lunch." She turned and led the way to the kitchen.

I hung my coat and purse over the back of a chair and set my lunch sack on the small Formica table. Kayla was just reaching for the fridge handle when the doorbell rang.

Her eyebrows shot up. "I wonder who that could be?"

I followed as she hurried to open the front door. From where I stood behind her, I could see a thin middle-aged man standing on the porch twiddling his fingers and shifting his feet. He had stringy black hair and wore a shabby corduroy coat.

The roofer? I thought. What a weird coincidence

that would be.

"Can I help you?" Kayla asked.

The man stopped fidgeting and smiled, revealing stained, crooked teeth. "Hi. Are you Ed's daughter? He talked about you all the time. I'm Arthur Bailey. I live next door. I saw you were here and just wanted to come over and pay my respects and tell you how sorry I was to hear about Ed. He was a great guy."

"Thank you, Mr. Bailey," Kayla said. "I appreciate that."

He glanced down at his hands and shuffled his feet again. "I suppose you'll be disposing of your dad's things now." He pinched his lower lip and took a deep breath. "Well...um...before you do, I...um...I need to get my lawn mower back. I loaned it to Ed, see, and he never returned it." His eyes held a pleading look.

"Oh, sure," Kayla said, "no problem. Meet me out front. I'll go through and open the garage door."

As she closed the front door and headed downstairs, I said, "How do you know he's telling the truth? He seemed awfully nervous. He may just be looking for a new lawn mower." I'd seen cases where grieving survivors had been bilked out of heirlooms and other valuables by fast-talking relatives and so-called friends of the family.

"I don't know. But it sounds like something Dad would do. Anyway, it's no big deal, it's just a lawn mower."

"I know, but be careful about giving away expensive things." I knew that Kayla was feeling fragile after the sudden death of her father. Wading through probate was difficult enough without people using the opportunity to take advantage of her. Jason's affairs had been fairly straight forward, but it had still taken months to get it all settled.

The garage was a dank cavern smelling of chemicals and fertilizer; the irregular outlines of workbenches, shelves, tools, and garden implements loomed in the shadows. One small, dirt-encrusted window let in a modicum of light. Kayla wove her way through the clutter to the front of the garage, and with an effort, shoved on the door until it swung heavily overhead.

The neighbor, Arthur Bailey, stood just outside, waiting. He gave a grunt of thanks as he went into the back and dragged out an old gas-powered push mower. I doubted the thing was worth more than fifty bucks.

Instead of rushing off as I expected, he stood fidgeting again, obviously wanting to say more.

"Is there something else, Mr. Bailey?" Kayla asked.

"Yeah...I...uh," he wiped a hand over his chin as he mumbled, trying to get the words out. "I was interested...that is...your dad showed me his stamp collection once, and I...well...I mean...I thought if you was thinking of selling it, maybe you'd let me have first crack at it." He looked hopeful.

"Oh," Kayla said, "I haven't run across his stamp collection yet, but when I do..."

I stepped forward and put a restraining hand on Kayla's arm. "We'll want to get it appraised first, and then we'll let you know. How does that sound?"

He gave me a look that was decidedly cool, but he nodded. "Sure, sure, I understand. Didn't mean to overstep. Just...whenever it's convenient, okay? Thanks. I'll see you later, Ms. Glassner."

"It's Kayla Donnelly," she corrected.

"Right," he nodded, "Ms. Donnelly." He turned then and pushed the lawn mower down the driveway, headed toward the street.

Kayla looked at me and gave a little laugh. "That was weird. I didn't even know Dad had a stamp collection. Do you think it might be valuable?"

I shrugged. "Probably not. I've had to get stamp collections appraised before, and they're never worth more than a couple hundred dollars at most. But you never know."

She sighed and swiped at a cobweb clinging to her sleeve. Her eyes took on a faraway look. "I still can't believe he's gone. He went fishing in that canoe every Sunday for twelve years and never so much as got his feet wet, and then he goes and falls into the lake and drowns. It just doesn't make sense. He was an excellent swimmer."

"The canoe tipped over, didn't it?"

"I guess so." Her creased brow and tight lips expressed uncertainty. "I just don't see why he didn't swim to shore."

I shook my head sadly, searching for something to say. "Hypothermia? The water had to be freezing. It was an accident. There's nothing any-one could have done."

"I know." She sniffed and wiped away a tear.

"Will there be a funeral?" I asked.

"No. His ashes will be buried next to my mother, but Dad always insisted he didn't want a funeral. I'm thinking I may just have a small gathering later for a few friends and family."

"That sounds nice."

She sniffed again and gave me a weak smile. "Well, we'd better go in and eat. I know you're on your lunch hour."

"Don't worry about that. This is business. But I probably should get back before too long."

We ate lunch in a hurry, then Kayla led me downstairs to the basement. The space had been divided into two halves, the front side facing the street having obviously been a cozy family room at one time. A couch faced an old TV sitting on a stand full of DVDs, a bar hugged one corner, and a brick fireplace matched the one directly above. Now the room appeared to have been given over to the storage of junk.

A wooden rocking chair with a broken leg leaned against one wall, and under the window was a shelf heaped with tattered fishing magazines, old games, and puzzles. His passion for gardening was evident in the flower pots, watering can, and soiled gloves piled on the floor. Random objects like an electric fan, a space heater, a couple of TV trays, and a set of golf clubs were wedged in among stacks of unlabeled cardboard boxes. On a table in the corner collecting dust sat a sewing machine that must have belonged to Kayla's mother.

"What a disaster," Kayla said, staring bleakly at

the mess. "After Mom died, Dad just sort of let things go." She pulled a dingy rag doll off a pile of old clothes that had been tossed carelessly on the couch. "I used to play down here, now I'll need a bulldozer to clean it out." She gave a rueful sigh. "I suppose I'll have to have a garage sale."

I glanced around, shaking my head. "Huh-uh, I recommend you hire a company specializing in estate sales. They'll do all the work—getting appraisals, setting things up, and handling the sale. You'll be amazed at the results they get. I'll give you the names of some good companies." I had seen professionals get thousands for estates full of things most people considered junk: toys, books, tools, furniture, clothes, dishes, movie posters, costume jewelry.

"I should probably throw a bunch of this stuff away first." She flipped through a pile of old magazines. "Nobody's going to buy these."

"You'd be surprised," I said. "Seriously, don't throw anything out. Now then, which way to your dad's office? I'll help you get started, then I need to get back to work."

Kayla opened a door in the partition wall. By comparison, the office was fairly neat and organized. The walls were covered in dark walnut paneling; a black steel desk, book shelves, and a filing cabinet crowded into the space.

"Look at this," she said, reaching for an object sitting on the corner of the desk. "I can't believe Dad kept this all these years." She held up an old black rotary dial desk telephone. "It's been sitting here for as long as I can remember."

I sucked in a breath of appreciation. "Oh, that's cool. It's vintage, probably from the '50s. Where'd he get it?" I laughed. "I'm sure your dad wasn't *that* old."

She smiled. "He told me it came out of the original office when he and his partner first bought the nursery over thirty years ago. The place had been up and running for years, but needed tons of work and renovation. The owner wanted to retire, so they got it for a great price. When they started updating, Dad brought this old telephone home. He loved it, but he always did like old stuff."

Her chin trembled as she studied the device. "I remember playing with this as a kid. I'm not sure he ever actually hooked it up."

"Lots of people buy stuff like this," I said. "Mid-century is very collectible right now." I thought of my friend Tamara Munroe, part fashionista, part bohemian, with just a smidgen of Louisiana Creole on her mother's side. She loved random, eclectic oddities. I smiled. She'd probably make it into a lamp.

Kayla handed me the old telephone and I turned it over in my hands, examining it closely. The unit was surprisingly heavy; the Bakelite plastic cover was scuffed but intact. The handset, attached to the body by fourteen inches of coiled cord, was stamped with the words "Western Electric." A couple of feet of cable hung off the back, apparently snipped with wire cutters. It was questionable whether it could ever be made to work, but it would make a great art deco piece.

"If you like it," Kayla said, "I want you to have it."

I looked at her in surprise. "Oh, no, I couldn't. It's an antique, worth at least a hundred dollars."

"Please, I insist. You said I should go through Dad's stuff and choose some personal items to keep. Well, I'm keeping this—and giving it to you. Consider it a thank-you for all your help. Besides, what would I do with it? I'd rather give it to you than sell it to some stranger."

"Thank you," I said. "I love it. I'm going to clean it up and put it on the shelf in my room above my desk."

We spent the next twenty minutes going through the filing cabinet. It was stuffed to capacity with both business and personal papers. Kayla didn't find the paperwork on the roofing job but she promised to keep looking for it.

Meanwhile, I instructed her on making a claim on her father's life insurance, and advised her that once she had the Certificate of Qualification from the court as executrix on her father's will, she'd be able to pursue her father's bank accounts and move forward toward acquiring her share of her father's business. I also gave her the names of a couple of reputable estate sales companies and encouraged her to call for a consultation.

Once she seemed confident, I left her to it and headed back to the office. I tucked the vintage telephone on the floor behind the driver's seat of my car.

Chapter Three

I was so wrapped up in my thoughts when I got home that night, I didn't notice Nancy Chumley next door puttering outside in her garden. The thickset woman was a retired teacher, local historian, and tireless busybody. As soon as I pulled my PT Cruiser onto the gravel strip in front of the house, she came bustling over. It was getting dark so I suspected she'd been waiting for me.

"Oh, *Brenna.*" Nancy's high-pitched voice cut through the air as I got out of my car. "I'm glad I caught you. Now that you're working, we never get to see you anymore. I just wanted to touch base and let you know everything's on track for the craft fair. Can you believe it's only two weeks away? And Thanksgiving's next Thursday! Where does the time go?"

Doesn't the woman ever breathe?

"I hear your family's coming from Arizona," she continued. "That's wonderful. I haven't seen your mother in goodness knows how long. You be sure to tell her to come over and see me, won't you?"

I opened my mouth to speak, but a strange look came over Nancy's face and she cut me off. "Your car is ringing." She peered around me and stared at the dilapidated old vehicle.

I listened, and sure enough, the loud jangle of a telephone was emanating from the back seat of my car. For a moment, all I could do was stare. I patted my coat pocket, feeling for the solid, reassuring shape of my cell phone.

Once more the strident ring sounded from my car.

"Aren't you going to answer it?" Nancy asked.

I realized I'd been holding my breath, and I let it out in a rush. "Yes, of course." I turned and yanked the back door open, reaching inside for the vintage telephone. *This is impossible,* I thought as I pressed the receiver to my ear. "Hello?"

Through heavy static I thought I detected a faraway voice, but the words were too faint to make out. *A trick phone?* It had to be. Had Kayla known this when she gave it to me?

Nancy stared, wide-eyed.

I jammed the handset onto the cradle. "Gotcha!" I said, looking at my neighbor and forcing a laugh. "It's not a real phone—just a joke."

Nancy howled. "Marvelous! Where'd you get it? I want one."

I thought fast. "You can't buy them, I got it at a

garage sale. The guy said he builds these gimmicks himself, said he likes messing with wires and stuff."

She clapped her hands together. "What a great gag for a party. Maybe I could borrow it sometime."

"Uh...sure. Well, I'd better get inside. Feels like it's starting to rain. It was nice seeing you, Nancy."

I turned and hurried toward the house, carrying the curious telephone.

Buster met me at the door as usual, barking and wagging his tail. He noticed the strange object in my arms and began to bounce on his back legs, pawing at me and whining plaintively as he attempted to get a good sniff. He seemed inordinately interested in the antique phone and followed closely at my heels as I took it to my bedroom and set it on the desk.

"What do you make of it, Buster?" I asked the chubby hound. I knew his senses were far more acute than mine, but I couldn't imagine what he found so intriguing about this chunky old relic.

I decided that as soon as I had a chance, I would grab a screwdriver and take the thing apart. There had to be a battery inside and some sort of electronic mechanism. There was no other way it could have rung on its own. The whole thing was unnerving.

Just then, Connie peered in. "What are you doing?"

"Looking at this old telephone," I said.

Buster snuffled noisily as he jumped up and put his paws on the desk, stretching his neck to get his nose as close as possible.

"Where'd it come from?" Connie asked.

"Remember Kayla Donnelly from the coffee shop next to your store? Her father died recently."

"Oh, I'm sorry to hear that. I'll have to take some flowers over to her."

"I'm sure she'd appreciate it. She's a client of ours—at least, her father was—and we've been helping her with his estate."

"But what's that got to do with this old telephone?"

"Kayla gave it to me. She's getting rid of most of her dad's stuff. I told her I thought it was cool—sort of a nifty antique—so she said I could have it as a thank-you for the help I've been giving her."

Connie gave me a sideways look. "What are you going to do with it?"

I laughed. "I don't know. Maybe I'll start collecting old telephones."

She gave a sharp *pfft*, then said, "Well, dinner's almost ready. Come on, Buster." She grabbed the dog's collar and dragged him out of the room.

Outside, I could hear the rain picking up. Sounded like we were in for a good drenching. With dismay, I thought of the roof leak at Kayla's father's house. Hopefully, it wouldn't get any worse.

When dinner was finished and the table cleared, I spread a towel on the dining room table to protect the surface, then retrieved the old phone from my bedroom. There was nothing unusual about it other than its old-fashionedness. My mouth quirked in a wry smile. *Kids nowadays probably wouldn't even know what this is.* But rotary telephones like these used to be common. I remembered a green one Grandma used to have on the kitchen counter when I was a child before she upgraded to a touch-tone.

I rummaged through the kitchen junk drawer until I found a screwdriver. I love these catchall drawers. Where else can you find a pair of scissors, a roll of tape, and a screwdriver all in one handy location?

The sturdy black Bakelite case showed wear around the edges and had a few scratches, but overall it seemed in pretty good shape. The handset, shaped like a small dumbbell, felt solid when I held it. *You could whack someone good with this thing,* I thought.

I turned the body of the phone over and examined the bottom. Two screws held the plastic top to the flat metal base. It didn't look as though it had been tampered with. I gripped the screwdriver and loosened the screws. I separated the Bakelite cover from the base and set it aside. The rotary mechanism, the bells, and a tangle of wires and other bits I couldn't identify remained screwed to the metal frame. The inner works appeared to be old, corroded, and original.

"*Now* what are you doing?" Connie asked, coming up beside me.

"I'm taking this old telephone apart."

She leaned forward for a better look, squinting through her glasses. "Why?"

I expelled a breath of frustration. As far as I could tell, there was nothing here to explain why the phone had rung. I set the screwdriver down and leaned on the table. "Because it rang in the car when it shouldn't have, and I'm trying to figure out why. I thought maybe someone had replaced the old insides with some sort of newfangled battery-powered ringer." I left off the part about hearing a faint, garbled voice.

Connie tapped on the brass bells with a fingernail producing a pleasing *tink tink*. "Naw," she said. "You're way overthinking this. It probably just got jostled in the car and sounded like it was ringing."

I sniffed and sucked my lower lip. The car had been parked and stationary when the phone rang. It wasn't jostled. And there had definitely been noise on the other end of the receiver when I'd put it to my ear. It didn't make sense, but this wasn't the first time I had encountered the unexplainable.

Would it ring again? I stopped and stared at the antiquated telephone. It was nothing but a worn-out old artifact full of outdated wiring. Maybe I *was* making too much of this. Maybe there was nothing weird going on at all and my senses were simply colored by my previous ghostly experience.

"Yeah," I said, "you're probably right."

I reaffixed the top of the phone to the base and carried it back to my room, placing it on the floor of the closet next to my shoes.

I jumped when the sudden jarring crow of a rooster erupted from my cell phone lying on top of my desk. Once more, I considered switching the text alert to something more pleasing, but as usual, I decided against it. Jason had installed the loudest ringtone he could find as a joke after I'd missed an important text. Two years later, I still couldn't bring myself to change it.

Grateful for the distraction, I closed the closet door and reached for my phone. It was Gage Moreland wanting to know if I was free for dinner tomorrow night. I smiled as a warm, fluttery feeling washed over me. With everything else going on, a relaxing dinner with a good friend was exactly what I needed.

Gage and I have known each other since we were kids, when this was Grandma's house. My mom used to bring me here every summer to visit. Gage and his sisters lived next door. Back then, Gage was a scrawny kid with big ears, a long nose, and dark hair that hung perpetually in his eyes. I used to torment him with the name "donkey face," and he would retaliate with a well-aimed water pistol. At nine years old, I would have died before admitting I had a full-blown crush on him.

But after my mom married Dennis and we moved to Phoenix, the Morelands had receded in my memory. Eventually I grew up, went to college, and met Jason, the man I married. Not until years later, after Jason and I moved back to Seattle and he was killed in a traffic accident, did I become reacquainted with Gage.

In the intervening years, Gage had grown from a gangling kid to a handsome, broad-shouldered man with dark, brooding eyes and a square, resolute face. While his nearness gave me a heady feeling, Jason's memory was still too tender and I wasn't ready to commit to a serious relationship.

Gage seemed content to remain good friends, which for now was exactly what I needed.

I sent back a reply telling him I'd love to go out, and we agreed that he'd pick me up at six.

In the living room, I heard Connie turn on the TV. She had a ritual of watching television every evening after dinner until bedtime. I would have loved to join her, but I still had papers from Mrs. Hansen's to go through. I sat down cross-legged on top of the bed and pulled the box toward me. I wanted to get these organized before I went back there on Monday for another boxload.

The pest control company would be coming then too. I didn't know what the operation entailed, but I didn't want the old woman getting unduly upset. Maybe afterward I should take her someplace nice to get her mind off the raccoons. I wondered when the last time was she'd been taken out to lunch.

As I mulled this over, I was suddenly startled by a muffled metallic jangling. My first impulse was to jump up and grab my cell phone off the desk. With a start, I realized the sound wasn't coming from there. The old rotary phone in the closet was ringing again.

For a moment I sat dumbstruck, but on the third ring I bounced off the bed and made a leap for the closet. I threw the door open and fell to my knees, grabbing for the handset. "Hello?"

I pressed my ear to the receiver, bracing myself. Again, a faint male voice was barely discernible through the static. Outside, the bushes beneath my window rattled in the wind making it impossible to hear. The dark, moonless night heightened the gloom and increased my feelings of foreboding.

Finally, the phone went silent and I found myself holding nothing but a cold, inanimate hunk of old plastic. I pulled in a deep breath, striving to slow my racing heart. For a full minute, I sat staring at the old telephone. *Please, God, not another ghost!*

Hands shaking, I replaced the handset and shoved it once more into the closet. Then I climbed back into the center of the bed and tried to concentrate on Mrs. Hansen's box of papers.

I slept fitfully that night, dreaming of ghosts and haunted telephones. As it was Saturday, I allowed myself the luxury of drowsing in bed a little longer than usual. When I finally got up, I put on my black knee-length leggings, a t-shirt, and my purple running shoes. Connie had already left for the flower shop so I shooed Buster into the back yard, then scarfed downed a piece of toast in the kitchen. After that, I grabbed my jacket and headed out the front door.

The day was cool and cloudy, typical of late November. Wet grass and mud puddles were evidence that heavy rain had fallen during the night. I turned left at the street and jogged toward Bill Prescott's house. He knew I liked to run in the morning and often stood by his fence waiting to give me a little salute in greeting as I went by, so it was no surprise to see him standing there in his bathrobe with the morning paper tucked under his arm.

"You're late," he called, a jovial grin on his whiskery face. I thought his salt and pepper beard added a certain rakish quality to his brawny good looks.

"It's Saturday," I said, slowing down. "I slept in."

"Have you had breakfast?"

"A piece of toast," I replied. "But I could stand a cup of coffee if you've got any. In fact, I want to talk to you. How about if I stop on my way back?"

"Bacon and eggs it is," he declared with a wave of his hand. "Go build up an appetite and I'll see you in a few."

I didn't bother arguing—it would do no good. Stuffing me with food was one of the methods he used to make up for all the years he'd missed being a father. So I simply nodded and took off running again.

Thirty minutes later, Bill had exchanged his bathrobe for jeans and a faded plaid shirt. He shoveled three crispy bacon strips and a perfectly fried egg onto a plate next to a slice of whole wheat toast and set these on the table in front of me along with a glass of orange juice. The kitchen had a warm cozy feel with its rustic shaker cabinets, gingham curtains, and floral wallpaper.

"Mmm," I inhaled with pleasure. "Smells delicious. You'd make a great short order cook."

He chuckled. "I've always liked to cook. Nothing fancy, but it's pretty hard to go wrong with plain old bacon and eggs." He filled his own plate, then set the coffee carafe on a trivet in the middle of the table and took the seat opposite. Crunching on a piece of bacon, he said, "Now then, you wanted to talk to me?"

I washed down a bite of egg with a swig of steaming coffee. I licked my lips and took a breath. "My family is coming from Phoenix this year for Thanksgiving, and I'd love it if you would join us."

His face sobered. "You want me to come for Thanksgiving dinner with your parents?"

"And Connie and my two brothers."

He rested his right hand on the table, gripping his fork. His eyebrows drew together as he frowned. "They okay with it?"

"Of course," I said. "You're my father. That makes you part of the family."

He leaned back and chewed thoughtfully. Outside, the rain had begun a soft patter on the porch steps. "I'm not sure your stepfather would see it that way."

I gave a little shrug. "Dennis has always known he's not my real father, and it's not like you're a big secret anymore. He knows all about you. He's a great guy, and my parents have a solid marriage. I think the two of you would get along just fine." In fact, Dennis was a teddy bear. Everybody liked him. It was my mother I was more worried about.

As though reading my thoughts, he said, "What about your mom? I doubt she'd be happy having me horn in on your Thanksgiving dinner. We haven't exactly been friends since I left her 'holding the bag,' so to speak."

I frowned at his choice of words.

"I'm sorry, Brenna," he said. "No offense. But the truth is I was a jerk in those days, doing stupid things, getting into trouble. Your mom and I both knew I'd make a terrible father. It was better for everybody to have me out of the picture." He reached across the table and touched my hand. "But I hope you know it's a decision I've come to regret."

"So, be a part of my life now," I said. "Come for Thanksgiving—meet the rest of the family."

He stuffed another piece of bacon in his mouth, then downed the rest of his coffee. "No, I'm no good at big family gatherings. I'd just make everyone uncomfortable."

I was disappointed, but knew he was right. It would be hard to relax and enjoy my parents' visit if I had to constantly be running interference between Bill and my mom—or worse, my brothers who would undoubtedly view my biological father as a curiosity, somewhere between sci-fi anomaly and circus freak.

"Besides," he went on, "you know there'd be questions...things I don't want to talk about. It could get real awkward."

I tried to reassure him. "I've talked to my parents. They'll be discreet, I promise."

He looked away, then after a moment shook his head. "I don't think so, Brenna. I'm sorry."

I nodded and picked absently at a spot on the table. "That's okay, I understand."

"They staying the whole weekend?"

"They're arriving Wednesday afternoon and

leaving Saturday morning."

He rubbed a hand over his jaw, smoothing his beard. "Tell you what, if it's okay with them, why don't you bring them over Friday morning after breakfast? That way I can say hello and meet Dennis, tell him what a great job he did raising you."

I looked up and smiled. "I like that idea."

He stood and started clearing the dishes. "Now then, can I get you anything else? More coffee?"

I groaned and patted my stomach. "No, thank you. I couldn't eat another bite. But, um, could I ask you kind of a dumb question?"

He gave me a wide grin and leaned back against the kitchen counter, his sinewy hands gripping the edge like the talons of a great bird. "Of course, dumb questions are my specialty."

I took a deep breath. "Okay, so I was recently given an old rotary dial desk phone, probably from the 1950s. The weird thing is, it sometimes rings by itself and when I pick up the receiver I hear static. Does that make any sense to you?"

He stroked his beard. "Well, they used to say ham radio signals would sometimes bleed over onto phone lines. More likely it's just a wrong number, or a telemarketer in one of those damn boiler rooms. Half the time they don't answer right away when you pick up—but you oughta just hang up on those anyway." He narrowed his eyes. "How'd you manage to get the phone hooked up? You still have a landline?"

"Um, no." I bit my lip and drummed the table with my fingernails. "I guess I forgot to mention that it's not actually hooked up. At the moment, it's sitting on the floor in my closet."

"Hmm, I see." He paused, one eyebrow lifted slightly. "Then there's only one answer."

I waited, willing my hands to stop fidgeting, hoping his years of experience could somehow make sense of this puzzle.

He leaned toward me and said in a low conspiratorial voice, "The phone is haunted."

My mouth dropped open. The look of shock on my face must have been hilarious because Bill gripped his sides and threw back his head in a roar of laughter.

"I'm just messing with you, kid." He waved his hand like he was batting at a fly. "Don't look so serious. Come on, you know there's no such thing as ghosts."

I forced a laugh and pushed back my hair in an effort to recover my composure. "Of course. You just caught me off guard."

"Those old ringers are mechanical," he said. "Nothing fancy. Just brass bells. They'll ring at the slightest bump. Drop 'em, or knock 'em against something, they'll ring. As for the static, it's probably just background noise resonating inside the plastic handset, sort of like how you hear the ocean when you put a seashell up to your ear."

"Sure. That makes sense." I smiled weakly, feeling foolish for even bringing it up. What had I expected? I placed my hands on the tabletop and rose from my chair. "I'd better get going. I've got things to do today. Thank you so much for breakfast."

I hurried home, anxious to get out of my running clothes and take a shower. But first I brought Buster inside. If left on his own in the back yard for too long the little hound tended to get bored which sometimes led to his digging under the fence and getting into trouble. One of these days, I intended to fasten chicken wire to the bottom of the fence as a deterrent to digging, but I'd just been too busy lately and hadn't had a chance to get to it.

I thought about my dinner with Gage tonight. Should I tell him about the mysterious ringing telephone? I could just see him rolling his eyes and telling me I was imagining things. I could talk to his sister Maureen. She was the only other person I knew who had seen a ghost. But she was in therapy, working through years of emotional trauma. Her life was just starting to approach normal, with a new relationship and happy prospects. The last thing I wanted to do was burden her with a new crisis.

A short time later, as I was toweling my hair dry, the old telephone in the closet began to ring. My chest tightened and my breath caught in my throat. I swallowed hard. Nothing could have bumped the phone. I hadn't even been near the closet.

What would happen if I didn't answer it?

As I dressed, the phone kept ringing, the shrill metallic noise grinding insistently into my head. In the hallway outside my bedroom door, Buster began to bark, a deep relentless howl. Finally, I tore open the closet, grabbed the phone, and flung it onto the bed where it bounced, sending the handset flying off the cradle. Eerily, it continued to ring.

I grabbed the receiver and pressed it to my ear. "Hello?" I feared no one would answer, but worse, I dreaded someone *would*. At first all I could make out was static, then faintly, as though from a great distance, I heard a man's voice. Holding my breath, I strained to distinguish his words from the popping and crackling in the background.

"Hello," I said again into the mouthpiece. "I can't hear you. There's too much interference." My hands trembled as I gripped the handset, but after a moment the sound diminished and the phone went dead.

I hung up and sank down on the edge of the bed, pressing my fingers to my face as my knees jittered beneath me. I had no more doubts—*the phone was haunted*. What other explanation could there be?

I gulped and tried to think. The phone had belonged to Kayla's father. Was his spirit trying to make contact? But why? Why hadn't it crossed over? Had something important been left undone or unsaid?

My friend Tamara had once told me that her grandfather's ghost came back to tell his widow where he'd hidden some money, a secret stash no one else had known about. And Hannah's spirit had lingered for years until her killer was found and her body recovered.

But Kayla's father had died in an accident; there were no suspicious circumstances. He'd been fishing alone on a small lake in his canoe like he'd done a hundred times. The boat had tipped over and he'd fallen into the freezing water. Hikers had discovered his body, as well as the overturned canoe floating in a mess of cattails by the shore. The police and coroner had determined the cause of death to be accidental drowning.

My parents were arriving on Wednesday for Thanksgiving, and the craft fair was the week after that. I let out a big sigh. *I don't have time for this.*

Chapter Four

Gage arrived promptly at six. I felt a tickle of pleasure as I opened the door and saw him standing there, an imposing figure silhouetted against the velvety twilight. His casual jeans and leather bomber jacket gave him an air of virile self-assurance. I smiled as I recalled a conversation we'd once had where I'd accused him of being stodgy and conservative.

The corners of his mouth turned up in appreciation as he ran his eye over my pink and blue midi dress. It had a deep v-neck and flared skirt with a flounce that I thought looked ultra-feminine.

"How does Frankie's sound?" he asked. "Or would you rather go someplace fancier?"

"Frankie's is fine." In fact, I had a certain

fondness for the Italian restaurant where we'd had our first date. Red and white checkered table-cloths, red brick walls, and rough hewn beams on the ceiling created just the right mood.

Calling a hasty good-bye to Connie in the kitchen, I pulled a warm coat on over my dress and followed Gage out to his sporty blue SUV. It was Saturday night and Frankie's was buzzing when we got there. After a twenty-minute wait, we were seated at a private table in the corner. I ordered the shrimp scampi with angel hair pasta, and Gage chose the house spaghetti and meatballs.

"So, what have you been up to?" Gage asked. "Still enjoying the new job? You look amazing, by the way."

A warm flush spread over my cheeks. "Thank you. And yes, I love my new job, but it has its quirks. For instance, I am now the official guardian of an eighty-six-year-old lady who lives alone, has raccoons in her attic, and apparently hasn't opened her mail in years."

He crunched on a bread stick. "Fascinating. I assume you mean *actual* raccoons and not some euphemism for..." He twirled a finger beside his head.

I snorted. "Yes, I mean *actual* raccoons. I have to get rid of them before she gets bitten or they destroy her attic. I've got an exterminator coming on Monday to remove them, preferably as far away as possible."

"Uh-huh, and what do you do when you're not harassing raccoons? Sit with the old lady and sip tea while you open her mail?"

"Don't laugh. That's pretty much it. She's got mail piled up all over her house. First thing I did was put her utilities on auto-pay. Luckily, her Social Security check is automatically deposited so she has money in her checking account, but it hasn't been balanced in years. I also discovered she owns some stock because I've found statements and dividend checks lying all over the place. It's going to take me ages to sort through it all."

"At least you won't get bored."

I gave a quick laugh. "No chance of that. What about you? Any plans for Thanksgiving?"

He nodded. "That's why I wanted to see you tonight. Maureen and I have decided to fly to Florida to see our folks. We're leaving for Tampa on Monday. We'll be gone all week."

Gage and Maureen's mother and stepfather had moved to Florida years ago. Since then, they had scarcely set foot back in the state. I knew there was no love lost between Gage and his stepfather, but lately they had called a truce and were trying to make a go of it for Gage's mother's sake.

I kept my eyes on the table. It wouldn't do for him to see my disappointment. I guess in some parallel universe I had envisioned introducing him to my parents.

"That's great," I said, looking up. "Just shows how far Maureen has come. Can you imagine her making the trip a couple of months ago? It'll be good for you both to see your parents, clear the air, make amends."

"Yeah, I guess so. Maureen's looking forward to it. What about you and Connie?"

"My family's arriving from Phoenix on Wednesday. They'll be staying till Saturday."

"That'll be nice..." he caught the look on my face. "Won't it?"

I shrugged. "Yes and no. I haven't seen them in awhile. Not since I found out..."

Gage nodded sagely. "Not since you found out about Bill. Is that going to be a problem?"

"Well, let's see." I pressed my hands together and stared at the ceiling. "Thanksgiving with my mom, her husband, and the guy down the street who got my mom pregnant when she was eighteen, then shirked his duty, pretended to be dead, spent time in prison, and never paid a penny of child support. And on top of all that, throw in my two idiot brothers What could possibly go wrong?"

He laughed. "I see what you mean. So, you invited Bill for dinner?"

"It was actually Connie's idea, but I agreed with her. I thought he should be included in the family. But he's smarter than me and declined the invitation. Instead, he said I should bring my parents over to his place on Friday so he could meet them and say hello."

The waiter brought our orders and we both dug in with relish. Candles on the tables and soft music in the background produced a cozy atmosphere. Sitting here with Gage in this setting gave me a warm, contented feeling. I could feel my resolve against a romantic entanglement slipping.

Twirling pasta on my fork, I said, "You know, as much as I'm looking forward to seeing my family, I'll be glad when Thanksgiving's over and they go back home. I have so much going on right now. The following Saturday is the craft fair, and after that my birthday, and before you know it, it'll be Christmas. Talk about not getting bored."

Gage looked up abruptly, focusing on my face. "What? Wait a minute. Your *birthday?* When?"

"Oops, did I say that out loud?" I sipped my water to keep from breaking into an embarrassing grin. Okay, maybe I'd let it slip accidently on purpose.

"After the craft fair? What date is it? I have dibs on that night."

I raised my eyebrows.

"I mean taking you out. Dinner and a movie or whatever."

"It's the ninth. I'll have to check my appointment calendar to see if I'm free."

He snorted, then his mouth widened in a grin.

Time to switch gears. I thought fast and made a quick decision. "Changing the subject, our office is probating the will of one of our clients who died recently, drowned when he fell out of his canoe while fishing alone on a deserted lake."

"Sorry to hear it," he said.

"I've been helping his daughter navigate the rigors of settling the estate, and she gave me a thank-you gift."

"That was nice. Do all your clients give you presents?"

"Not usually, but I went a little above and beyond in this case. Turns out we knew each other from when I worked at Connie's flower shop. She and her husband own the bakery-slash-coffee shop next door. I used to go over there on my breaks all the time. She remembered me and we just sort of clicked. I went to her house for lunch yesterday to give her some advice, then helped her get started organizing her father's papers."

"Great. So, what'd she give you?"

I poked at a piece of shrimp on my plate with studied nonchalance. "A vintage telephone. One of those old rotary dial desk phones from the 1950s. It's pretty cool-looking."

His mouth twitched in amusement. "Uh-huh. What are you going to do with it?"

"I don't know yet. It has one major flaw."

"What's that?"

I leaned toward him. "It's haunted."

Gage nearly choked on his spaghetti. He stared at me like a second nose had sprung from the middle of my forehead. Then he glanced around to see if anyone had heard. The neighboring tables were full of chatty patrons, deeply absorbed in their own conversations; no one showed us the least bit of interest.

He took a deep breath and blew it out again. "I'm probably going to regret this," he said, keeping his voice low, "but what makes you think it's haunted?"

"Because it's not hooked up, and it rings all by itself." He opened his mouth to say something, but I cut him off. "Don't say it's because it got jostled. It wasn't bumped, kicked, shaken, or stirred. The last time it rang, it was sitting on the floor in my closet. When I answered it, I swear I heard a man's voice, very faintly, through a lot of background noise, like static."

His expression sobered. "What did he say?"

"I couldn't make it out."

Gage leaned back in his chair and drained his glass of beer.

"Do you believe me?" I asked.

He put the glass down. "Honestly, Brenna, I don't know. I believe you think you heard a voice, but whether it was a ghost..." He expelled a breath. "I'm just trying to keep an open mind, okay?"

That was probably the best I could expect. "I think I need to talk to Kayla, the daughter of the man who died—it was *his* phone."

"You think that's a good idea? She's likely to think you're crazy. You don't want that getting back to your boss."

He had a point.

"What do *you* think I should do?" I asked.

He gave a short laugh. "I don't know. Bury the thing in the back yard? No, scratch that. Just give it back. Tell her...tell her you've got no place to put it. Let *her* deal with it."

"Yeah, I know—but I can't shake the feeling that this ghost has something important to say."

"But why does it have to be you? Why not the daughter? Wouldn't it rather speak directly to her, anyway?" He glanced around again and muttered, "I can't believe we're having this conversation."

I gave him a pointed look. "What if Kayla can't hear it? Not everyone is open to listening to ghosts, as you well know."

It had taken years to get Gage to finally acknowledge the presence of his little sister's ghost.

Even now, after seeing with his own eyes, he resisted the notion of spirits communicating with the living.

He frowned and leaned across the table. "You didn't know this guy, did you? I thought you told me you had to have a connection with the dead person, like you had with Hannah?"

"Could be I was wrong. I don't know. But I *do* know Kayla, *and* I have an open mind. I'm willing to listen. Maybe that's all it takes."

The look on his face was skeptical, concerned.

"Don't worry," I said. "I won't say anything to her until I feel her out, find out how broad-minded she is."

Gage sighed and wadded up his napkin. "Just be careful. Now, it's getting late. We should go. I've got to get home and start packing."

He drove me home and walked me to the front porch. When I started to thank him for the evening, he took my hand and drew me close, placing a warm kiss on my lips. The night was wet and cold, but I didn't notice. His nearness provided more than enough heat.

"Have a nice Thanksgiving," he murmured in my ear. "Enjoy the time with your family. Don't let it stress you out."

"You too," I whispered back.

I watched as he trotted down the steps toward his car. When I went inside, I was greeted by a capering beagle.

———

Later, I sat in my room chewing over my conversation with Gage. Connie was in the living room watching TV as usual. I told her I still had work to do on the box of papers I'd brought home, but in truth, I just wanted to be alone to think.

Gage still balked at the thought of ghosts, even after all we'd been through. I needed to talk to someone who wouldn't dismiss the notion of a haunted telephone, someone who wouldn't automatically think the idea was crazy. Besides Maureen, there was my friend Tamara.

Suddenly, the telephone in the closet began to ring. Taken off guard, I hesitated, gritting my teeth. But the last thing I needed was for Connie to hear and come in asking questions. Somehow, I couldn't picture having a rational discussion with her on the existence of ghosts, let alone haunted antiques, and I wasn't in the mood to handle more skepticism. So I jumped up and flung open the closet door, grabbing the receiver and pressing it to my ear.

"Hello?" As expected, I got an earful of static and unintelligible mumbling. The hissing and popping grew louder until finally the voice faded and the receiver went dead.

I stared at the device in my hand. The ghost was obviously trying to tell me something—but what? A sudden spasm of goosebumps ran up my arms. Maybe Gage was right. I should give the phone back to Kayla and be done with it. I replaced it in the closet and pushed it way to the back, smothering it with a pillow off the bed.

It was just past nine o'clock; Tamara was

probably still up. I knew she didn't work on Sundays, so I grabbed my cell and sent her a text: *Free tomorrow? Need to talk.*

Ten minutes later, my phone's familiar *cock-a-doodle-do* announced her reply: *Sure. Where and when?*

We settled on brunch at a favorite café midway between downtown and Shoreline, then I set my cell phone on its charger and went to join Connie in front of the TV.

———

"A haunted telephone?" Tamara's smooth brown face broke into a grin as she covered her pancakes with boysenberry syrup. She looked chic as usual in a flaming orange off-shoulder tunic embellished with a rope of turquoise beads. Her mass of dark hair was held back with a matching satin headband. I felt very plain in my blue sweater and jeans.

"The guy who owned it just died," I said. "My office is probating his will. His daughter is a friend of mine. I met her when I worked at the flower shop. She gave me the phone as a sort of thank-you for helping her deal with her dad's estate. It's one of those old black 1950's rotary dial desk phones."

Her eyes sparked with interest. "Cool."

I gave a wry scoff. "That's not the word I'd use. It's creepy—and it rings at the most inopportune times."

She grinned. "I saw one in a magazine once

that had been made into a candle holder. It was very retro."

"I'm sure it was, but *this* one has a ghost living in it. It's got to be the guy who just died. I think he's somehow trying to use it to communicate. It was his old phone. According to his daughter, it sat on his desk for years."

"Like I said, *cool*. So, what does he say?"

I loved how Tamara just accepted my statement that the phone was haunted. No questions, no cynicism, no eye rolling.

"I can't make it out. There's definitely a man's voice, but it's drowned out by a lot of noisy interference."

"So you don't know what he wants."

"Huh-uh. Could be anything."

Tamara chewed a bite of pancake and looked thoughtful. "Have you asked the dead guy's daughter? The one who gave it to you? She might have an idea."

"Right. And how am I supposed to do that?" I grimaced. "I can't very well tell her there's a ghost in the phone she gave me, and I think it might be her father."

"Why not?"

"Seriously? Her father just died, she's in mourning. It would be tactless, not to mention shocking. And remember, I work for the law firm handling her father's Last Will and Testament. I'm supposed to be all levelheaded and professional. The last thing I need is for her to think I'm deranged and not fit to handle her legal affairs. What if she tells my boss? I can't have it getting around that I'm some sort of nut job."

She laughed, then pulled a questioning face. "Okay, so what's your plan?"

"I don't know, just give the phone back, I guess."

"If you've already decided that," Tamara said, "why'd you call me?"

I shrugged and poked at my omelet. "I don't know. I just wanted to talk to somebody who doesn't think I'm crazy."

She smirked. "Oh, I think you're crazy all right."

"Thanks a lot."

"I suppose this means you don't want to hear my other brilliant idea."

I lifted an eyebrow. "Go ahead, hit me."

She put down her fork and leaned toward me, her dark eyes brimming with excitement. "We should hold a séance!"

Chapter Five

When I got home, I parked my car on the gravel margin along the fence and hurried next door to Morelands'. I wanted to wish Maureen a happy Thanksgiving, and congratulate her on the progress she'd made overcoming the debilitating agoraphobia that had kept her a prisoner in her home for so long. The upcoming trip to visit her parents was a real milestone.

Maureen greeted me with an exuberant smile. After the trauma she'd endured, I was thrilled to see her looking so cheerful. Of course, much of the credit was due to her budding romance with Nick Donato across the street, as well as her growing fondness for his two lively little girls.

"Come in," she said, "it's so nice to see you."

I gave her a warm hug. "Gage tells me you're

leaving for Tampa tomorrow. I wanted to wish you a happy Turkey Day and *bon voyage*."

"Thanks," she said. "I'm excited, but also scared to death." She sucked air in through her teeth and gave a couple of little bounces on the balls of her feet.

"Don't worry," I said, "you'll be fine. Just focus on having a good time and re-connecting with your parents."

She took a deep breath and blew it out slowly. "I'm trying."

"You'll have a lot to talk about," I said.

She gave me a wry smile. "That's for sure." Then she brightened and said, "Gage tells me your parents are coming from Phoenix on Wednesday. That's wonderful, but I'm sorry I'll miss your mother. It's been ages since I've seen her."

"I can't wait to show her the rag rugs you've been helping me make," I said. "She'll be so pleased someone is following in Grandma's footsteps, keeping those old skills alive."

The rest of the afternoon I spent at home with Connie preparing for Thanksgiving. I had to admit our housekeeping had gotten a bit lax lately and the place was overdue for a good tidying up, but apparently out-of-state guests, even family, qualified as a state of emergency, calling for extraordinary measures.

Connie went into panic-mode. She became obsessed with dusting, vacuuming, and disposing of clutter, while the task of scrubbing the kitchen and bathroom fell to me. Even Buster was forced to submit to a bath.

I filled the bathtub with about four inches of water then plunked the whining, protesting beagle into it and lathered him up with sweet-smelling doggy shampoo. He seemed to enjoy the brisk rubdown as I scrubbed him from head to tail, but he was less enthusiastic about the rinsing I gave him with the hand-held shower wand. He kept pulling away, shaking and drenching me while throwing soapy water all over the walls. *People do this for a living?* I sent silent kudos out to all professional dog groomers.

Later, as I picked clumps of beagle hair out of the bathtub drain, my mind turned to Tamara's suggestion that we hold a séance to communicate with the ghost in the old telephone. The idea sounded so ridiculous—like something out of a cheesy old horror movie—I had a hard time taking it seriously.

I remembered in sixth grade, my friend Heather Anderson had had a slumber party where we'd tried having a séance. As eleven-year-old girls, we'd gotten a delicious thrill out of sitting around her kitchen table in our pajamas at midnight with the lights turned off. A single candle in the center of our circle had created an air of spookiness that had set us all to giggling and shrieking every time it flickered. We had scared ourselves silly, but never did manage to raise a ghost.

By the end of the day, tired and sweaty, Connie declared the house clean enough. We took turns in the shower, then collapsed in front of a brainless sitcom on TV. Connie was drowsing when the faint jangle of a telephone wafted from the direction of my bedroom. She looked up, bleary-eyed. "Do you hear that?"

"Um, hear what?" I said, nerves on edge.

She gazed around. "Sounds like a phone's ringing."

"Oh, *that*—it's on the TV." I slumped down and made a deliberate show of ignoring it. After several more rings, the phone went silent.

"Huh," Connie said and closed her eyes. "I would've sworn it was in the next room."

———————

Nine o'clock Monday morning I was back at Norma Hansen's. She welcomed me with her usual good humor and offered to make a pot of tea.

"Let's hold off on the tea for now," I said. "The exterminators will be here in a few minutes."

She frowned. "Exterminators?"

"To get the raccoons out of your attic. Remember?"

"Oh yes, of course," she said in her soft quavery voice, "the raccoons."

I donned an expression that I hoped was both firm and sympathetic. "Don't worry, they won't be harmed, but we want to encourage them to leave the neighborhood and go back to the woods where they belong. They'll be much safer there, away from cars and dogs."

A few minutes later, a knock at the front door

announced the exterminators' arrival. The team consisted of a man and woman in boots and coveralls. I explained the situation and they nodded like they'd heard it all before.

"First," the man said, "we'll have a look around and see if we can find where they're getting in. Fortunately, there shouldn't be any new babies this time of year, so we can simply remove them and block up the hole." He caught the look on Norma's face. "Don't worry, I promise we won't hurt them. The traps we use are very humane. And once they're out, there are things you can do to discourage them from coming back: motion sensor lights, smelly rags, even a radio kept on in the attic. Basically, the idea is to make it uncomfortable for them to live there. You want to convince them to go someplace else."

"And you'll clean up any mess they've made in the attic?" I said.

He nodded. "Yep. Once we've trapped them, we'll clear out the nest and remove the droppings, then sanitize and put down new insulation if necessary."

Norma directed them to the attic access in the garage, then I sat with her in the living room while the two got busy. We could hear them scraping and knocking about overhead. With each bump, the elderly woman scanned the ceiling, fingertips touching her lips.

"They seem nice," I said with a reassuring smile. "I'm sure they know what they're doing."

She just nodded and sat wringing her hands in her lap.

"I have an idea," I said. "After they leave, why don't we take a little drive, maybe go out and get a treat. I know a nice coffee shop near here that has wonderful pastries."

Her face lit up. "I'd like that. I haven't been out of the house in ages."

"How long have you lived here, Norma?"

"Oh, a long time. Carl and I moved here from Michigan nearly forty years ago."

While she talked, I took the opportunity to fill two boxes with more of the unopened mail from the piles stashed around the living room. An hour and a half later, the woman exterminator came to inform us that they had finished for the day.

"Looks like you've got three coons," she said. "Probably two adult females and a young one. Looks like they've been getting in through a hole in the fascia board under the eaves on the north side. When they heard us coming, they took off running. So we put three live traps in the attic baited with cat food. Once we catch them, we'll block the hole and seal the attic. Then there's quite a mess up there that will need cleaning. We'll be back in the morning to check the traps."

Norma stood by and listened while I thanked the woman and assured her I would be here again in the morning. Just then, her partner came in holding out two earthenware bowls.

"I found these on the back porch," he said. "Somebody's been putting out food." He cast an accusing glance at Norma.

I tilted an eyebrow in the old woman's direction. "And that's going to stop right now. No more feeding the raccoons, Norma. It's important." I was fond of the lady—she reminded me in many ways of my grandmother—and I didn't want her getting sick or hurt.

She sighed and gave a contrite little nod.

The exterminators left, and fifteen minutes later we were in my car headed for Kayla Donnelly's bakery and coffee shop. I hoped the outing would be a pleasant distraction to get Norma's mind off the raccoons.

By the time we arrived it was mid-morning and the early rush was over. For the moment, we were the only customers in the place. Leaning on her cane, the eighty-six-year-old worked her way to a small table in a corner by the window. I pulled the chair out and helped her get settled.

Kayla hurried to greet us. Her face was flushed and her words spilled out a mile a minute. "Brenna, I'm so glad to see you. I've been dying to tell you what happened Saturday night."

"You'll have to excuse her." A man's voice came from behind the counter. Kayla's husband, garbed in hair net and white apron, was busy arranging chocolate éclairs on a tray in the glass display case. "She's been a basket case all morning."

"Hi, James," I said.

"I'm sorry," Kayla said. "James is right—don't mind me, I'm totally messed up. What can I get you?"

I turned to my elderly companion. "Norma, this is my friend Kayla. She isn't always this flustered. She's usually a very capable barista."

"Nice to meet you, Norma," Kayla said with an

apologetic smile, smoothing the front of her pink gingham apron. The words, *The Good Stuff*, were embroidered across the front.

"Would you like an espresso?" I asked. "Or do you prefer tea? And maybe a donut or a scone? My treat."

"I'll have some tea," Norma said, then peered toward the display case, "and one of those."

"Sounds good." I aimed a nod at Kayla. "Tea and an éclair for each of us."

Once we were settled, Kayla pulled a chair over. "Okay if I join you? I've got to tell you what happened on Saturday."

I glanced at Norma. She smiled assent, then gave her tea a sip.

"Sure," I said to Kayla. "Tell us what happened."

She leaned forward, eyes wide. "My dad's house was broken into! It was so scary."

"Oh, my god," I said.

"His office downstairs was completely ransacked. The desk, the filing cabinets, the bookshelves—everything was on the floor. I spent all day yesterday cleaning it up, putting the books back on the shelves..."

"Where was your father?" Norma asked with concern.

I turned to her and explained. "Kayla's father passed away recently. She's been sorting through his things, dealing with the estate."

Kayla said, "Luckily, thanks to Brenna, I'd already removed most of the important papers I needed."

The old woman murmured sympathetically and reached across the table, touching Kayla's hand. "I'm so sorry, dear."

Kayla smiled at her and took a steadying breath.

"Was anything taken?" I asked.

"Not that I could tell," Kayla said. "But everything was such a mess."

"Sounds like they were looking for something."

"I know, but what? It doesn't make sense. My dad didn't have any money. I just went over there to pick up a couple of things. We'd given him this nice espresso machine for his birthday—it was still practically new—so I thought we might as well take it back, right? But then I went inside and I could hear someone in the basement, shuffling around, moving things—"

"You mean he was inside the house while you were there?"

"Yeah, so I yelled *get out of here, I'm calling the police!*"

"Geez, Kayla, you're lucky he didn't come upstairs. You could have been in real danger."

"I know, it was stupid, but it must have scared him because there was a crash like he dropped something, and then I heard the basement door slam."

"You did call the police though, didn't you?" I said.

"Of course. But before they even got there, the neighbor—Arthur Bailey, remember him?—he showed up to see if I was all right. He said he'd seen a light moving in the basement—like maybe a flashlight—and then he saw my car pull up, and a few minutes later he said he thought he saw someone running away."

"Did he see who it was?"

"No, it was too dark."

"It was nice of him to check on you."

"Yeah, that's what I thought too, at first. But it turns out all he was really interested in was my dad's stamp collection. He wanted to know if I'd found it yet."

I gave a humorless laugh. "Maybe he was afraid that if something happened to you, he'd never get his hands on it."

Kayla exhaled through her teeth. "Yeah, that stupid stamp collection. I wish I knew why he wants it so bad. I'm starting to wonder if it's really valuable. Maybe that's what the burglar was after. Trouble is, I don't know where it is. I looked through Dad's dresser, his desk, all the book shelves..."

Norma spoke up then. "Does your father have a safe? That's probably where he'd keep it if it were valuable."

Kayla's forehead furrowed as she concentrated. After a moment, her face lit up. "Of course, now that you mention it—there's a small safe on the floor in the back of his closet. I forgot all about it. He bought it years ago at a government surplus auction. I didn't think he ever actually used it."

"It might be worth checking out," I said.

We were interrupted when a couple came into the shop and ordered caffè lattes and pastries to go.

Kayla jumped up to wait on them while Norma and I finished our tea and éclairs. Morning was slipping away and I was getting antsy to leave. There was a pile of work waiting for me at the office, and this was a short week.

But once the customers were out the door, Kayla hurried back, eager to resume our conversation. "I've been thinking about that safe," she said. "How do I get it open? I don't know the combination."

"Well, most people use numbers they can easily remember," I said, "like birthdays or anniversaries."

"There's always dynamite," piped up James from behind the counter.

"You're not helping," Kayla fired back.

"What's your mother's name?" Norma asked.

The question was unexpected, and we all turned to look at the elderly woman.

"Mary," Kayla said. "Why? She passed away a long time ago."

"But she was important to your father, wasn't she? What was her full name?"

"Mary Winifred Glassner," Kayla said, "but what's that got to do with anything?"

Norma's aged brow knit as she repeated the words. "Mary Winifred Glassner: M, W, G. What a fortunate name. M is the thirteenth letter of the alphabet, and G is the seventh: 13 and 7—two powerful numbers."

"I thought 13 was unlucky," I said.

The old woman shook her head. "In some cultures, maybe. But in truth, no number should be singled out as lucky or unlucky. Each has its own strengths. And 13 is a composite number, containing elements of the numbers 1 and 3, which, when added together, result in the number 4. It can represent pragmatism, focus, and creative self expression."

"Oh, come on," Kayla said. "That's just superstition."

Norma continued, unfazed. "And W is the twenty-third letter, my personal favorite. The number 23 signifies harmony, creativity, and abundance. And as a random number, 23 turns up more frequently than any other, did you know that? Why don't you try using those three numbers? Thirteen, twenty-three, seven."

Kayla laughed. "Sounds like a stretch, but I'll give it a shot."

I stood up then and put on my coat. "It's getting late, I think we should be going. Come on, Norma. Sadly, my boss does expect me to occasionally show up at the office. See you later, Kayla. Let me know how things go, okay? And don't go back to your dad's house alone. If that robber was looking for something and didn't find it, there's a chance he might return."

"I'm not too worried. The police didn't make much of it. They figured it was just kids." She sighed and gave a shrug. "Empty houses can be kind of a target, I guess."

On the drive back to Norma's house, I took the opportunity to question her further. "Norma, I'm curious. Where'd you get the idea to change the first letters of Kayla's mother's name to numbers?"

The old woman's laugh was soft and throaty. "I guess you could say I'm an amateur numerologist. I look for numbers in everything. I believe numbers possess a lot more meaning than most people realize."

I gave her a sideways look. "I know lots of people believe certain numbers are lucky or unlucky, but that's just superstition."

She smiled. "Think about it. What's more consistently logical in this world than numbers."

"Let me guess, you used to be a math teacher or an accountant."

"Far from it," she said, shaking her head. "Actually, I was a librarian for many years."

"Ahh, so your love of numbers started with good ol' Dewey Decimal."

She laughed again. "No, credit for that has to go to my husband. Carl was passionate about numbers. He thought they influenced every part of our lives. He was a big believer in the existence of realities beyond our perception. But then, his mother was something of a mystic, a proponent of spiritualism, so you might say he was raised in a rather unconventional way."

"Spiritualism?" An icy tingle rippled up my spine. This was definitely beyond mere superstition.

Norma nodded. "The belief in spirits and the ability to communicate with them. Carl's mother was a medium—so was his grandmother. They used to hold séances in the parlor, usually for grieving widows, calling up the spirits of fallen soldiers after the world wars." She put up a knobby hand. "Oh, I know, you probably think I'm crazy, and believe me, I was a skeptic too at first, but over time, I became convinced. I saw things that would make your hair stand up. Carl's mother often used a Spirit Board. Do you know what that is? You might have heard them called Ouija Boards."

"I've heard of Ouija Boards, but I've never seen one." This whole conversation had veered off in a very bizarre direction. There was a lot more to this sweet, grandmotherly old woman than I ever would have imagined. *I wonder what she'd make of a haunted telephone.*

"Carl's mother left me hers when she passed," Norma said. "I'll have to show it to you some time. Spirit Boards were very popular a hundred years ago, but nowadays people lump them in with the occult. They say they're evil, a tool of the devil or some such twaddle."

"I suppose all the horror movies of the last century didn't help," I said, offering a crooked smile.

The old woman gave a snort of contempt. "Stuff and nonsense."

Parking the car in her driveway, I turned to look the old woman in the face. Her striking jade-colored eyes were clear and bright. I no longer saw her as doddering, but instead as someone who had lived an interesting life and knew her own mind.

"I feel like I've come to know you a lot better today," I said, "and in some ways, I think we may be kindred spirits." Should I tell her I believed in ghosts, had seen one, talked to one? Maybe, but not yet.

She smiled. "Thank you, dear. I feel the same."

"Would you mind if I asked you a personal question?"

"No, go right ahead." She gave her head a curious tilt.

"You seem like a smart lady. Why do you need me? I get the impression you'd be perfectly capable of managing your own affairs if you wanted to."

"Thank you, Brenna, it's sweet of you to say so. But the simple fact is, I find all that paperwork tedious. Most of the mail I get these days is junk anyway. I'm eighty-six years old and I just can't see wasting a precious moment on things that don't make me happy."

"But I thought you liked numbers," I said.

She sniffed. "Don't confuse my appreciation for the mystic power of numbers with mundane bookkeeping. Actually, it was Carl who really enjoyed working with numbers and managing finances. He was quite good at it. He played the stock market and made all sorts of lucrative investments. He always said we had plenty of money and I would never have to worry after he was gone." She reached over and laid a hand on my knee, her face breaking into a blissful smile. "I feel his presence with me all the time, you know, watching over me. I often hear his spirit at night, roaming the house, and it gives me comfort."

Oh, geez, I thought, *I hope it's not the raccoons.* Then I smiled. She called me Brenna.

Chapter Six

When I got to the office, I set to work transcribing some correspondence Mr. Cavendish had dictated, letters to clients regarding cases we were currently handling. The attorney himself was in court and not expected back till later in the afternoon.

Around three o'clock, Kayla called. "Brenna, help...I need some advice. Mr. Thurmond's been pestering me to sell him my half of the garden store. He just called and offered me a hundred thousand dollars in cash. That's an awful lot of money. James thinks we should take it. What do you think? Is that a good deal?"

"Kayla, I can't answer that. I have no idea what the business is worth. You need to get an appraisal."

"How do I do that? Can you recommend somebody?"

"Sure," I said, "I'll text you the names of a couple appraisers Mr. Cavendish has used before. Once you have the appraisal, you'll be in a better position to negotiate. Mr. Cavendish can help you with that too." I hoped Mr. Thurmond wasn't in too big a hurry. With the holidays approaching, there was no telling how long an appraisal might take. It would just depend on how busy everyone's schedules were.

It was nearly five by the time Mr. Cavendish made it into the office. He flipped through the mail, listened to his messages, and signed the letters I had printed out for him. We spent a few minutes discussing cases, and just before I left, I reminded him that I had one more late morning at Norma Hansen's scheduled for tomorrow.

"Hopefully, by then the raccoons will be captured and removed," I said. "The exterminators said they would patch the hole in the fascia and seal up the attic so nothing else can get in, but then there will be the added expense of cleaning up the mess the raccoons made."

The lines on the lawyer's face deepened as he grimaced. "Yeah, nothing like the aroma of raccoon filth to spoil your day. Do what you've got to do, and come in when you can. Tomorrow we'll be busy tying up loose ends before the holiday. I know you're picking up your parents at the airport on Wednesday which won't be a problem since we're planning to close early that day anyway. Then, of course, we'll be closed Thursday and Friday."

All the way home, I thought about Mrs. Hansen and her belief in numerology and spiritualism. I'd never been superstitious, and I'd never given much credence to mysticism or alternate realities, but I couldn't deny the existence of ghosts. Apparently, spirits whose mortal lives had ended abruptly with business left unfinished, lingered on earth waiting for someone to come along with the ability to communicate with them and help them find peace. To my consternation, I seemed to be one of those people.

The old telephone Kayla had given me which now resided in the back of my closet posed a conundrum. Obviously, it was haunted. By Kayla's father? Probably. But what did he want? How was I supposed to help him? My first ghostly encounter had been with Hannah Moreland, Gage's little sister, who had been my childhood friend. We had had a strong connection, and communication between us had been almost telepathic.

But I had never met Kayla's father, and I'd really only known Kayla for a few months. Even though we'd quickly become friends, it wasn't the sort of bond I'd had with Hannah. Was that why it was so difficult to converse with the ghost in the phone? Did our lack of a personal relationship somehow create interference?

Should I involve Kayla? Tell her that her recently deceased father was trying to communicate through his old office desk phone? What would she say? She was still in mourning, coping with her father's sudden death while struggling to deal with his estate. How would any normal young woman in the twenty-first century react?

I snorted and rubbed my forehead. At the very least, she'd assume I was crazy. Worse, she'd think me deplorable for making such cruel, insensitive assertions in her time of bereavement.

I thought again of Mrs. Hansen and her calm, self-assured acceptance of the supernatural. By the time I got home, I had made a decision.

———

After dinner, I went to my room to call my mother. She confirmed their itinerary and told me they had booked a nice room at a local motel. She asked about renting a car, but I assured her they could use mine while they were here. She said the boys were fine with sleeping in the living room; one would take the couch and the other the floor. I told her I still had sleeping bags from when Jason and I used to go backpacking, so we agreed the sleeping arrangements were sorted to everyone's satisfaction.

"Do the Morelands still live next door?" Mom asked, out of the blue. "I read about their little girl in the news. What a terrible tragedy."

"Mr. and Mrs. Moreland moved to Tampa a few years ago. Their older daughter Maureen lives there now, but she and her brother will be visiting their parents over Thanksgiving so they won't be here."

"Maureen—yes, I remember her," Mom said.

"She used to babysit you when you were little. Her mother and I were friends years ago. Where did you say they moved? Tampa? I ought to send her a card."

"That'd be great, Mom. I'm sure she'd love to hear from you." I wanted to get through this conversation before she started asking questions about Hannah. The case had been resolved, with details widely publicized. It wasn't something I wanted to talk about. "So, it sounds like we're all set," I said. "See you day after tomorrow."

I hung up and set my cell phone on the nightstand, relieved to have that out of the way. Then I got on my knees, took a deep breath, and steeled myself. I pushed open the closet door and pulled the old telephone toward me. I took a quick glance over my shoulder to make sure the bedroom door was closed tight. Connie, as usual, was in the living room watching television.

Sitting cross-legged on the floor, I put the old phone in my lap and studied the bulky black instrument: the rotary dial with its ring of finger holes around a central disk, and the sturdy handset that looked like droopy Mickey Mouse ears. An archaic device, well past its days of usefulness. I could almost imagine a gloomy face looking up at me.

Could I use it to call the ghost of Kayla's father? Would it speak to me if I initiated contact? *Only one way to find out.* Fighting against the trembling that threatened to unnerve me, I picked up the receiver and placed it against my ear. There was static in the background.

"Hello?" I said. "Are you there? I want to help you."

More static. I waited, keeping my breathing shallow, straining to hear.

At last, a man's voice in the background, too faint to make out.

"I can't hear you," I said. "Speak louder. Who are you? Are you Kayla's father?"

The static lessened. The voice sounded hoarse and far away. *"Find the letter."*

My heart lurched. These were the first words I'd been able to hear, but they made no sense to me. Urgently, I gripped the handset and pressed my mouth to the transmitter. "My name is Brenna. I'm Kayla's friend. I want to help you. What letter? Tell me how to find it."

The noise was increasing again, making it hard to hear. *"Find...the...letter."*

"How?" I tried to will the voice louder, but it was weakening. "What letter? Tell me how to find it."

The voice faded into the background as the crackling swelled up and overtook it. With a frustrated growl, I slammed the receiver back into the cradle on top of the phone. I sat and stared at it. What was this mysterious letter? How was I supposed to find it? I felt helpless. Again, I was tempted to simply return the telephone to Kayla. Would she be able to connect with the ghost?

I expelled a deep breath and chewed absently on my lower lip. Experience had taught me that skeptics made bad receptors. But I had one more idea.

"Well, we got them," said the pest removers. "Three raccoons, just as we thought. Two adult females and a young male, this year's kit. We'll take them up in the hills east of here and release them."

I stood with Mrs. Hansen in her living room the next morning while the workers explained the procedure for removing the traps from the attic and relocating the animals, followed by the steps required to patch the hole under the eave. They assured us they'd be out of the house in no more than an hour. After the holiday weekend, they'd be back to remove and replace the soiled insulation in the attic.

The old woman stood quietly listening, her gaze focused out the front window. I hoped she was imagining the raccoons running free, climbing trees in their new home in the wooded hills well away from the city and all its dangers.

"Norma," I said, "why don't we go into the kitchen and have some tea? We don't want to get in the way while they work." I feared that the sight of the animals in cages might upset her.

She nodded, then said, "Come to my room first. I have something to show you."

I followed as she hobbled down the hall, leaning on her cane. I hadn't been in this part of the house, but found it unremarkable with beige walls and dull olive carpet like the rest of the house. The only embellishments were a framed photograph on the wall of an elderly man and another of a smiling family. Her late husband and some other relatives, I presumed.

She pushed open the bedroom door and I stopped, gazing around with my mouth open.

Her room was a feminine sanctum reminiscent of old Hollywood. Lace curtains covered a wide window beneath which stood a round tea table adorned with a floor-length crocheted table scarf. Beside it were two lavish antique chairs with embroidered cushions, and upon the table rested an old-fashioned hurricane lamp with a jeweled shade. Against the opposite wall was an elegantly carved mahogany dresser with a silver candelabrum perched on top. The floor was polished hardwood, partially covered with an elaborate Persian rug. But the focal point of the room was a canopy bed spread with a coverlet of emerald green damask. The spiral corner posts were carved of the same dark wood as the dresser. Gold-flocked wallpaper covered the walls, and a glittering crystal chandelier hung from the ceiling, completing the effect.

"You have an amazing bedroom," I finally managed to say.

"Thank you," Norma said. "Carl always said a woman should have an elegant boudoir. It's taken me years to find just the right pieces."

And you've obviously spared no expense. As her court-appointed legal guardian, I'd spent the last few days slogging through this lady's financials— bank statements, stock certificates, dividend checks, credits and debits—trying to get them all balanced and organized. It occurred to me that Norma probably had more money stashed away than she knew what to do with.

Kudos for spending it on yourself, I thought. *After eighty-six years, you deserve it.*

I grinned. "I hope when I'm your age, I have a room half as nice as this."

She waved her hand in an embarrassed gesture, then tottered over to a large antique steamer trunk sitting on the floor at the end of the bed. Like everything else in the room, the sturdy wooden chest with its curved top and decorative tin embellishments displayed a bit of bygone elegance. Putting aside her cane, she bent and unfastened the latch, lifted the lid, and began rummaging through the contents.

"Ah, yes, here it is," she said, grasping something at the bottom. "My mother-in-law's Spirit Board."

Dislodging countless odds and ends—mementos and collectables, I guessed, accumulated over the years—she pulled out a flat, rectangular piece of wood about sixteen-by-fourteen inches. Closing the trunk, she propped the board on top so that I could get a better look.

In an old-fashioned font, the letters of the alphabet were silk-screened in black ink on the smooth surface in two wide arcs: **A** through **M** on the first line, and **N** through **Z** on the second. Beneath the letters in a straight line were printed the numbers 1 through 0, and in a smaller font across the bottom were the words "GOOD BYE." In the upper left corner was printed a small sun graphic and the word "YES." In the upper right corner was a crescent moon and the word "NO." The whole thing was faded and worn from decades of use.

Everything necessary for the contacting of spirits, I thought with an uneasy gulp. I was starting to feel seriously creeped out.

"Does this really work?" I murmured. *Now who's being a skeptic?*

"In the right hands," Norma said, "with the right mindset. I have seen some amazing results with this Spirit Board."

I dragged my eyes away from the mystical object and fixed them on the elderly woman's face. "And speaking of keeping the right mindset," I said, taking a deep breath, "I've brought something to show you."

The wrinkles in the old woman's forehead deepened as she gazed at me quizzically.

"It's in the car," I said. "Wait here, I'll be right back."

She nodded and took a seat in one of the antique chairs by the window, folding her hands in her lap.

In the garage, at the other end of the house, the exterminators were still busily removing the traps from the attic and carrying the unfortunate raccoons to the back of a large white van parked on the street in front of the house. I acknowledged them with a nod as I opened the back door of my car and reached in for the paper grocery bag I'd stowed there that morning.

Moments later, I was back in Norma's bedroom placing the black Bakelite telephone on the tea table between us. In a breathless rush, I said, "Remember Kayla from the coffee shop? This belonged to her father. She was going to get rid of it along with a bunch of other stuff in his basement, but I told her I thought it was cool—sort of mid-century chic—so she gave it to me."

Norma leaned forward, studying the old phone curiously. "May I?" Without waiting for an answer, she put a finger into one of the holes of the rotary dial and gave it a tentative spin. When she removed her finger, the dial whirred back into place. Her face took on a nostalgic, faraway look. "Oh my, that takes me back," she said.

"I was going to put it on the shelf in my office. It's such a collector's item—" Suddenly I felt awkward. What I saw as an intriguing antique had once been a common household object, a familiar part of this woman's life. The last thing I wanted was to make her feel she was obsolete, or that her memories were no longer relevant.

I cleared my throat. "But when I got it home, it started to ring."

She said nothing, but her green eyes were bright and piercing.

"It wasn't hooked up," I continued. "There's no way it should have rung." I watched for her reaction. Did she truly believe in ghosts, or had she just been embellishing old tales she'd heard the way my grandmother often used to do?

The old woman pressed her palms together and rested them against her lips. Then she tilted her head and looked me in the eye. "Did you answer it?" she asked earnestly. "Was anyone there?"

I realized I'd been holding my breath, expecting her to say I was just imagining things. "I could barely hear," I said, "there was so much interference. But there was a man's voice. He sounded far away. I think it was Kayla's father."

She nodded, looking thoughtful. "Very likely. Could you make out what he said?"

I smiled. "First, I want to thank you for not telling me I'm crazy."

She reached over and gave my hand a grandmotherly pat. "Nothing wrong with being a little crazy, my dear. The world would be an awfully somber place without a little bit of craziness."

I gave a soft laugh, but couldn't help wondering just what she meant. I hoped she wasn't humoring me, playing along for her own amusement.

Before I could say anything, there came a light tapping on the bedroom door. The woman exterminator called out, "We're all done. We're getting ready to leave."

I rose and hurried to the door, meeting her in the hallway. As I escorted the pair to their van, they explained what they had done, how they had nailed a board over the loose fascia, and secured the attic inside from further unwanted visitors. The traps and all their paraphernalia had been removed, but the attic still needed a thorough cleaning which they would come back and tackle after the holiday weekend.

Inside the house, I found my elderly friend in the kitchen putting the tea kettle on the stove to boil. The old black telephone sat on a placemat in the middle of the table.

"I know you have to return to your office soon," she said, "but you surely have time for a quick cup of tea. Besides, you have to finish telling me about your strange phone call." She gave me a serious look and intoned, "I believe you have been contacted by a departed spirit. That is a rare privilege."

"So, you believe me?"

Her eyes widened in surprise. "Of course I do. It's not the sort of thing one makes up, is it? Now, tell me what the voice said."

I dropped into one of the chrome and vinyl kitchen chairs, then I told her what I had heard.

"Hmm...and you don't know what letter he was referring to or why he wants you to find it?

I shook my head.

Norma placed the tea pot on the table, along with cups, the sugar bowl, and a small pitcher of milk. Last, she set down a plate of homemade oatmeal cookies and took the seat facing me.

"Did he say anything else?" she asked.

I poured a cup of tea and stirred in a spoonful of sugar. "No—he probably thinks he's talking to Kayla."

She pursed her lips. "Possibly, or maybe he tried and found her unreceptive. You seem to be more attuned than most people."

Lucky me.

"Would it be possible to ask Kayla about this letter?" Norma continued. "Maybe she knows something about it."

"How would I ask her? 'Received any odd letters

lately?' I can't very well tell her I've been talking to her father's ghost. She really *would* think I'm crazy." I grimaced and shook my head. "No, I have to maintain my credibility. I work for the attorney handling her father's will, remember? Chances are she wouldn't be as understanding as you are. Not many people actually believe in ghosts."

I took an oatmeal cookie and munched on it as I thought about my neighbor Maureen, and how for years people had accused her of being mentally disturbed because she insisted she could see her dead sister's ghost. It wasn't until I had seen the ghost too and convinced Maureen she wasn't insane that she had finally been able to recover and get her life back. Even her brother Gage, who thought maybe, he *might* have seen the ghost—and insisted he was keeping an open mind—still looked askance at me when I mentioned her.

Kayla's bakery café was right next door to Connie's Pretty Petals florist shop. They talked all the time. All I needed was for Kayla to tell my cousin I'd been speaking to ghosts. Next thing I knew, it would get back to my boss, or worse, my *mother*.

I shook my head again. "For now, I want to keep this to myself. I'm hoping to be able to talk to the ghost again, get him to tell me more so I can figure this out myself. I told him I want to help."

Norma looked pensive, her eyes focused somewhere over my shoulder. After a moment, she gave her chin a little rub and swung her gaze back to me. "There's something else we could try."

I raised my eyebrows, inviting her to continue.

"We could use the Spirit Board."

I bit my lip and stifled a groan. "You mean have a séance?" Tamara would jump all over this. A séance had been her idea from the beginning. If I agreed to do this, I would definitely have to include her.

"Let me think about it," I said, feeling suddenly like I was back in the sixth grade.

The old woman nodded. "I think you'd be amazed at how well it works."

I expelled a deep breath. "If we do this, it'll have to be after Thanksgiving. My parents are coming from Phoenix tomorrow and I'm going to be up to my eyeballs."

"Of course, dear. I understand. This is a busy time."

I looked at her with sudden concern. "What about you? Do you have any plans?" I hated the thought of this sweet old lady spending Thanksgiving all alone.

"Oh, yes," she said, waving her hand in the air in a don't-worry-about-me gesture. "The senior center has a big Thanksgiving Day feast planned. They'll probably show a movie, and then we'll play bingo till it's time to come home."

"How will you get there?" *I'm starting to sound like my mother.*

"They have a bus. They'll pick me up and bring me home afterward. You needn't worry, I'll be fine. Now, you'd better head off to your office before they start wondering what happened to you."

I stood and began to gather my things. "I'll call you next week to make a plan."

I smiled encouragement. "You should sleep better now that there are no raccoons living in your attic, scratching and thumping around in the rafters."

She sighed softly and nodded. "Yes, I suppose so."

Chapter Seven

Wednesday morning Kayla called me at the office. "Hey, Brenna, sorry to bother you at work, but I wanted to invite you to a small reception I'm having Saturday afternoon at the coffee shop. I know this is kind of short notice and it's a busy weekend, but I was hoping you might be able to make it. It'll just be a small gathering for a few friends and family, sort of a wake to remember my father."

My first impulse was to decline. I had so much going on right now. My parents were arriving from Phoenix today, and I had to leave soon to go pick them up. Then tomorrow was Thanksgiving, followed by the whole awkward get-together with Bill Prescott. The last thing I needed was another obligation. Besides, spending an afternoon with

Kayla's relatives mourning her father's passing just sounded depressing, not to mention weird since I was convinced he'd been speaking to me through the old antique telephone.

"You know I never met your dad, right?" I said. "He was a client at the office way before I started working here."

"I know, but that doesn't matter. You've been such a good friend lately, helping me wade through all that estate business. I'd really love it if you could come. Connie, too. You wouldn't have to stay long." With a short laugh, she added, "All the free food you can eat."

She sounded almost pleading, and I thought again. She was reaching out, friend to friend, asking for support. How could I refuse? *So much for decompressing after my parents' visit.*

"Sure, I'll be there," I said. "I'm pretty sure Connie's planning to work at the flower shop on Saturday, but I'll let her know. What time? I have to drive my folks to the airport Saturday morning."

"Starts around five. The shop closes at three so that gives me a couple hours to get ready. My daughter Ruby is going to spend the day at a friend's."

"Okay, see you then."

I prepared to hang up the phone, but Kayla wasn't finished.

"Brenna? Just one more thing..."
There's more?

"...I was wondering if you'd mind asking Troy to come."

"Troy? Why don't you ask him yourself? Aren't

you old friends?" He had told me they used to date in high school. It made sense that he would have known Kayla's father.

"Yeah, he was my boyfriend a long time ago. My dad always liked him. They were both into sports so they got along really well. Trouble is, James is kind of jealous..."

"So you need me to call him?" *Because that wouldn't be awkward for me at all.*

"I just thought Troy might like to come and pay his respects."

I opened my mouth to reply, but in a rush she added, "I'm pretty sure he likes you, and I think you kind of like him, so I thought maybe you wouldn't mind asking him to come along as your plus-one?"

Wait a minute. *Is she playing matchmaker?* Troy and I hadn't even had a first date. Sure, I'd thought about it, imagined it, played it out in my head, but to actually make the first move...

"Then if he's with you," Kayla continued, "James can't object."

I swallowed and licked my lips. So, I would be doing her a favor? Put that way... "Okay, I guess I could do that." Then I thought of something else. "Oh, by the way, have you heard any more from the guy who did your dad's roof? You know the weather's only going to be getting worse as we get closer to winter."

I heard her sigh into the phone. "No, I haven't had time to look for that contract."

"That's okay," I said. "Don't worry about it. I know you've been busy."

I left the office at two o'clock and headed straight for the airport to pick up my family. I hoped they hadn't brought a lot of luggage. While my PT Cruiser generally had plenty of room for me and my stuff, this morning I realized with chagrin just how crammed we were going to be.

An hour later I met them at the curb. I hadn't seen my family since I'd gone to Phoenix for Christmas almost a year ago, so their arrival naturally precipitated an onslaught of squeals and crushing embraces. Mom had barely changed, though she had put on a couple of pounds which I thought gave her attractive figure a softer, rounder look consistent with a contented life. I also noticed that her dark brown hair, so like my own, was starting to reveal streaks of gray.

Dennis was a typical middle aged desk jockey: clean-shaven, thinning hair, slightly paunchy. But his average looks were more than made up for by his friendly, outgoing personality, keen sense of humor, and even temper. In my whole life, I had never seen him get riled over anything.

My brothers, Paul and Michael, attired in jeans and Arizona Wildcats hoodies, stood nearby smirking. After submitting to a hug, Paul stood back and eyeballed the purple hatchback with something like amusement mixed with distaste. "Is this your car?"

"Yeah," I said. "Like it?" I swung the rear door up and started loading the luggage. Fortunately, they had packed light; my parents shared an upright rolling suitcase, while the boys each carried a backpack.

My brother gave a derisive snort, making his opinion clear. Muscle cars were more his style. Paul was the family jock: tall, good-looking, and athletic. He'd been a starter on the Wildcats football team for the last two years, but was looking ahead to graduating in the spring with a degree in business. What his plans were after that, I had no idea, but he was plucky and ambitious, and I knew he'd be fine no matter what he did.

Michael smacked his palm on the roof of the car and exclaimed, "Hey, they don't make these anymore. It's practically a collector's item." He turned to me with a grin. "Gotta be twenty years old, am I right?"

Younger than Paul by two years, Michael was shorter and stockier. The more studious of the two, his idea of a team sport was chess club.

I returned the grin. "Yep, same age as you and almost as cute." I reached out and ruffled his hair. I'd been fourteen when he was born and I still thought of him as my baby brother.

"As much fun as this is," Mom interrupted, "we need to get going, it's getting late. Dennis, you sit up front with Brenna and I'll crowd in with the boys in back."

The budget motel was on the highway a couple of miles from Connie's house. Funny that I still couldn't call it *my* house. I was paying rent to my cousin and still considered the situation temporary. My eventual plan was to get a place of my own now that my condo downtown had sold. But with starting a new job and the holiday season approaching, the thought of house hunting was daunting.

I pulled up in front of the motel office and Dad went inside to check in. A large three-story affair with a covered drive-through, large windows, and attractive landscaping, the overall façade was modern and inviting. A few minutes later he came back bearing the key.

He handed it to me and said, "Why don't you guys go open up the room while I move the car."

"Okay," I said. "See you in a few minutes." I unloaded the suitcase, the boys grabbed their backpacks, and we headed inside.

The third floor room was clean and well-appointed, with a queen-size bed facing a wide TV on the wall above a sleek wooden dresser. In one corner sat a mini-fridge along with a table holding a coffee pot and all the accoutrements. Paul and Michael made a point of trying out the mattress by whooping and throwing themselves onto the bed. Mom rolled her eyes and went into the bathroom to freshen up.

I shook my head and drilled my brothers with a sisterly look of mock disapproval. "I see you boys haven't let the rigors of academia alter your intrinsic puerile behavior."

Paul propped himself on his elbows. "Say *what?*"

"I mean," I said, fighting to keep a straight face, "I see that you haven't allowed yourselves to become ruled by the dictates of conventional decorum."

He stared back, his mouth slack.

"She means we're immature," Michael supplied

matter-of-factly.

"Ahh," Paul said, addressing his brother. "Why didn't she just say that?"

"She works for an attorney," Michael replied with a shrug. "That's how they talk."

Paul gave a nod. "She's *right*, you know. We *are* immature."

"Certainly. And proud of it."

Their faces broke into impish grins reminding me of the little boys they had been not so long ago.

I gave a snort and crooked my mouth in a benevolent smile. "You guys are such dorks."

Paul turned to Michael with a serious expression. "I think she's calling us dorks."

I was about to deliver a snappy comeback when the door swung open and Dad sauntered in. He glanced around and nodded. "Nice room. All set?"

Mom came out of the bathroom then, one eyebrow lifted slightly, looking from me to my brothers. "If you children are finished getting reacquainted, we should be going."

I turned to her with an expression of total innocence. "Yes, absolutely. We should be going. Connie will be expecting us for dinner."

Indeed, I knew that Connie had prepared an elaborate feast of pot roast and onions with potatoes and carrots. She had gotten up early that morning and loaded everything in the slow cooker to simmer all day. Left to me, dinner would probably have consisted of pizza or Chinese take-out.

When we walked into the house, Buster ran around eagerly from person to person, barking and howling for attention. Paul and Michael were happy to oblige, lavishing the playful hound with rubs and pats, and throwing toys across the room for him to chase.

Connie emerged from the kitchen and my mom rushed to give her a hug. "Connie," she said, "it's so wonderful to see you. It's been *ages*. How's your mom? I haven't seen her since your folks moved to Sacramento. Do they like it there?"

Connie's mother was my mom's older sister. Like my mom, Aunt Peggy had grown up in this house. She and Uncle Frank had lived in the Seattle area until a year ago when they had been lured away by California's drier climate.

"Yeah, they love it there," Connie said, straightening her glasses. "They just bought an older home somewhere in the hills that they want to renovate." She shook her head. "Sounds like a huge project. I don't know when they're going to find the time. Mom just got a job at a dentist's office doing bookkeeping or something."

My mother responded with a grin. "Oh, I'm sure they'll find a way. Peggy can be pretty determined once she's made up her mind to do something." Then she stepped back and looked around, taking in the ambiance of the well-worn room. "And speaking of older homes..."

"Yeah, I know," Connie broke in. "This place could use a bit of renovation."

"No," Mom shook her head. "I was going to say how glad I am that you girls are living here, how well you've kept the house up and retained all the wonderful mid-century charm. Your grandmother would be so pleased. She loved this house. It's been in the family for a long time, and has always been such a happy place."

Connie smiled and nodded agreement. "Brenna and I practically grew up here, we spent so much time visiting every summer." She turned to me. "Remember when we built a fort in the back yard out of sheets and cardboard boxes? We were going to sleep out there. We took pillows and blankets—"

"Uh-huh," I said, "and as soon as it got dark, we got scared and ran back inside."

Mom laughed, then ran a critical eye around the living room. "You know, I don't think Grandma would mind if you wanted to replace the carpet. It's been pretty well used over the last fifty years. I can hardly believe it's still holding up so well."

Oh no, I thought with an inner groan, here comes the "Brenna spilled chocolate milk on the rug" story.

I tried not to roll my eyes as my mother began recounting old stories we'd all heard a hundred times before. My brothers, of course, were highly amused by the retelling of the time I ran naked out the front door after a bath. The fact that I was three years old at the time did nothing to diminish their hilarity. Connie managed to insert a few tales of her own while my stepdad stood by, chuckling softly when appropriate. At one point, he caught my eye and gave me a sympathetic smile.

After a while, Connie excused herself and disappeared once more into the kitchen. I could tell Paul and Michael were losing interest when they started edging toward the living room, cell phones in hand.

Mom took Dennis and starting showing him around the house. I was just thinking I should go help Connie when my mom turned and asked, "Brenna, do you mind if we poke our heads into your room for a second? I want to show Dad my old bedroom."

I gulped, suddenly unable to breathe. *My room? The room with a haunted telephone stashed in the closet?* What if the ghost chooses that moment to call?

They stood in the hallway waiting for my answer. I couldn't very well refuse.

I swallowed and licked my lips. "Sure Mom, go ahead." I gave a stuttering little laugh. "Just don't look in the closet, it's a disaster."

Fortunately, Connie saved the day.

"Dinner," she hollered. "Everyone come and eat."

Mom pushed open the bedroom door and Dad took a quick peek around. Then they turned and joined Paul and Michael at Grandma's old wooden table in the dining room. Breathing again, I hurried to help Connie carry dishes of hot food, taking care not to trip over Buster. The beagle ran back and forth, tail wagging furiously, hoping some morsel would find its way to the floor.

"I didn't have time to bake bread this morning," Connie said as she set a plate of warm rolls in the middle of the table. "I'm afraid we'll have to make do with store-bought."

"Oh, Connie, don't be silly," my mother said. "This is all just wonderful. You shouldn't have gone to so much trouble. We would have been perfectly happy with pizza."

Mom and I still have a lot in common.

I set the platter of savory meat next to Dad's elbow and he helped himself to a huge portion. Passing the plate to Mom, he murmured, "Speak for yourself. I'll take pot roast over pizza any day."

He shot a look at his sons. Paul and Michael immediately erupted with enthusiastic agreement and boisterous thanks. I suspected they had been coached before the trip.

Connie gave a dismissive laugh and waved a hand in the air. "Really, this was no trouble. I just threw everything in the crock pot this morning and it took care of itself."

"If you think this is good," I said to my stepfather. "Wait till you see what Connie's got up her sleeve for tomorrow. Nobody does Thanksgiving dinner like she does. Connie's a true master."

Connie's cheeks pinked prettily as she demurred. She loved cooking for people. She owned a successful florist shop, but she could just as easily have run a restaurant.

"Grandma would have been so proud of you girls," my mother said, looking at each of us in turn.

Suddenly I felt sentimental and choked up. I cleared my throat. "Speaking of Grandma, I've been learning how to make rag rugs like she used to do. I found out that she taught Maureen Moreland next door how to do it, and Maureen's been teaching me."

"You're doing something crafty?" Michael piped up. "Will wonders never cease?"

"Well, it is *rags*," Paul said reasonably. "Makes perfect sense."

"Hush," said Mom, frowning in his direction. She looked at me again. "Honey, that's wonderful."

I nearly stuck my tongue out at my brothers, then remembered in time that I was the mature, sensible big sister who couldn't be dragged down to their level. Instead, I gave them each a cloying smile.

Connie said, "Brenna and I have been helping to organize a neighborhood craft fair for the holidays. In fact, it's a week from this Saturday."

"Everybody's been helping," I said. "We're holding it at the elementary school down the street. I think it will be a huge success. We've got signs up everywhere, and we've started a neighborhood Facebook page."

"Sounds like fun," Mom said. "I'd love to see the rugs you're making."

"Connie, what are you making?" Dad asked.

"Yule logs," Connie said. "Real birch logs decorated with holly and ribbons. You can use them for decoration or burn them in the fireplace for good luck on Christmas."

"What a great idea," Dad said. "Where do you get the logs?"

She grinned. "The internet, of course. I ordered a small bundle and they were delivered in two days. One of our neighbors donated sprigs of holly off a tree in her yard."

Dinner progressed as we continued catching up

on family news. Then suddenly Michael raised a hand, signaling for silence. He cocked his head.

"Do you hear that?" he said. "Sounds like your phone's ringing."

Oh no, not now.

Connie looked at me, a puzzled look on her face. "That's not your regular ringtone, is it?"

"I like that ring," Mom said. "Sounds like an old-fashioned telephone."

The room went silent as everyone listened. *Think fast.*

"Just ignore it," I said. "That's my old phone. I changed carriers and got a new phone last year. The old company keeps sending me spam trying to get me to come back."

"Why don't you just turn it off?" Michael asked.

"You still keep it charged?" Paul eyed me like I'd lost my mind.

"Um, yeah...I mean...I just threw it in the closet...and...um..." I could feel my face burning. I was getting flustered. Too many questions. No good answers. I pushed back my chair and jumped to my feet. "I'll go take care of it."

I rushed to my room, closing the door behind me.   I lunged for the closet and dove for the telephone stuffed in the back under a pillow. I grabbed the receiver and growled into it, "This is not a good time."

As usual, I got an earful of crackling static.

The knob on the bedroom door jiggled and I barely had time to shove the old phone back into the closet before Paul stuck his head into the room. "You coming? Connie's dishing up dessert."

He peered around me, angling for a glimpse at whatever I was fiddling with on my knees in the closet.

"I'll be right there," I said. "I'm getting one of the rugs I made to show Mom."

He grunted and withdrew. I blew out a breath and rubbed my hands vigorously over my face. I should have listened to Gage. He said I should bury the phone in the back yard. My mouth twisted in a wry smile. The thought conjured an image of my brothers in the yard fruitlessly searching the bushes for the source of the mysterious ringing.

I pulled out one of the rag rugs I had made with Maureen's help. I had never been very artistic or crafty, but now I found that I really liked making these rugs. I couldn't explain why, but there was something therapeutic about braiding the colored strips of fabric together to create something that was both beautiful and useful. So far, I had finished three in widely diverse colors: an earthy one in browns, greens, and yellows; a blue one in various shades of sky and sea; and last, my favorite, an autumn rug in blacks, oranges, and reds. My goal had been to have something to sell at the neighborhood craft fair and then maybe even something to give as Christmas gifts.

But now what I needed was a conversation piece, something to get everyone's mind off the ringing telephone in my bedroom closet. I knew it wouldn't take much prompting to get Connie to show off her decorated Yule logs as well.

"These are gorgeous," Mom gushed a few minutes later as I spread my colorful creations over the back of the couch for inspection. "Your grandmother would have been so proud."

"Very impressive," Dad agreed, fingering the material, feeling the heft of the woven mats. "You won't have any trouble selling these. Great work."

As usual, Buster was underfoot, weaving nimbly to avoid being stepped on, his keen beagle nose snuffling curiously as he went from person to person. I purposely kept the new rugs off the floor to keep Buster away from them. Clean as he was, I didn't want to risk dog hair clinging to the fabric before the sale.

"Nice," Paul said.

"You made these?" Michael added. "Cool."

"Thanks, guys," I said, aiming a crooked smile in their direction.

Count on my brothers to keep a rein on their enthusiasm.

Connie presented her festively decorated Yule logs and was met with raves from my parents, even receiving kudos from Paul and Michael. The evening was filled with more talking and horsing around while Connie and I cleared the table and loaded the dishwasher. Tomorrow would be a busy day and we still had some prepping to do. Everyone pitched in, and as we worked we talked, laughed, and bandied jokes between us. I'd almost forgotten how much fun my family could be. Before long, it was nine o'clock.

"Well, Mother, I think it's time we called it a night," Dad said, looking at his watch. "It's getting

late and we've still got to find our way back to the
motel." He started pulling their coats out of the
hall closet.

I looked up, concerned. "Do you need help with
directions?" It was dark outside and a light rain
was falling.

He grinned and held up his phone. "Nope. Got
it all in here. Mom's going to navigate."

"We're not as old-fashioned as you think," Mom
quipped. "I figured out that GPS stands for *Get
Places Sooner*, right?"

I laughed. "Something like that."

Mom looked past me to Paul and Michael
sprawled in the living room deeply engrossed in
checking their phones. "You boys behave
yourselves and don't stay up too late." She turned
to Connie. "Thank you for a lovely dinner. We'll be
back in the morning."

"I'm just going to set out fruit and muffins for
breakfast," Connie said. "Nothing fancy. It'll be
ready whenever you get here."

"Please don't go to a lot of trouble for us."

Funny, I thought, how people always say that,
knowing full well that their very presence is cause
for a lot of trouble. But that's the nature of family
get-togethers. You do the work, enjoy the company,
then spend the next few days getting back to
normal.

I went to the linen closet and pulled my old
sleeping bags from the top shelf where I'd stashed
them, along with a couple of pillows, then took
them into the living room and dumped them on the
couch between my brothers.

"Here you go," I said. "You can figure out where you want to sleep whenever you're ready."

"Thanks," Paul said, barely looking up from his phone.

Michael made a noise that I interpreted as "thanks," then he reached for the TV remote on the coffee table.

I left them to it and went into the kitchen to help Connie.

She had made pies the day before and wouldn't let me near the turkey, but apparently she thought me capable of constructing a fruit salad. On the counter waiting for me was a large mixing bowl, a knife, and a pile of various fresh fruits.

"Just chop them and dump them together in that bowl," Connie said. "Then cover it and put it in the garage. I'm going to start on the candied yams."

Because the kitchen was fairly small and refrigerator space limited, we had set up a card table in the garage where we could keep things cool overnight. This necessitated the use of sturdy plastic containers with lids. Buster was usually in charge of dispelling mice from the premises, but with the pumpkin pie and fruit salad at risk, we weren't taking any chances.

As I began the tedious task of coring and chopping apples, I said, "Kayla called me this morning. She's having a small reception at the coffee shop Saturday afternoon around five to honor her dad and she's asked us both to come."

Connie puckered her lips as she thought about

it. "I'll be working on Saturday, but I should be able to come over for a few minutes."

"She wants me to ask Troy to come as my plus-one. She seems to think I'm interested in him." I popped a small slice of apple in my mouth and gave her a sideways look. "I wonder where she got that idea."

She smiled crookedly as she said, "I may have mentioned to her that you like him."

"I do like him," I said, "as a friend. He's very nice. But we've never been on a date, and you know I'm sort of seeing Gage."

"So don't ask him." Her tone carried a hint of irritation. "I didn't think you and Gage were that serious. You *are* still wearing your wedding ring, after all."

She was right. I'd been saying all along I wasn't ready for a serious relationship. Besides, asking Troy to come with me to Kayla's reception for her father could hardly be construed as a date.

"No, you're right. It's not a big deal. Kayla thinks Troy should be there, so I'll ask him. It's too late tonight. I'll call him tomorrow."

I went back to chopping apples, and my mind drifted to the old telephone in the closet. The sudden ringing during dinner had nearly thrown me into a panic. How much longer could I take this? Something had to be done to banish the ghost. But what? I had to know what the ghost wanted. Crazy as it sounded, that séance was starting to feel more and more like a viable option.

Chapter Eight

The next morning I rose early as usual, tiptoeing past my brothers still asleep on the living room floor. With Buster in tow, I eased out the front door and went for a quick jog around the block. By the time I returned, showered, and dressed, things were stirring. Connie put the coffee on while I set the table with muffins and sliced melon. My parents arrived around nine thirty and we enjoyed a leisurely breakfast.

The rest of the day was headache-free and everybody seemed to enjoy themselves. Connie kept a steady stream of snacks available on the coffee table in the living room while Dad and the boys sat fixated in front of the television watching football. Buster sat at Paul's feet, watching diligently for dropped tidbits. Somehow, that imploring doggy face seemed to cause an inordinate amount of accidental spills.

"If you make him sick," scolded Connie, catching Paul in the act of slipping the beagle a wedge of cheese, "you're cleaning it up."

Paul merely tipped his head toward the pudgy little dog and said, "Aww, but look at him—he's starving." Buster gazed at him with adoring eyes and wagged his tail in agreement.

Connie threw up her hands and emitted a loud, disgusted sigh.

At five o'clock, amid oohs and ahhs, Connie presented the turkey roasted to a perfect golden brown. She brought it to the table and Thanksgiving dinner began in earnest. Plates were filled and conversation carried on, barely hampered by the din of scraping cutlery, clinking glasses, and spontaneous laughter.

I gave a momentary thought to the haunted telephone hidden in my closet, fervently praying it wouldn't ring and disrupt the mood. But as the meal progressed and nothing happened, I relaxed and threw myself into the festivities. Dad told his usual dumb jokes, Mom talked about her job at the book store, and Paul and Michael regaled us with tales of college life.

An hour and a half later, groaning and holding their stomachs, the men adjourned to the living room for more football while Mom, Connie, and I chatted and cleared the table. Suddenly, my cell phone rang and my shoulders tightened. Taking a breath, I willed my racing pulse to slow down.

I can't start freaking out every time a phone

rings. I glanced at the caller: Tamara.

I caught Connie's attention with a quick wave, then took the phone into my room and shut the door. "Hey," I said to my friend. "How was your Thanksgiving? Done already?"

"Dinner's over," she said. "Curtis and his dad are watching football and his mom fell asleep in her chair, so I thought I'd just give you a quick call and see how things were going with you."

I laughed. "Well, no major catastrophes so far."

"No calls from the beyond?"

I made a scoffing noise. "Funny you should ask. The ghost did call yesterday while we were having dinner. It took some quick sleight of hand to come up with a semiplausible explanation for a phone ringing in my bedroom closet. As it is, I think my credibility has become suspect in the eyes of my family."

"They're leaving Saturday morning, right?"

"Yeah, but I'm supposed to take my parents over to meet Bill Prescott tomorrow." I rubbed a hand over my face as I pictured all the ways that could go wrong.

"Bill...? Oh, right—your bio-dad. That should be interesting."

I snorted. "No kidding. I can't believe I wanted to invite him for Thanksgiving dinner. What was I thinking?"

"You were thinking he's your father," Tamara said reasonably.

"Yeah, and I'm glad I've gotten to know him, but..."

"But?"

"Somehow putting him in the same picture as the rest of my family just doesn't feel right. They don't sync—sort of an 'apples and oranges' thing. Does that make sense?"

"Sure, but I think you're making too much of it. Just do the introductions, smile a lot, and pretty soon it'll all be over.   Awkward, but not life-threatening."

I let out a soft laugh. "I like how you can put things into perspective."

"Hey, that's what friends are for."

"Thanks.   Now I'd better get back to helping Connie clean up.   Thanks for calling.   Enjoy the rest of your weekend. I'll talk to you later, okay?"

"Yep. Call me if you need me."

I was about to set my phone on its charger and leave it there when the rooster crowed announcing a new text message.   When I saw it was from Gage, I relaxed and a happy feeling enveloped me like a warm hug.

He wrote: *Happy Thanksgiving. How's it going?*

I replied: *So far so good. How about you?*

Better than expected. Lots of talking, hugging, and crying

Sounds like a good thing, I wrote. *Give Maureen my love*

He replied: *I will. Take care and enjoy your family. Eat lots of turkey*

I smiled and texted back: *When do you get home?*

Do you miss me?

Maybe. A little. I inserted a silly smiley face.

We get back Sunday. Can't wait to see you

Me too. Gotta go now and help Connie with dishes. Have fun. See you soon

I dropped the phone on the charger and left to go help in the kitchen. It occurred to me that I hadn't called Troy yet, but it was Thanksgiving Day and he was probably busy. Nothing to do with procrastinating.

———

The next morning, my parents arrived from the motel just as the sun was poking out of the clouds. It promised to be a beautiful day and I decided this was a good omen. After breakfast, I suggested to my parents that we walk over and see Bill Prescott. I knew my mom had already talked to Dennis and prepared him for this meeting. Paul and Michael naturally wanted to come too, but Mom told them firmly to stay put. She and I had agreed beforehand that we didn't want this turning into a circus sideshow.

I knocked at Bill's front door and he greeted me with his customary good-natured smile. He looked especially handsome in a tan chambray shirt with long sleeves that covered the flamboyant tattoos on his arms. His jeans were clean and pressed, his boots were polished, and his beard was trimmed. Obviously, he had put some effort into making a good impression.

"Happy Thanksgiving," I said, giving him a quick hug.

"You, too," he said. Then his eyes swung past

me and riveted on my mother. "Lisa—been a long time."

"Hello, Bill." My mother greeted him the way one might approach a strange dog. She gave him a courteous smile, but stayed at arm's length. Then she introduced Dennis, and the two men shook hands.

Bill motioned us to come in. "Brenna's told me what a great dad you are," he said, "and I'm truly grateful. I'm sure it's not easy raising another man's child, but it's clear she loves you and you've done a wonderful job. She's grown up to be a fine young lady."

Dennis nodded and fixed me with an appreciative smile. "She's an amazing girl and I've always been proud to call her my daughter."

This is getting seriously mushy.

Embarrassed, I laughed and said, "Let's just agree that I'm perfect and move on."

Bill invited us to sit at the kitchen table while he rounded up mugs of coffee and a plate of assorted cookies. Mom loosened up and the conversation turned to other topics. I suggested to Bill that he show my parents his woodworking shop and some of the items he'd built for the upcoming holiday fair.

"He has a real way with wood," I said. "Don't tell Connie, but she's getting one of his handmade jewelry boxes for Christmas."

Pleased, Bill led us to the garage where he proudly pointed out the handcrafted birdhouses, toys, rocking horses, and other wooden objects he had lined up on a shelf, artfully painted and decorated, ready to sell. I knew Dennis had done a bit of woodworking himself, so I figured he'd be particularly impressed.

Gazing around at the tables and benches covered with various saws, drills, clamps, and tools, Dennis gave a low whistle and said, "Wow, you've got a real Santa's workshop going on here."

Bill shrugged modestly. "Well, a few years ago I decided I needed a hobby, something to keep me busy"—he chuckled—"out of the pool halls, you know? So I started cutting up pieces of wood and gluing them together to make things. Turned out I had kind of a knack for it. I'd get an idea for a toy and I'd come out here and fiddle with scraps I had lying around. If it looked good, I'd cut some templates out of cardboard. There's a stack of templates up there on that shelf."

We all turned to look.

Bill continued. "I got that tabletop scroll saw there for a bargain from a guy online. It's great for doing rounded shapes. That old saw's gotten a real workout lately."

Dennis nodded appreciation. "You've really gotten into this."

"Yeah, I guess so," Bill said. "It's one of those things, ya know, where you get into the zone and it's hard to quit. I'd start working on something after lunch, and the next thing you know it'd be dark. But once I had the template cut for a certain toy, I'd want to keep going till I had enough pieces for a whole batch. Then I'd spend the next day sanding, gluing, and painting." He reached up and pulled a wooden race car off the shelf, turning it over in his hands. "Before long, I'd have a dozen cars rolling off my assembly line."

"Yeah, I can see that," Dennis said. He reached up to another shelf and pulled down a wooden robot. It had a blocky head and body cut from 2x4s, with 2x2 cubes strung together on a length of heavy cord for arms and legs. "This is cool. I never would have thought of making a robot."

"I had some leftover pieces from another project," Bill said. "I started playing around with them and before you know it, voilà, I had a robot. I used the table saw to make the cubes, and in no time I had enough pieces cut for a dozen robots. I set the blade on the table saw at about a quarter inch to cut a slit for the mouth, then used a Forstner bit on my drill press to drill the eyes."

"What's a Forstner bit?"

"Let me show you," Bill said. He removed a plastic case from a drawer and opened it, pulling out a metal drill bit about the size and shape of a pencil with a wide head at one end. "Here, you can see it has flat cutting edges around the center point. It's designed to make holes with a flat bottom instead of the cone shape that a regular drill bit makes."

"I see," Dennis murmured as he inspected the thing. "I always wondered how those holes were cut. I've got to get one of these."

Mom and I stood aside while the two men hunched together over the workbench discussing the finer points of scroll saws, coping saws, and routers. The visit was going better than I'd hoped; the two men really seemed to have hit it off, but I could feel Mom getting antsy.

Bill picked up another toy and handed it to my stepfather. "Remember these?"

Dennis broke into a grin. "Yeah, I had a toy boat like this when I was a kid. Used to play with it in the bathtub all the time. See this, Brenna?" he said, demonstrating. "You wind up this paddle wheel on the back with a rubber band and it'll go clear from one end of the tub to the other."

"That's cool, Dad," I said, smiling at his enthusiasm. "But maybe we should be getting back. It's almost lunchtime and we don't want the boys to come looking for us."

"One more minute," he said. "I want to take a look at some of these birdhouses. What a great idea to use old license plates for the roof. I never would have thought of that."

Bill nodded. "Yeah, I had a stack of old license plates I couldn't bring myself to throw away. Then I figured if you fold them in half like that, they're the perfect size for the roof. Now I pick them up wherever I can get them. And how about this one? I designed it to look like an old outhouse, complete with a half moon painted over the door."

Dennis laughed. "Maybe if I put this up by the garage the birds would get the hint and quit pooping on my car."

"Here, what do you think of this one?" Bill pulled another birdhouse off the shelf. The roof of the wooden structure was covered with shiny copper shingles.

"Pennies?" Dennis exclaimed. "You must have almost five bucks worth glued on there."

"Close," Bill said. "I was sitting at the kitchen table counting out the pennies I'd been dumping in a jar, and came up with a brainstorm. I thought I'd rather use them on a birdhouse than mess with taking them to the bank."

"These are all very impressive, Bill," my mother interrupted. "I'm sure you won't have any trouble selling them at the craft fair. But now we really ought to be going. Thank you for the coffee and the tour." She gave him a crooked smile. "I have a feeling Dennis is going to go right home and start building birdhouses."

Bill grinned. "I'm glad you came over. It was nice seeing you again—and Dennis, it was great meeting you. I hope you'll keep in touch."

––––––––

The minute we walked in the door, I knew something was up. Paul and Michael were huddled over the dining room table, and even Buster barely spared us a glance. His attention was fixed on whatever the boys were doing.

Hearing us come in, Michael turned and said, "Brenna, where'd you get this nifty old telephone?"

My heart gave a jolt and I froze, staring in horror. They had the old black rotary phone lying in pieces between them on the table.

"What are you doing?" I cried.

Paul looked up, screwdriver in his hand. "We're trying to figure out how this thing works."

"It *doesn't* work," I said. "And what were you doing in my closet anyway?"

"We heard a phone ringing in your room," Michael said. "It just kept ringing and ringing, and then Buster started barking like crazy and scratching at your bedroom door."

"Yesterday, you said it was just your old cell phone sending you spam," Paul said, "so I didn't think you'd mind if I just went in and turned it off. But there wasn't any cell phone, just this cool antique."

"You had no business rooting around in my closet," I said hotly.

"You should have seen the way Buster was acting," Michael continued. "You'd have thought the thing was cursed or something."

"Oh, for heaven's sake," Mom said. She went to hang her coat in the closet.

"So, did you answer it?" Dad asked, cracking a broad smile. "Was anyone there?"

If you only knew, I thought, gritting my teeth. I was fearful the ghost might ring the phone again at any moment, even with it disassembled.

"That's the weird thing," Michael said. "I thought for sure I heard a voice at first, then it just turned into static. How is that even possible?"

"Hmm," Dad murmured as he leaned in for a closer look.

"It's not," I said, growing frantic. "It's a trick phone. It doesn't work."

"What's a trick phone?" Michael asked.

Mom looked around. "Where's Connie?"

"She said she needed something at the store," Paul said. "She should be back any minute."

My nerves were starting to fray. I took a deep

breath and dug my fingernails into my palms. "Would you please put it back together, *now.*"

Would tampering with the device upset the ghost? I'd taken it apart and nothing had happened. And even if it got mad, what was the worst it could do? With a shudder, I decided I didn't want to find out. Horror movies were full of angry poltergeists wreaking havoc on unsuspecting mortals. Things never ended well for them.

With a reluctant sigh, Paul began to reassemble the pieces. "But if it's broken," he persisted, "how did it ring?"

"Where'd you get it?" Michael asked. "What did you mean by *trick phone?* Can you hook it up, make it work?"

"A friend gave it to me," I said, talking fast. "It's old, it doesn't work, and I'm *not* planning to hook it up. I've taken it apart myself and found nothing more than a weird mechanical gadget with clunky brass bells. Sometimes it rings, okay? I don't know why. A faulty mechanism or something. I don't care. I think it looks cool and I'm going to put it on a shelf in my room as a decoration. Now, *will you please put it back together before you wreck it.*" I could feel my face burning.

"Geez, Brenna, take it down a notch," Paul said, tightening a screw to reattach the top to the base.

"Yeah," Michael said, frowning. "We can't break it any worse than it already is."

"Well, you shouldn't have been in my room going through my closet in the first place." I felt like I was sixteen again, bawling out my little brothers for touching my stuff.

"Brenna," interjected my mother. No further words were necessary. She was giving me the *look* she had perfected years ago when we'd squabbled as kids.

I felt a twinge of shame. It's not like they'd actually hurt anything, and I didn't want Thanksgiving to end on a sour note. I heaved a sigh.

"Look, never mind," I said to my brothers. "I'm sorry I overreacted, okay? I just...I was surprised, that's all. If you hear it ring again, please just ignore it."

Paul and Michael both nodded, but they continued to stare at the old phone. I knew they were bemused. They had enough technical knowledge between them to know that none of my explanations made sense, but I wasn't about to tell them the phone was possessed by the spirit of my friend's dead father. The very absurdity of it almost made me laugh outloud.

Dad reached out and spun the dial absently. He shook his head. "It would take a lot of monkeying to get this old thing working again. Besides, I assume you don't have a phone line to the house anymore."

All of a sudden, Buster gave a yip and bounded to the front door. Connie came in carrying a bag of groceries. "I can't believe I was out of mayonnaise," she said, striding past and disappearing into the kitchen.

"Who's ready for lunch?" she hollered a moment later. "Turkey sandwiches coming up."

Grateful for the distraction, I swept up the old

telephone and hurried with it to my room. I stashed it once more in my bedroom closet, carefully swathing it in a blanket and smothering it with a pillow. I knew now I had to do something. I couldn't continue this way. I either had to dispose of the thing or find out what the ghost wanted and help it find peace so it could move on.

My imagination bombarded me with crazy ideas: I could take the telephone on the ferry and drop it overboard in the middle of Puget Sound, or I could hike to the top of Mount St. Helens and drop it into the center of the crater. I stifled a laugh under my breath. What would that accomplish? *You can't kill a ghost.* With my luck, it would take up residence in my cell phone and haunt me relentlessly for the rest of my life.

I pulled out my cell and looked up Norma Hansen. I glanced over my shoulder to make sure the bedroom door was firmly shut, then punched in the number.

After three rings, the elderly woman answered. "Hello?" Her voice sounded soft and brittle.

"Norma? This is Brenna Wickham, the one who's been helping you with your papers and finances?" My fingers fidgeted as I fought to keep my nerves under control.

"Why, yes, Brenna, how nice of you to call. How was your Thanksgiving?"

"It was very nice. How about you? Did you make it over to the senior center?"

"Yes, and they served a lovely meal, turkey and gravy with all the trimmings. I saw lots of my friends, and they showed an old Cary Grant movie,

Arsenic and Old Lace. I've seen it before, of course, but it was very enjoyable."

I took a deep breath. "Norma, the reason I'm calling..." I hesitated. Was I really doing this?

She finished for me. "You've decided to do the séance. You want to communicate with the spirit in the old telephone. I knew you would. I've been expecting you to call."

I didn't know whether to be stunned or grateful. "Yes... um," I stammered, "it keeps ringing, and..."

"It's all right, dear," the old woman said in a soft pleasant voice. "I understand completely. How does tomorrow night sound? Saturday at midnight has a nice ring to it, don't you think? And you won't have to go to work the next day."

"Tomorrow?" I gulped. "Give me a second to think."

My parents were leaving in the morning, so that wouldn't be a problem. I thought about Tamara. She would kill me if I didn't include her. She didn't work on Sundays, either, so that worked out perfectly. I'd have to make up some story for Connie, but that was doable.

I took another deep breath. "Okay, let's do it. And I'd like to bring a friend if that's okay. Another believer who knows the whole story and wants to help."

"Certainly," she said. "The more energy, the better."

"Okay then, we'll be to your house around eleven thirty or so tomorrow night, ready to commune with the spirits." I gave a shaky laugh. "And thank you so much, I really appreciate it."

At that moment, Paul pounded on my bedroom door and shouted, "Hey, Brenna, lunch is ready. Are you coming?"

"Just a minute," I hollered back. Then into the phone I said, "I've got to go, Norma. I'll see you tomorrow night."

I hung up and quickly sent a text to Tamara: *Séance tomorrow night at midnight! You still game? I'll call you later.*

Her answer was almost immediate: *Count me in! Waiting for your call.*

At lunch I told Connie I'd been invited to a friend's tomorrow night for a late "stargazing party." I concocted a fantastic story about using a telescope to look at planets and constellations. I felt terrible lying to her, but it was the only moderately believable story I could think of.

Better than the truth, I thought with an inward wince.

Connie simply shrugged and said, "Sure, whatever."

Chapter Nine

I spent the rest of the day doing touristy things with my family. They wanted to see the waterfront so we drove into Seattle and spent the afternoon at Pier 57, Miner's Landing. The wharf smelled heavily of fish, brine, and creosote, and the sidewalks were bustling with holiday visitors. All around, flocks of screeching seagulls vied for position along the docks, swooping down occasionally to snatch French fries dropped by passing sightseers.

Paul and Michael braved the giant Ferris wheel, while Mom and I rode the carousel with its bright lights and painted horses. Dad strolled around shooting picture after picture of the city, the water, and the scenic surroundings. We lucked out on the weather. Clear skies and sunshine set the surface of the water alight with millions of glittering sparkles, though the chill breeze dutifully reminded us that winter was fast approaching.

While the others wandered toward the gift shops, I took a moment to call Tamara.

"Tomorrow night," I said when I had her on the phone. "If you can be to my house by eleven we can go together."

"Go where?"

That's when I realized I hadn't told her about Norma and the Ouija Board. "There's this eighty-six year old woman, Norma Hansen," I said, "for whom I've been made legal guardian through the court. I oversee her welfare and look after her finances. She's a sweet lady, but kind of unusual. She believes in numerology and spiritualism, and has a Ouija Board that she says can be used to contact the dead. She calls it a Spirit Board. I told her about the haunted telephone and she's all onboard for having a séance at her house."

"Hmm," Tamara said dubiously. "You sure she's not some sort of con artist out to get your money? You're not paying her, are you?"

"No," I said. "She doesn't want money, she just wants to help. She told me her mother-in-law was a medium. The Ouija Board belonged to her. Norma said that widows of soldiers killed overseas used to come to her hoping to contact the spirits of their dead husbands. I showed her the phone and she believes what I said about it being haunted. I thought you'd be more excited."

"Oh, I am. I just want to be sure you aren't being taken in by some charlatan."

"What, you mean some crazy person who actually believes ghosts are real?"

Tamara laughed. "You know what I mean—mystics, fortune tellers, mind readers. There are all sorts of cranks out there happily willing to take your money."

I paused a moment to think as a group of noisy children ran past me on the sidewalk. Could Norma be a fraud, a crackpot leading me on for some nefarious reason of her own? No. I mentally shook my head. I refused to believe it. She was a kindly old woman who fed raccoons, didn't bother with money, and happened to believe in ghosts.

"Huh-uh," I said to my friend. "Norma might be a little flaky—eccentric for sure—but certainly not dishonest or underhanded. We're going to hold a séance tomorrow night at midnight to contact the spirit in the telephone. So, the question is, are you going to join us?"

"Absolutely," Tamara said emphatically.

"Good," I said. "I knew I wouldn't have to twist your arm. If nothing else, it'll be fun, right? Like junior high."

Tamara made a snorting noise into the phone. "Okay, so what's the plan?"

"I told Norma we'd be there about eleven thirty. She doesn't live too far from me, so if you get to my house by eleven, that should be plenty of time. It'll be late, so bring your toothbrush and jammies. Then you can crash on my couch and go home Sunday morning."

"Ooh, slumber party."

I laughed. "What did I tell you? Junior high all

over again. Oh, and I told my cousin we're going to a friend's to look at the stars through her telescope. Just play along."

Tamara gave a soft chuckle. "Okay, whatever you say. I guess you couldn't exactly tell her what we're really doing. See you tomorrow."

I hung up and expelled a deep breath. With that out of the way, it was time to call Troy. I pulled my coat tight against the chill breeze as I punched in his number.

He answered on the third ring. "Hey, Brenna, what's up? How was your Thanksgiving? Dad tells me your folks came out from Phoenix. Did you have a good visit?"

"We did. In fact, we're still having it. They're leaving in the morning, but they wanted to see the waterfront so we're currently in Seattle down at the pier. My parents are off exploring the souvenir shops. How about you? Good Thanksgiving?"

"It was great," he said. "As usual my mom made enough food to stuff an army. Some aunts and uncles came over and we played cards. My mom's a demon when it comes to canasta."

Nearby, the long low blast of a ship's horn cut through the air. Seagulls cried, and waves sloshed against the pilings.

"Are you free tomorrow afternoon?" I asked.

"Should be. Why?"

"Kayla Donnelly's having a small reception at the coffee shop for family and friends to remember her father—sort of a wake in celebration of his life. Kayla asked me to ask you. She said you and her dad were friends, and she'd like you to be there.

Sorry this is such short notice."

"What time?"

"It starts around five. I thought maybe you could pick me up about four thirty and we could go together."

James won't have a reason to be jealous if we arrive together.

He gave a small laugh. "Not exactly how I pictured our first date."

I echoed his laugh. "What, you don't find funerals romantic?"

"I'll make it up to you," he said. "How about if I take you to dinner afterwards?"

I thought for a second. I had the séance tomorrow night at Norma's, but not until late. There should be plenty of time. I'd been fantasizing about a date with Troy, and the timing was fortuitous since Gage was out of town. I felt a momentary twinge of guilt, but pushed it away. Troy and I were just friends, nothing to feel guilty about.

"Okay," I said. "I'd like that. I'll text you my address and I'll see you tomorrow at four thirty. Now, I need to go find my parents before they buy up all the souvenirs in Seattle."

I hung up feeling stressed and excited at the same time. I had pictured relaxing and getting back to normal after my family left. But tomorrow was shaping up to be another hectic day. Airport in the morning, Kayla's reception at the coffee shop in the afternoon, followed by dinner with Troy, and—I gave a quick laugh—a séance at Norma's to top it all off. I would barely have time to breathe.

I turned and scanned the storefronts, looking for signs of my parents. It was getting late and I thought we ought to decide on a place to have dinner. Ivar's Acres of Clams at pier 54 was a favorite of mine and just a short walk up the street. I knew my mom was crazy about fresh seafood. I headed toward the Pirates Plunder gift shop.

Suddenly, a loud voice at my shoulder caused me to jump and nearly bump into a guy careening by on rollerblades. His angry invective was muffled by traffic noise as he swerved and disappeared down the sidewalk.

I whirled on my brother. "Don't sneak up on me like that."

"Come on," Paul said, grinning widely. "We're getting hungry. Dad's ready to wrestle the seagulls for a French fry."

Saturday morning started slowly, then erupted into chaos as my brothers scurried to gather their strewn belongings and stuff their backpacks in preparation for leaving. Pillows, sleeping bags, and carelessly folded blankets were heaped on the couch while the kitchen counter lay hidden under piles of empty pop cans, crumpled napkins, and dirty dishes.

When my parents arrived from the motel we wolfed down a hasty breakfast, then made for the airport. Connie had said her good-byes the night before as she had to leave early for work at the flower shop. Holiday traffic on the freeway moved at an aggravating crawl, but we managed to arrive at the departure doors with minutes to spare. After a rush of hurried hugs and well-wishes, the family turned and proceeded to the gate. As soon as they were out of sight, I heaved a sigh and headed back to the house to prepare for the evening.

As I did my makeup in front of the bathroom mirror, my eye caught the quick flash of my diamond ring as it reflected in the light. My wedding ring, the symbol of my love. I stopped and stared at it, the breath catching in my throat as emotions I had been suppressing roiled to the surface. Jason's sweet face rose in my mind. I had vowed to love, honor, and cherish. I took a deep breath and wiped away an unbidden tear. *Till death do we part.*

Now I was preparing to go out with another man. I had already been out with Gage, even kissed him. Part of me cried "traitor," but another voice whispered that it was time. Time to move on, to have a life. It's what Jason would have wanted. I pulled off the ring and slipped it into the jewelry box on my dresser.

Troy arrived at four forty in a sporty red Nissan, looking sharp as usual. He had swapped his familiar tortoiseshell glasses for a pair in shiny dark blue, and was dressed in a gray suit with a navy shirt open at the collar. He might have been meeting colleagues for drinks after work. Of course, with that body, wavy blond hair, and chiseled face, he would have looked classy in anything.

"Come in," I said, swinging the door open. I had chosen a simple navy blazer over a straight-cut floral dress with a plain gold necklace. Staid enough for a memorial, but dressy enough for an evening out.

He looked me up and down with an appreciative smile. "You look lovely."

Teasing, I replied, "I'll bet you say that to all the girls."

Buster approached and gave him the requisite beagle once-over, snuffling noisily around Troy's ankles before giving him an approving tail wag.

"Nice doggy," Troy said. He reached down and gave Buster an ear rub. The dog's tail went into high gear.

"Looks like you've passed the sniff test," I said with a laugh. "Buster's a great judge of character."

He grinned, adjusting his glasses. "Yeah, dogs and babies love me."

I slipped my purse strap over my shoulder and straightened my jacket. "Shall we go?"

"After you." He held the door open and stepped aside so I could slip past. The sun was setting and the night was clear and cold. Overhead, several bright stars could already be seen twinkling among a few scattered high clouds.

When we arrived at the coffee shop, Kayla met us at the door, her face bright and welcoming as she gave us each a hug. "Thank you both so much for coming," she gushed. "I'm so glad you could make it. Troy, I would have called you myself, but I've just been so busy lately."

And this gave me the perfect opportunity to push you and Brenna together, I thought wryly to myself.

"That's okay," he said. "I know things have been tough."

"There's coffee and goodies over there," she said, pointing to a table spread with a white lace cloth and covered with plates of pastries and finger sandwiches. A large commercial coffee urn sat at one end, along with a sugar bowl, small pitcher of cream, and a stack of disposable cups.

"Help yourselves," she continued. "Look around, enjoy yourselves. I don't want this to be a gloomy affair. Dad wouldn't have wanted that. Oh, and look at the flowers." Her words came in a flurry. I could see she was keyed up with nerves and emotion. "Aren't they gorgeous, Brenna? Your cousin donated them. She's so sweet. She said she'd come over for a minute if she gets a chance."

Troy leaned toward her and said softly, "Take a breath, Kayla."

I looked at the large arrangement of colorful blossoms on top of the bakery counter. *Beautiful. How like Connie.*

Beside the bouquet, in pride of place, was a framed photo of a lean, dark-haired man with a pencil mustache. Ed Glassner, of course. Kayla's father. She bore a strong resemblance to him through the eyes and the shape of her chin. With a jolt, it occurred to me that this was the face of the ghost who had been reaching out to me through the old telephone for the past week.

The unblinking eyes of the man in the picture seemed to hold me in an imploring gaze. A shiver ran up my spine and I gulped, struggling to keep my composure.

Troy leaned close and whispered, "You okay? You're trembling."

I took a deep breath and nodded. "I'm fine." I gave him a reassuring smile and repeated, "I'm fine—just a little chilly." I readjusted the purse strap on my shoulder and brushed back my hair. "Everything looks wonderful, doesn't it?" I turned and focused my attention on the table laden with pastries.

Get ahold of yourself. There are no ghosts here.

Behind us, the door opened letting in a rush of cold air and a middle-aged couple. Kayla turned and greeted them warmly. "Uncle Simon, Aunt Lilly," she exclaimed, "I'm so glad you came. I wasn't sure you'd make it."

Troy and I stepped back as Kayla and her aunt embraced. We started to move away, but Kayla took hold of my arm and steered me around to face the newcomers. Troy stayed at my elbow.

"Brenna, Troy," she said, "I'd like you to meet my aunt and uncle, Lilly and Simon Howard. Uncle Simon is my mother's brother."

The man reminded me of a bulldog, short and stocky, with a barrel chest and broad, fleshy face. His expression was grim and humorless. His wife was plump and rather plain-looking in a loose purple sweater with gray slacks; her pale hair hung to her shoulders. She wore no makeup or jewelry, but had a rosy face, dimpled cheeks, and bright sympathetic eyes.

"Pleased to meet you," Aunt Lilly said. Then she turned to Kayla. "We're so sorry for your loss."

"I'm not," the uncle grumbled under his breath.

"Oh, Simon, none of that," scolded his wife, giving him a quick nudge. "We're here for Kayla. This is a hard time for her and we're here to be supportive."

Uncle Simon grunted. "Sorry for your loss. Your dad and I didn't get along, but it's nothing to do with you."

If that was intended as contrition, I thought, *it was a flimsy attempt.* His words came off sounding like a growl.

Troy and I exchanged uncomfortable glances.

"We're going to go get some of those delicious pastries," I said quickly to Kayla, then grabbed Troy by the arm and pulled him away.

"What was that all about?" I murmured.

"No idea," Troy said, shaking his head.

We edged over to the buffet table. *James has been working overtime.* I studied the plates mounded with delicacies. I wavered between a chocolate brownie and a maple bar. Who was I kidding? I went for the chocolate. Selections made, we angled for one of the small tables out of the way.

Six café tables with chairs were arranged against the walls to provide seating, but also to maximize space for mingling in the center of the room. There were a dozen or more guests of varying ages—relatives and friends of the family. I looked around for James and saw him across the room deep in conversation with a heavyset man in a tan sports jacket and jeans.

"Nice party," I said to Troy in a lame attempt to make conversation.

One side of his mouth quirked up. "Beats a funeral."

"Do you know any of these people?" I noticed Simon and Lilly Howard had filled plates and taken a seat near the door. Kayla had moved on and was now conversing with another couple.

"Huh-uh. But I think that guy talking to James may be Ed's partner at the nursery. I met him a couple times, years ago, when Kayla and I were going out."

James wrapped up his conversation and sauntered in our direction. When he saw me, he broke into a smile and pulled up a chair.

"Hey," he said. "Brenna, isn't it? Thanks for coming." He gave Troy a nod. "You, too. It means a lot to Kayla that you're both here."

"It had to be hard losing her father that way," I said. "Such a terrible accident."

"Yeah, for sure," James said. "It hit Kayla hard. She and her dad were really close." He expelled a breath and leaned his head back, running a hand over his hair. "And now we have to deal with the estate—the house, the car, all his stuff, and the *paperwork*. Plus we have to decide what to do with Kayla's share of her dad's business."

"Was that Ed's partner you were just talking to?" Troy asked.

"Yeah, Ward Thurmond. Nice guy. He's been talking to Kayla about selling him her half. He's made a very generous offer, and frankly I wish she would take it and be done with it. The bakery is just holding its own and an injection of cash right now sure wouldn't hurt."

"I told Kayla it would probably be a good idea to get an appraisal first," I said.

Troy nodded agreement. "It's in a great location, been there a long time. Have you seen the books, what kind of business they do?"

James sighed again. "Yeah, Ward brought us a stack of spreadsheets he printed out, but we haven't really had time to go over them. In just flipping through, though, I get the idea they were doing okay. I know Kayla feels sentimental about her dad's business, and I get it—he put his heart and soul into that nursery, he had a real green thumb—but the last thing we need is another weight around our necks."

Chapter Ten

Suddenly, Kayla's voice called out. "James, would you come and join me?" She was standing alone in front of the bakery counter, her hands clasped in front of her as she smiled at her guests.

James gave us a quick thanks and hurried to join his wife.

When he was by her side, she began. "I want to thank all of you for coming, for sharing your memories, for offering your support." She paused and took a breath. "My dad was a wonderful man. He worked hard all his life as a horticulturist, growing and nurturing plants. He loved nature and being outdoors."

Her voice caught once or twice as emotion overtook her, but for the most part I was impressed at how well she kept it together. My eyes drifted involuntarily back to the photograph on the counter behind her. This time, to my surprise, the image seemed to be smiling, the eyes shining with paternal pride. I suddenly saw the ghost in a new light, and felt more determined than ever to help it if I could.

"We used to do a lot of camping when I was little," Kayla continued. "We'd go up in the mountains and Dad would always bring along empty buckets so he could dig up wild native plants to bring home. I thought this was perfectly normal. Other campers took home rocks and pine cones. We took home shrubs."

Soft laughter rippled around the room. Many were obviously familiar with this quirk of Glassner's to collect native plants wherever he found them.

Kayla smiled. "I remember one time when he dug up a cascara sapling and tried to fit it into the back of the car with the camping gear. Of course it tipped over and got dirt all over the sleeping bags. Needless to say, Mom was not happy."

More laughter, along with a few sniffles.

"Most of all, he loved his family," Kayla said. "He was a caring father and a devoted husband."

At these words, a derisive snort erupted from the crowd. I looked in time to see Kayla's Aunt Lilly turn and say something to her husband. She looked angry.

Something's going on there, I thought. Obviously there had been a conflict between Kayla's uncle and her father. I thought about the ghost. Was it possible that an unresolved argument between the two men had been so distressing that it was keeping Ed Glassner's spirit from going to its final rest? Did Kayla know what it was?

She kept speaking, tears streaking her face as she told how her father had taken her to piano lessons after school every day when she was in fourth grade. She laughed as she recounted how he had bravely endured hours of listening to her practice.

"When Mom got sick, Dad was devastated," Kayla said. "She was the love of his life. After she died, Dad started taking his canoe out every Sunday to a remote lake near the mountains. He liked the peace and solitude. He said he could feel Mom's presence when he was out there communing with nature. I like to think her spirit was with him at the time of the accident, holding his hand, reassuring him."

This elicited another snort accompanied by the scraping of a chair as Kayla's Uncle Simon stood up suddenly and stomped out the door, leaving his wife behind looking mortified. The room went quiet as people stared. The embarrassment was palpable.

Poor Kayla, I thought. Why did her crotchety old uncle have to spoil everything? Whatever the disagreement he'd had with her father, this wasn't the time to air it.

Aunt Lilly rose and went to Kayla, giving her a hug. "I'm so sorry, Sweetheart," she mumbled. "We never should have come." Then she turned and followed her husband.

Pushing open the door, she nearly collided with Connie. My cousin entered and looked around, bemused. People were whispering, shaking their heads. I waved at Connie and she came over to join us.

"What did I miss?" she asked as she pulled up a chair.

"I'll tell you later," I said.

Kayla and James still stood at the front of the room. James cleared his throat and clapped his hands for attention. The group quieted and turned their eyes back to Kayla.

She brushed the tears from her cheeks and fixed a smile to her face. "Well, that's Uncle Simon— always has to be the center of attention."

Chuckles burbled through the crowd as people relaxed and nodded agreement. I reminded myself that most of these folks were Kayla's relatives. They were probably familiar with Uncle Simon, and knew about the rift and what had caused it. Perhaps the blowup hadn't been as big a surprise to some as I'd thought.

When she finished speaking, Kayla opened the floor to anyone who wanted to contribute memories of her father.

The man I recognized as Ward Thurmond, the business partner, came forward and told how he and Ed had purchased the rundown nursery thirty years ago, how after loads of hard work and determination they had brought it back to life and turned it into a successful venture. He turned to Kayla and said, "You should know your dad was always very proud of you and what you've achieved here.   He never missed an opportunity to brag about this place you've built." He smiled broadly. "Best coffee and donuts in town."

Connie took the opportunity to lean over and whisper, "Did your parents make the plane all right this morning?"

Was that just this morning?

"Yep, no problem," I replied in a low voice. "Mom said she'd let me know when they got home."

Then I remembered I'd put my phone on silent; nothing like a rooster crow in the middle of a solemn occasion. I dug it out of my purse and, sure enough, there was a text from my mom saying they'd made it to Phoenix and reiterating their thanks. I texted back a quick "smiley face" and dropped the phone back into my purse.

"Seems like I've hardly talked to you in days," Connie said with a quiet laugh.

"Yeah, we've got some catching up to do," I said. "First of all, I don't think I told you, I'm having dinner with Troy after we leave here."

Troy moved in closer and put an arm around my shoulder, flashing Connie a cheesy grin.

Her eyebrows rose. She looked at me, then back at him. Her lips pulled into a wide smile as she gave him a thumbs up. I rolled my eyes. Clearly we would have to talk before she started getting ideas. I liked Troy of course, but I also liked Gage. I liked them both and I enjoyed their company, but at present I had no interest in committing to a serious relationship with either one.

"Wait a minute," Connie said, "didn't you say you were going to some kind of party tonight? To look at stars or something?"

Troy gave me a quizzical look.

"It's me and a couple of girlfriends," I said, repeating the story I had told Connie. "One of them is into astronomy. She has a telescope and she's invited us to come over at midnight and look at the stars."

"Do you want to postpone dinner?" he asked. The gleam in his eyes dimmed slightly.

"No, if I'm home by ten I should have plenty of time."

Troy's expression was dubious. "You do realize it's November, right? It'll probably be too cloudy to see anything."

"Not to mention cold," Connie added.

"I think it's supposed to be clear tonight," I said, then gave a little laugh and shrugged. "Doesn't matter. My friend's getting over a bad breakup and this is just an excuse to have people around to commiserate."

This fib was getting more complicated by the minute. A line from an old poem my mother used to quote popped into my head: *Oh, what a tangled web we weave...*

I was saved from having to elaborate further by a woman sitting at the next table who turned to us with a finger to her lips uttering a stern *"shhhh."* We turned our attention back to the speaker, a previous employee at the garden store who had lots of humorous anecdotes to share.

He was the last to speak, and people were soon mingling again. A few were putting their coats on, preparing to leave. I wanted to get going too, but I hadn't had a chance to talk to Kayla. I glanced around and saw her coming toward us.

"Brenna, Troy," she called out. "I'm so glad you came. Connie, thank you again for the beautiful flowers." Her face beamed as she gave us each a hug.

"It was a lovely reception," I said. I was dying to ask about the obvious grudge harbored by her uncle. I thought it would give me some insight into the ghost, but it would have been tactless so I bit my tongue.

As it turned out, Kayla brought it up herself. "I'm so sorry about Uncle Simon's stupid outburst." She frowned. "I'm not even sure why he came. Aunt Lilly made him, I suppose."

"What's his problem?" I asked.

She sighed and pressed her lips together in a rueful frown. "It's a long story—but my uncle has it in his head that my dad was responsible for my mother's death."

Connie gasped, expressing the shock we all felt.

"It's ridiculous, of course," Kayla said. "My mom died of breast cancer. It was nobody's fault. But my mother was Uncle Simon's little sister and he just couldn't accept that she was going to die. For some reason he blamed my father. He thought Dad should have done something more." She shrugged. "I don't know what he thought Dad could do, but he's been mad about it ever since."

"Oh, wow," I said. "Kayla, that's awful. I'm so sorry."

She waved a hand dismissively and reaffixed the smile to her face. "Hey," she said, "forget it.

It's Uncle Simon's problem. I don't want it to ruin this day."

"Nothing is ruined," Troy said. "Seems to me your Uncle Simon is just a grumpy old man looking to cause trouble."

I nodded. "I think that was pretty much the consensus."

Troy looked at me. "Well, on that note, I think it's time we got going." He grinned. "Wouldn't want you to be late for your midnight rendezvous."

Kayla's eyebrows rose.

Before she could ask, I said, "Troy and I are going to dinner, but afterwards I'm going to a friend's for a midnight stargazing party. She's into astronomy and has invited a few people over to look at the stars through her telescope."

"That sounds like fun," Kayla said. "I hope the clouds cooperate."

"I'd better be going too," Connie interrupted. "I need to make sure things get closed up at the store." She shouldered her purse. "Kayla, I'll see you next week. Hang in there."

As we turned to go, Kayla suddenly exclaimed, "Oh, Brenna, wait. I almost forgot. I have something to give you. I found my dad's stamp collection. You said you could get it appraised."

"You got the safe open?" I asked. Had Norma's deciphering strategy with the letters and numbers actually worked?

Kayla laughed. "Turns out it wasn't that complicated. The combination was Dad's birthday. Like you said, a number he could remember. But there wasn't much in it: birth certificates, marriage license, the deed to the house. In fact, the stamp collection wasn't in there at all. Turns out it was under his mattress, of all places. I never would have looked there, except I was pulling off the sheets and spotted the corner sticking out. I brought it with me. I don't know if it's worth anything, but I'll be glad to get that neighbor, Mr. Bailey, off my back. He's constantly asking me if I've found it yet. It's in the back room. Wait a minute while I run and get it."

"Do you think it's valuable?" Troy asked when she had gone. "But if it is, you would think he'd have put it in the safe, wouldn't you? Under the mattress seems sort of cliché, like something your grandparents might have done."

I gave a little shrug. "I don't know, we'll see. I've had all kinds of collections appraised and I've never yet seen a stamp collection worth more than a couple hundred dollars."

Troy laughed. "Well, a couple hundred is a couple hundred, I suppose. If someone needs the cash, it's better than nothing."

Kayla returned and handed me a slim hardcover book. Inside, it resembled a photo album with plastic pages containing pockets for inserting stamps. Flipping through, I saw stamps in a multitude of shapes, sizes, and colors. There were pictures of people, plants, animals, and edifices from countries all over the world. Impressive collection, I thought. Maybe there *is* something to it.

"I'll take it to an appraiser I know in Seattle as soon as I get a chance." I pursed my lips thoughtfully. "Might not be right away, though. I'll take it with me next time I go to the courthouse."

"Why don't you let me take it?" Troy chimed in. "I can drop it off on Monday. Just let me know where."

"That would be great," I said. I dug out my phone and texted him the name of the appraiser I'd used many times at the law firm where I'd previously worked. They'd always proven to be very knowledgeable and usually had a quick turnaround. I didn't expect the stamps to come back with any real value, but just getting this done would help take one more thing off Kayla's mind.

"Thank you so much," Kayla said again. "Now I'll let you go. Have a wonderful evening."

———

Troy drove us to the Edmonds waterfront. He parked the car and we went for a stroll along a walkway that overlooked the marina. The sun had long since set, but lights along the pier illuminated the rows of pleasure boats moored at the docks below.

"Beautiful, aren't they?" Troy said. "Do you like boats? I've been thinking of getting one."

"The only boat I've ever been on is the ferry," I said, "but I do love the water." Growing up in Phoenix, the closest I'd ever gotten to a boat was when Jason and I went paddleboarding on Bartlett Lake. After moving to Seattle we'd only ridden the ferry twice, but I'd found the trips exhilarating.

I shivered. Frigid breezes gusting off the water were sending goose bumps up and down my arms. I hadn't dressed for the outdoors. My lightweight polyester blazer did nothing to keep out the chill. Troy put his arm around me and pulled me close as we leaned on the railing. I welcomed the warmth of his body, but the move created an intimacy that took me off guard.

Getting back into dating was going to be harder than I thought. I wanted to shake myself. *What's wrong with me? The guy is perfect.* He's handsome, intelligent, and rich. Most girls would kill to be in my place. But it felt so awkward. Troy and I were good friends. I didn't want to spoil that. Then I remembered something Tamara had said to me once—*Nobody's telling you to marry the guy. Just go out and have some fun.*

She had been talking about Gage at the time, but the words still applied. I smiled up at Troy and leaned closer, determined to relax, have a good time, and enjoy the evening.

"Let's go inside," he murmured. He turned and led me toward a nearby steak and seafood restaurant perched at the edge of the marina facing west over the shimmering waters of Puget Sound.

Inside, the dining room was both lively and seductive as breathtaking views and candlelight vied with boisterous voices and clinking glassware. Waitstaff in white coats carrying trays and wine bottles scurried back and forth among the tables.

Fancy. I couldn't help comparing this to Frankie's, the quiet little Italian bistro in my neighborhood where Gage and I liked to go. It wasn't bustling or pretentious, but the food was good and the atmosphere warm and friendly.

As we followed the hostess, our attention was suddenly diverted by a shrill feminine voice.

"Troy!" A shapely hand reached out and grabbed his coat sleeve. The hand belonged to a radiant blonde in evening attire seated with two equally attractive young women.

Troy halted and turned to face her. "Mandy," he said with surprise.

"Where have you been?" The blonde affected a pretty pout. "You promised to call me after Bobby's party."

"I've been busy," Troy said, casting an embarrassed glance my way.

"Did you hear? Kristy's getting married." She grasped the left hand of the girl next to her and held it out so we could all get a good look at the flashy diamond resting there. "We're celebrating." She held up her champagne glass to prove it.

"Congratulations, Kristy," Troy said, edging away.

I noticed that the hostess had continued walking, oblivious to the interruption.

As we turned to go, Mandy yelled, "Call me." This was followed by a barrage of giggles.

Hope they're not driving, I thought.

Once we were seated at our table by the window, well away from the partiers, Troy attempted a clumsy apology. "Sorry about that. Mandy and I dated a couple of times. She seems to think—"

I put up a hand to stop him. "It's okay. You don't have to explain. It doesn't matter. You can date whoever you want. You and I are just friends, okay? No promises, no commitments."

It was the same spiel I'd given Gage. I wasn't ready for a new relationship. So why had I taken off my wedding ring? Mentally, I sighed. I didn't know what I wanted.

Troy nodded, his expression inscrutable.

I changed the subject. "Tell me what kind of boat you'd like to get."

Chapter Eleven

It was after ten o'clock when Troy brought me home. He walked me to the front door, then drew me tight, his arms encircling my waist. A giddy flush of heat coursed through my body as he bent and pressed his lips to mine. Unbidden, my subconscious compared his hot, ardent kiss to Gage's soft, tentative one. I thrust the thought away, determined to keep this night about Troy.

My heart pounded as I stood on the porch and watched has he backed down the steps and trotted to his car. No doubt about it, he was one sexy hunk of a man.

Inside, I found Connie dozing on the couch in front of the TV. She woke at the sound of the door latching behind me.

"How was your date?" she asked, levering

herself upright.

"Fine," I said.

"Just *fine?*"   She rubbed her eyes and straightened her glasses.

"It was nice. What do you want me to say? We went to Edmonds and walked around the marina looking at boats. Then we went to a restaurant overlooking the water and I had the grilled salmon. We did a lot of talking. Like I said, it was nice."

"Did he kiss you goodnight?"

I gave a little snort. "That's none of your business."

She laughed. "Will you go out with him again."

I folded my arms and tightened my lips. "For heaven's sake, Connie, why do you care? Why is everybody so eager to throw us together?"

She shrugged. "I like Troy, that's all, and I think he's perfect for you. He's a lawyer. You have things in common. Plus, you've got to admit he's awfully good-looking."

I knew Troy was a favorite of my cousin's. He'd been coming into her shop on his way to work every Monday morning for years to buy flowers for his office. He was witty and engaging, and she was thoroughly taken with him. By contrast, Connie had mostly seen Gage at his worst: moody, ill-tempered, and impatient with his neurotic, agoraphobic older sister. But that had ended when the mystery of his younger sister's disappearance had been solved and her spirit set free. Now that Maureen was on the mend and the stress between them removed, Gage was proving to be charming and fun-loving, like the mischievous boy I remembered as a child. The boy I'd had a crush on.

"Sure," I said, "I like Troy and I'd probably go out with him again. But for the millionth time, I am not looking for a new relationship, so stay out of it."

She tilted her head and arched her eyebrows. "You took your ring off."

I heaved a sigh and tossed back my hair. "You're hopeless. Now, I've got to get my clothes changed. My friend Tamara will be here soon. She's coming with me to the party tonight, and then she's going to sleep here afterwards so she doesn't have to drive home in the middle of the night."

"Fine," said Connie, rising from the couch. "Have a good time. Now I'm going to bed, and I plan to sleep late in the morning." She turned and headed to her room with Buster trailing at her heels.

I don't know what current fashion dictates as appropriate dress for a séance, but Tamara arrived looking exotic in a silky peach-colored caftan with a maroon and gold paisley print that perfectly complemented her dark skin. Soft suede boots, a single gold chain at her throat, and matching hoop earrings completed the ensemble. She wore a wide knit shawl around her shoulders for warmth against the cold night.

"Oh, my god," I said, gazing at my friend. "You look gorgeous. The ghost won't stand a chance." I looked down at my casual beige sweater and jeans. "I think I need to change."

Tamara laughed, her dark eyes glistening with humor. "You look fine. I wasn't sure what to wear, so I just threw this on 'cause it's comfortable. I'm not out to impress any ghosts."

"I'm not sure what to expect," I said. "My experience with séances is pretty limited."

"Yeah," my friend agreed. "I saw one once in an old horror movie. Scared the bejeezus out of me."

I laughed. "Norma assures me she knows what she's doing."

Tamara lifted an eyebrow and puckered her lips. "Uh-huh. From what I've read, séances were a big deal over a century ago, popular with the upper class. But they were also popular with hucksters, and a whole lot of gullible people got conned."

"I know, and I fully intend to keep a clear head." I pulled on my coat. "Besides, aren't you the one always telling me you believe in ghosts and we should listen to what they have to say."

She nodded. "I do, and we should. I just don't want you getting roped in by some old shyster selling you a bill of goods. It's pretty rare to run into someone who actually believes in ghosts." She narrowed her eyes at me. "Why else would you keep your 'talent' to yourself?"

"My *talent?* You mean my curse. I never asked to see ghosts."

"I know, but you do. And you keep it secret because you're afraid people will think you're crazy."

Yeah, like Maureen.   For twenty-five years people called her crazy because she insisted she was being haunted by her sister's ghost.

I expelled a breath. "Well, come on. Let's get going, and you can decide for yourself whether you think Norma's a crank or not."

———

Norma Hansen greeted us warmly at the door. She had gone all out, donning a long black gown decorated with abstract splashes of deep red. On her head was a matching red turban with gold spangles. Her neck was draped in beads, and her fingers sparkled with an array of jeweled rings. She was barely recognizable as the demure old woman who had served me tea while I sorted through her heaps of neglected mail. I introduced her to Tamara, and she led us inside.

Heavy curtains were drawn over the windows and the living room lay in velvety darkness. The only light came from a vintage hurricane lamp on a corner table and four flickering candles arranged on the mantle. Embers of a dying fire glowed hot in the fireplace radiating a stifling heat, and the cloying scent of incense hung heavily in the air.

I looked around in amazement. In the center of the room three chairs had been placed at a card table covered with a scarlet cloth. A human skull sat on the table, and next to it the strange Spirit Board compelling us with its cryptic mysticism. The whole effect was nightmarishly eerie.

A little over the top, I thought. *She's really got*

this medium thing down to a tee. What a departure from the homey, unpretentious living room I had seen in daylight. It must have taken the old woman hours to clear the clutter and prepare for this gathering.

Tamara looked around and gave a little shiver. "If Bela Lugosi shows up," she said, "I'm outta here."

Norma laughed, a soft crinkly sound. "I apologize for the theatrics," she said. "It's what most people expect. Sort of sets the mood, you know. The darkness helps with concentration—blocks out distractions."

"I'll bet you're a real hit at Halloween," Tamara said.

I lifted an eyebrow and nodded toward the table. "The skull?"

"Looks real, doesn't it?" said Norma. "I've had it for years; I forget where I bought it. But the important question is, did you bring the telephone?"

Whether it was the chill of the evening, the dark room with its flickering candles and gothic trappings, or mention of the haunted phone, an icy shiver ran up my spine and sent a shudder coursing through my entire body. Goosebumps prickled my arms.

"You okay?" asked Tamara.

Norma looked at me with concern. "Close proximity to the supernatural can be unnerving for anyone," she said. "But as one who has actually communed with spirits, your sensitivity is heightened. You feel their presence more acutely.

Perhaps we should adjourn to the kitchen for some tea, take a few minutes to relax and prepare emotionally."

I gave a dismissive little laugh. "No, no, I'm fine. Just a little edgy. This whole business is so bizarre. It's hard to believe we're actually having a séance and trying to invoke a spirit. It all seems so...surreal."

Tamara gave me a pointed look. "You did remember to bring the phone though, didn't you?"

"Got it right here," I said, holding up a brown paper grocery bag. Thankfully, the ghost had remained silent in the car on the way over. If the phone had rung suddenly while I was driving, I probably would have run off the road.

Norma looked at the gold watch on her wrist. "Well then, if you're ready, perhaps we should get started. In three minutes it will be midnight. Lay your coats over there on the couch, then take a seat at the table."

We did as instructed, happy to follow the elderly woman's lead. I took the chair facing the fireplace and Tamara sat to my right. I took the old telephone out of the bag and set it on the corner of the table to my left with the dial facing me. The severed cord hung halfway to the floor. My throat felt dry, and my knees jittered nervously under the table. I had no idea what to expect.

Norma picked up the grinning skull. "Let's move Seymour out of the way." She placed the gruesome prop on the fireplace mantel alongside the candles.

Great, I thought, *now he's looking right at me.*

The old woman took the chair to my left, facing Tamara across the table. She reached out and we all clasped hands. Embers in the fireplace cracked and popped; the burning candles fluttered, sending fey shadows shimmying across the walls.

Norma closed her eyes and began to speak in soft, supplicating tones, urging the spirits to come to us and share their wisdom. "We especially wish to reach out to the one among you who has been seeking to communicate through this telephone." Norma opened her eyes and looked at me. "What is the man's name, dear?"

Startled, it took me a second to remember Kayla's father's name. "Um...Ed Glassner. Kayla Donnelly's father."

The old woman gave me a reassuring smile, then pinched her eyes closed once more and continued. "Ed Glassner," she intoned, "father of Kayla Donnelly, come to us tonight and let us help you find peace. Ed Glassner, we call on you. Whatever deeds you left undone, whatever cares you left unresolved, please speak to us now and let us help you alleviate those concerns. If you have a message for your daughter, we can pass that on, too. We are here to help you achieve eternal rest."

Like a cheesy low-budget movie. I looked at Tamara. She was staring at Norma, deeply engrossed. I wondered what she was thinking.

Suddenly the antique telephone rang. The brass bells resounded with such a loud, brazen clang that we all jumped in our seats.

That's enough to wake the dead, I thought stupidly.

I turned to Norma, and she nodded encouragement. Taking a deep breath, I picked up the receiver and put it to my ear. "Hello?"

As before, the man's voice was crackled and indistinct as though he were talking through a swarm of hornets. But this time it was louder, like he was close by. "Find...the...letter..." Then the buzzing increased, muffling the words, and once again the voice faded out.

I heaved a frustrated sigh and jammed the handset back onto the cradle. "The reception's no better than it was before. All I can make out is 'find the letter.' But I don't know what it means. I don't know what letter he's talking about or how to find it."

Norma was quiet, contemplative as she gazed at the tabletop. "We're not finished yet," she murmured. "We still have the Spirit Board." She indicated the strange wooden board on the table with its curious rows of numbers and letters. "Place your fingers on the planchette," she said, demonstrating as she rested her gnarled fingertips lightly on the movable device sitting in the middle of the board. It was triangular in shape and had a small round window in the center so that the markings on the board underneath could be read through it.

"A friend of mine used to have a Ouija Board," Tamara said. "It was great fun at parties, but everyone just pushed the thing around till they got the answers they wanted. There was nothing spiritual about it."

Norma tightened her lips and even in the dim

light I could see her eyes spark. The embers in the fireplace glowed red like dragons' eyes, casting the old woman's face in weird florid hues.

She really takes this seriously, I thought as another ripple of nerves coursed up my spine.

"I am confident there will be no need to push it," Norma said. "We know there is a spirit here trying to make contact. By combining our wills and our energies, and letting them flow through us, we should enable the spirit to use the board to give us a message. Now, place your fingers on the planchette and concentrate."

Without speaking, Tamara and I both reached out and touched our fingertips lightly to the top of the smooth, triangular device. No larger than a saucer, I could tell that it had once been highly decorated with cabalistic symbols, though now, after countless years of use, it was worn and faded.

Once more, the old woman closed her eyes and began to murmur supplications. The candle flames jumped and writhed as though teased by a passing breeze, though the air in the room was still as a tomb. My heart pounded in dread anticipation.

Then the planchette moved. It lurched under my fingertips and traveled across the board, centering itself over the letter "M."

Keeping my fingers on the moving device, I glanced at my companions. Norma's gaze was fixed on the planchette, but Tamara was looking at me with an expression that clearly said, "Oh, crap."

I arched my eyebrows and gave her a feeble smile. *In for a penny...*

The planchette moved again. It hovered for a

moment over the "U," then slid once more and came to rest above the "R."

I repeated the letters outloud, "M...U...R..." The device kept moving.

"Oh, my god," Tamara exclaimed. "Is this for real? Do you see what it's spelling?"

The atmosphere was charged with tension. The darkness was oppressive.

"D...E..." I continued.

The planchette stirred one last time.

"R." As I said this, the thing stopped moving altogether.

"Murder," Norma whispered in a low, barely audible voice.

Abruptly, the candles went out and the night closed in. Only the hurricane lamp on the side table and the dying embers in the fireplace kept us from plunging into total darkness.

I heard Tamara give a faint gasp.

Chapter Twelve

"Murder," I echoed. "But Mr. Glassner drowned when his canoe tipped over. It was an accident."

Tamara turned her eyes to mine. "Maybe it wasn't," she said.

I looked at the board, then at Norma in her full-blown fortune teller regalia. I had thought calling up the dead with candles and a Ouija Board to be slightly hokey, the construct of a less educated, more superstitious culture. I hadn't needed such contrivances in my first ghostly encounter.

Yet obviously there was something to this arcane mysticism. But what was I supposed to do now? Ed Glassner's death had been ruled an accident. Death by drowning. Had the police conducted an investigation? Or had they just assumed it was an accident based on circumstances? Kayla had told me her father went out alone in his canoe every Sunday to commune with nature. The solitude had helped him feel closer to his dead wife. But *had* he been alone? Or had someone gone with him this time? Someone capable of murder?

I turned to Norma. "Can we call the spirit back? He needs to tell us more. He can't just spell out 'murder' and leave us hanging. If he was murdered, he must know who it was."

The spangles on the old woman's turban glittered as she shook her head. "The candles were snuffed out by the ghost as he departed. I suspect it took all the energy he had to influence the planchette. Moving a tangible object is not easy for a non-corporeal being."

Her satin gown swished as she stood to go turn on the lights.

I sighed and sat back in my chair, dropping my hands heavily into my lap. "Then we should probably go," I said, suddenly exhausted. "It's awfully late. Thank you so much for all your help, Norma. We could never have done this on our own."

Norma pulled the gaudy hat off her head and dropped it on the table. She jabbed her knobby fingers into her tightly curled white hair and scratched her scalp. "I'm pleased I could help, Brenna. It's been a long time since I've invoked the spirits. I know it must have been unsettling for you. I hope you haven't been put off."

"Not at all," I said. "This ghost needed someone to listen to him. The police wrote his death off as an accident, but if he was murdered he probably won't rest until the murder is solved."

Tamara groaned and rolled her eyes. "Oh no, here we go again."

I ignored my friend and said to our hostess, "Can we help you put things away?"

"The chairs go in the kitchen," Norma said in her soft, reedy voice. She had reverted back to her sweet, eighty-six-year-old grandmotherly self.

Twenty minutes later, Tamara and I were in the car headed back to my place. The old telephone was stashed once more in a grocery bag on the floor behind me. The night was cold and dark. The headlights did little to dispel the ominous aura that lingered around us.

"That was intense," my friend said, stating the obvious.

I gave a quick snort. "No kidding."

"You don't think she, you know...?"

"What, pushed it? Pretended it was the ghost? Huh-uh, no way. She's the real deal, I'm sure of it." I gave Tamara a meaningful glance. "She didn't make the phone ring either."

"True. So, what are you going to do now?"

"I don't know. Poke around, ask a few questions."

She glared at me. "This isn't a twenty-five year old cold case, you know."

"I know."

"Could get dangerous," Tamara said. "The murderer might not like you nosing around. You should turn the whole thing over to the police."

My laugh was sharp and humorless. "And tell

them what? That we had a séance, and used a
Ouija Board to summon Ed Glassner's ghost, and
he told us he was murdered? Uh-huh. I'm sure
they'd get right on it."

She sighed noisily. "Yeah, yeah, I see your
point. So, what's the plan?"

"I don't know," I said. "For now, I just want to
go home and get some sleep. We can come at this
in the morning with fresh eyes."

Gage would be home tomorrow. I was eager to
tell him what we'd discovered, but I knew he would
try to dissuade me from getting involved. But how
could I not get involved? Now that I knew there'd
been a murder?

When I came out of my bedroom the next
morning, I found Tamara still lounging on the
couch, her arm dangling from beneath the blanket
stroking Buster's velvety head as he sat blissfully
leaning against the makeshift bed. The beagle
never missed an opportunity to exploit the
attention of strangers.

"How'd you sleep?" I asked.

"Well enough," she said, sitting up. "I was just
telling your cousin about the party last night."

"What?" I said, alarmed. I locked eyes with my
friend, giving her a warning look.

Connie was in the kitchen frying bacon. She
didn't work on Sundays and often took the
opportunity to whip up something extravagant for
breakfast. I wasn't sure how she'd react to our

attending a séance.

"Good morning, sleepyhead." Connie appeared from the kitchen wiping her hands on a towel. "Tamara tells me the stargazing was pretty much a bust. Too bad, but I could have told you. It was too cloudy last night."

"But we had a nice visit with friends," Tamara put in, "so it wasn't a total loss."

I blew out a breath and relaxed. "Right—the stargazing party. I guess we'll have to try it again some other night."

"But not right away," Tamara said, lifting an eyebrow. "It was kind of exhausting."

I joined her in a laugh. This would be our private joke. Neither of us ever wanted to experience another séance.

After breakfast, I motioned for Tamara to follow me to my room. The haunted telephone was still in my car. I had left it there, fearful it might ring again and force me to contrive another explanation. My hope was that the ghost would see me working the case and quit calling. His calls weren't very helpful anyway since I could barely understand anything he said.

I shut the door and said to Tamara, "Call your husband and tell him you're spending the day with me. It's time to start sleuthing."

She clasped her hands together. "You've got an idea."

I gave a quick nod and began to pace as I laid out my plan. "Okay, if we believe what we learned from the ghost last night—that he was murdered—then we have to assume there was someone else with him on the lake that day, right?　He didn't throw *himself* out of the canoe."

"Absolutely," Tamara agreed.

"I'm thinking that if the police wrote the death off as an accident, they probably didn't do much investigating.　So, I want to go check out the lake where it happened and look for potential witnesses. There must be houses and people in the area, right? Someone must have seen something."

"Returning to the scene of the crime," Tamara said eagerly.　"I like it."

"Either there was a second boat," I continued, "or there was another person with him in the canoe."

Tamara nodded, then looked down at her silky pajamas with chagrin.　"You'll have to loan me something to wear.　It's either these or my caftan, and neither is exactly suitable for outdoor field trips."

I laughed.　"I'm sure I can find you some jeans."

"So, where are we going?　Which lake is it?"

"I don't know yet.　But I got the impression from Kayla that it's not too far from here.　I need to find the news article with the details.　You call Curtis while I check the internet.　Shouldn't take more than a couple of minutes."

She went to retrieve her phone among her things piled in the living room while I searched the internet for Ed Glassner and was rewarded with a brief article on the obituaries page of the local paper about the unfortunate drowning incident. The local sheriff took the opportunity to remind readers to always wear a life jacket when boating.

"Got it," I said when Tamara had concluded her phone call. "Lake Langston, near the town of Carnation."

"Where's that?" Her face furrowed in a baffled sort of frown.

"Snoqualmie Valley, about an hour east of here. I've been there. It's a nice little town, way out in the country. Very picturesque. They have some neat antique shops."

"Mmm, and probably lots of bugs."

"Oh, don't be such a priss. Here, put these jeans on and let's get going."

Tamara dutifully changed her clothes, then turned and grimaced at the mirror.

I had to laugh at my friend. She didn't mind getting sweaty in the gym, but going out in public in anything but colorful, trendy attire was for her the height of slumming it.

"Before we go," I said, "let's take Buster for a walk. There's somebody I want you to meet."

Tamara's eyebrows rose curiously, but she agreed without hesitation and pulled on the heavy sweatshirt I had loaned her. Buster danced at my feet, eyes bright and tail wagging as I clipped the leash to his collar and headed for the front door.

Outside, the clouds were breaking up and patches of blue showed through in places. The air was crisp and cold, but the brightening sky hinted at a clear day ahead. Perfect for a drive in the country.

Down the steps and out to the street, I turned left and headed toward the house two doors down. Buster snuffled in the grass while Tamara gazed at all the tall fir, beech, and maple trees growing along the road and between the houses, branches spreading wide over roofs and lawns. Overhead, a squirrel scolded and a jay flew off in a flurry of feathers.

"It's a lot different from downtown, isn't it?" I said, laughing at her awed expression. Tamara's reaction was much like mine had been when I'd first moved here from the city.

Her mouth gave a twist. "Lots of grass to mow, leaves to rake, and weeds to pull."

I grinned. "Can't argue with that."

By the time we reached his yard, Bill Prescott was leaning on the fence waiting for us. I suspected he'd been watching for me from the window since my usual habit was to go jogging this way every morning. On weekends, I often stopped for a chat or a cup of coffee before returning home.

"Good morning," he called in a booming voice. A wide, welcoming smile split his bearded face ear to ear.

Buster let loose with his customary yodel and ran to greet him, leaping high on the fence to receive the ear rub he expected as his just due. Happy to oblige, Bill leaned over the rail to give the dog's velvety head a quick caress.

I grabbed Tamara's hand and pulled her forward. "Bill, I'd like you to meet my friend Tamara Munroe. She lives in the same building downtown where I had my condo before I moved out here." I pivoted to face my friend. "Tamara, this is Bill Prescott, my father." I couldn't help the feelings of pride that welled up as I introduced this robust, good-looking man as my father.

"Pleased to meet you, Tamara," Bill said, taking her slender hand in his beefy paw and giving it a shake.

"Same here," Tamara said. "I've heard a lot about you."

Cringing slightly, I tried to remember how much I had told her. That he'd been a wild hell raiser in his youth? That he'd been in prison for accidentally killing a man in a bar fight?

"You make birdhouses," Tamara said.

Bill threw back his head and laughed. "Yes, I do."

That was tactful. I slipped my friend a grateful smile.

"Do you have time to come in for a few minutes?" Bill asked. "I'll put on a fresh pot of coffee."

"Sorry—maybe another time," I said. "We've got a busy day planned. We're going to take a drive in the country. It's such a nice day, I thought it would be fun to get out of the city for a change and get some fresh air, maybe hit the antique shops out in the Snoqualmie Valley. Besides, Tamara has never seen an actual cow in its natural habitat." I threw her a teasing grin.

She made a face. "I prefer mine cut and wrapped at the grocery store, thank you very much."

Bill gave a chuckle and nodded. "I feel the same. Gimme a thick T-bone any day. Well, you girls have a good time. Tamara, it was nice meeting you. Maybe we'll see you at the craft fair next week. I'm sure Brenna's told you all about that."

"We'll see," Tamara hedged. "I might have to work that day."

I laughed. "Tamara's not big into handicrafts. Haute couture is more her style."

Bill took a half step back, fingering his chin as he made a show of sizing her up. The twinkle in his eye betrayed a roguish sense of humor. "Oh, I don't know. I think you'd look real cute in one of Selma Gunderson's gingham aprons."

Tamara grimaced, and we all laughed.

"We should probably get going," I said, giving Buster's leash a tug and turning toward the house. "Talk to you later."

"Brenna, when you talk to your folks," he called after us, "be sure to tell them I enjoyed seeing them."

"Will do," I called over my shoulder, making a mental note to be sure and give my mom a call. Since the family had come here for Thanksgiving, they might be expecting me to go back there for Christmas, but I wasn't sure my work schedule would allow a trip to Arizona at this time. I hadn't been at my new job long enough to accrue any vacation.

Back home, I told Connie we were going out for the day, but I didn't provide details. It would be too hard to explain and she didn't need to know. I did glance toward Morelands' as we headed out to the car, but Gage's SUV wasn't in the driveway so I assumed they hadn't returned yet from their Florida trip. Gage had said they would get home on Sunday, but I didn't remember him mentioning a time. Just as well. It would be easier to talk to him when we were alone.

As we drove, I filled Tamara in on my thoughts so far.

"I have two possible suspects. First is Kayla's uncle, her mother's brother. Kayla had a reception yesterday, like a memorial to honor her father, and this uncle acted like a total jerk. He made it real plain that there'd been bad feelings between him and Kayla's father. He practically came right out and said he was glad the guy was dead. His poor wife was so embarrassed."

"That's terrible. Do you know what their fight was about?"

"Kayla told me her uncle blamed her father for her mother's death, even though she died of breast cancer and there was nothing anyone could do."

"Hmm, they must not have caught it early enough," Tamara said. "I know there are treatments for breast cancer now. It's not the same sort of death sentence it was, say, fifty or sixty years ago."

"Yeah, maybe," I said. "I'm just telling you what Kayla told me. I'm sure there's more to the story, I just don't know what it is."

"And you think this uncle was angry enough about it to commit murder?"

I shrugged. "I don't know. Murders have been committed over lesser things. But if you'd seen the way he acted at the reception, you'd put him at the top of the list too. Problem is, I don't have any proof."

"Who's your other suspect?"

I took the exit off the freeway and merged onto the highway going toward the eastside.

"Well, this one's sort of a stretch," I said, "but I'm thinking maybe Kayla's dad's next door neighbor, a man named Arthur Bailey. He's been awfully keen to get his hands on Ed Glassner's stamp collection."

"What? You think he'd kill for a *stamp collection?*"

"Depends on the collection, doesn't it? Maybe it's worth a fortune. Troy's taking it to an appraiser this week to find out."

"Troy?" She gave me a quizzical look.

"My boss's son. I told you about him. I met him when I was helping Connie out in the flower shop. He helped me get my job."

"Oh, that guy." Tamara grinned. "Tall, blond, and gorgeous I think you described him. I remember."

I snorted. "Don't start. Connie's already determined to put us together."

"Have you dated yet?"

"Once. He took me to dinner last night right after the reception for Kayla's father. Before the séance."

"And you're just telling me *now?*" Her words came out as a high-pitched reproach.

"It wasn't that big a deal," I insisted. "Kayla sort of trapped me into asking him to go with me to the reception. Dinner afterward just seemed to follow naturally."

"Oh, my god," she said suddenly, pointing to my

hand on the steering wheel. "I just noticed—you took off your ring. You *must* like him."

"I *do* like him. He's a nice guy. But I've only known him for, like, five minutes. It's nothing serious, okay? And quit changing the subject. We're almost there."

Chapter Thirteen

Carnation is a small rural town east of Seattle located at the confluence of the Tolt and Snoqualmie rivers. Once home to several large dairy farms, it has lately become something of a bedroom community for people who want the country lifestyle but who commute to high tech jobs in nearby cities. At the eastern edge of town, the rugged Cascade foothills rise from the valley, providing habitat for a multitude of wildlife. Thick evergreen forests, pristine lakes and rivers, and amazing pastoral scenery bring visitors every year to enjoy the great fishing, hiking, and camping in the area.

Tamara consulted the map on her phone. "Okay, stay on the main road through town. The turnoff should be just ahead about half a mile."

We followed the directions and found ourselves on a long, winding country road. We drove past fields and farms, then through wide swaths of timber. Glimpses of the lake could be seen here and there through breaks in the trees. The further we went, the denser the forest became until we eventually entered a thick, undeveloped woodland.

I slowed when we reached the turnout to a gravel boat launch. The road widened to make room for parking, but today the area was deserted. I pulled the car over. We got out and walked to the water's edge. Except for the occasional bird, the place was utterly still. Broken clouds obscured the sun, giving the water a cold, gray cast.

What a lonely, desolate spot.

"I can see why Kayla's dad came here to be alone with his thoughts," I said. "There sure wouldn't be any distractions."

Tamara shivered and nodded, wrapping her arms tightly around her shoulders. "Great place for a murder."

I glanced up and down the shore, searching for homes overlooking the lake. We had come here hoping to find potential witnesses, but the trees and underbrush grew thickly along the bank, clear down to the water. If there were any houses nearby, I couldn't see them from here, but the lake curved around a bend out of sight. We would have to do a lot more exploring.

"Come on," I said. "Let's keep going. There must be houses further on or they wouldn't have put in a road."

"Good point," Tamara said.

We got back in the car and continued to follow the road through the trees.

A hundred yards ahead, a driveway emerged from the woods. Tamara straightened and pointed eagerly to a house set deep in a thicket of hemlock and vine maple. If it hadn't been November and the maples devoid of their usual heavy foliage, the dwelling would have been entirely hidden.

"Do you want to check it out and see if the owners saw anything?" she asked. "Looks like it's right on the lake."

This is what we came for.

I took a deep breath and turned the car down the narrow lane. We bumped along a rough dirt track through thick brush as we approached the house. It was a two-story cedar structure built on a rise overlooking the water. I stopped at the end of the driveway where a short sidewalk led to a wide covered porch. An old sedan was parked underneath a carport beside the house, and several hens scratched and pecked in a grassy enclosure nearby.

What a beautiful location, I thought, admiring the trees. *But just a tad too remote for me.*

"Here goes nothing," I said to Tamara, unfastening my seatbelt.

Together we mounted the stairs and I rang the doorbell. This was met with a burst of deep throaty barks inside. After a moment, a gray-haired woman dressed in jeans and a blue sweater opened the door and peered warily at us through the screen door. Beside her stood a large black dog with droopy ears, expressive eyes, and a long straight tail that swished side to side.

"Can I help you?" she said. "But if you're selling something or promoting some religion, you might as well know that we're not interested."

They probably don't get many strangers dropping by out here.

I gave her a friendly smile and shook my head. "No, no, nothing like that. My name's Brenna, this is Tamara. We're trying to find someone who may have witnessed the accident on the lake a few Sundays ago where a man fell out of his canoe and drowned. His daughter is a good friend of mine and she's very distraught. She can't believe her father would just fall out of his canoe. He's been coming here for years. We're hoping to find someone who may have seen something and knows what really happened."

She nodded slowly. "Yes, I remember hearing the sirens, but I was upstairs and didn't see anything. I saw in the news the next day that a man had drowned, but I didn't know him. The news article simply said the man fell out of his canoe. Such a tragedy."

My disappointment must have been evident because she seemed to take pity on us. Gripping the dog's collar, she leaned forward and pushed the screen door open.

"Why don't you come in out of the cold and we'll ask my husband. Maybe he saw something." She pulled the dog out of the way. "Don't mind Otis. He's really very friendly."

The dog sniffed at us as we edged past, but his tail wagged in a way that was more curious than

threatening.   My apprehension waned, but it
occurred to me that people coming to our house for
the   first   time   might   experience   the   same
misgivings about Buster.   The little beagle could
certainly put on an intimidating act with his
howling and jumping about, although he was half
the size of this fellow.

"Nice doggie," Tamara crooned nervously.

We followed the woman into the foyer and I
gazed   around,   admiring   the   beautiful   wood
finishes.   To the right through a cased opening lay
the living room.   A man sat ensconced in a recliner
in front of a wide television.   He had a plate of
sandwiches   and   chips   balanced   on   his   lap.
Sounded like he was watching a football game.

From where we stood in the entryway, it was
possible to see straight through to the dining room
where a sliding glass door opened onto a wide deck
overlooking the lake.   A narrow lawn sloped to the
water's edge and a wooden dock protruded from the
bank   a   short   way   into   the   water.   A   small
aluminum rowboat lay upside down in the grass
nearby.

"You have a beautiful home," I said.   "And what
a gorgeous view."

"Thank you," she said with a touch of pride.
Her   face   dimpled   kindly   as   she   smiled   and
motioned us to follow her to the huge window for a
better look.   The surface of the lake glistened as
shafts of sunshine poked here and there through
the clouds.   Heavy growths of trees and underbrush
formed impenetrable screens on either side of the
property.   The gravel boat launch down the road

was completely obscured from this vantage point.

"I'll bet you get lots of wildlife out here," I said.

"Oh, yes.   Deer   and   rabbits   mostly,   and
sometimes   coyotes   and   bobcats—even   the
occasional bear, although Otis does a pretty good
job of discouraging them, don't you, boy?"

The dog looked up and opened his mouth in a
wide grin, tail beating faster.

"But we do have to make sure the chickens are
locked up tight every night," she finished.

I slipped Tamara a covert smile. I didn't even
have to look at her to know what my city friend was
thinking. While she was fine with cats, dogs, and
ghosts, of all things, she had a real aversion to wild
animals up close. Once, when a wayward squirrel
had found its way into our downtown apartment
building, Tamara had totally freaked out, nearly
hyperventilating until the poor thing was caught
and removed.

"Do you take that little boat out fishing?" I
asked our hostess, indicating the small aluminum
dinghy.   "I understand the lake is stocked with
trout year round."

"Oh, our kids do sometimes when they come to
visit in the summer," she said. "It's a very popular
lake for fishing. But mostly our grandkids just like
to swim and feed the ducks." She paused and her
expression sobered. "You said it was your friend's
father who drowned? That's terrible, I'm so sorry."

I nodded. "The police believe he was alone on
the lake when he somehow tipped the canoe and
fell into the water."

The thin lines on the woman's face deepened as

she frowned. "And you don't believe that?"

I gave a little shrug. "Let's just say I have reason to doubt. But without physical evidence or an eye witness, I can't prove anything. That's why I'm here looking for someone who may have seen something."

With a determined nod, she led the way into the living room and confronted her husband in the recliner. The dog Otis ran over and sprawled next to the chair. He was rewarded with a rough caress and a piece of his master's sandwich.

"Richard," she said, blocking the TV. "These girls are looking for someone who might know something about the accident on the lake a few weeks ago when that man drowned."

I interjected the exact date of the incident.

The woman continued. "I remember hearing the sirens but I never knew exactly what happened. Did you see anything? I know you were home that day."

"Yeah, I was home," the man growled, trying to look around his wife at the screen. "I was sitting right here where I am every Sunday—watching the game, *not* the lake. I didn't see a thing." He looked up at me with hard, deep-set eyes. "Not a fan, I take it."

I smiled back at him. "Actually, I am. But I'm trying to help a friend. I work full time and this is the only day I have free. What's the score?"

His frown relented. "Seventeen, ten. Seahawks lead."

I grinned and pumped my fist triumphantly. "Go 'Hawks!"

The game switched to a commercial and he muted the TV, giving us his full attention. He looked at his wife. "You could try calling the Bannisters. They have a view of the lake. Maybe they saw something."

She shook her head. "They were at church. They drive clear into Redmond you know, and always go out for brunch afterward. Doris actually called *me* the next day to ask if I knew what had happened. They passed the ambulance on the road when they came home." She turned to me. "Bannisters have the only other house on the lake. Most of the property around here is undeveloped. It either belongs to the county or a timber company. There's a kids' camp on the other side but it's deserted this time of year."

I looked at Tamara and heaved a sigh, spreading my hands in defeat. "I guess that's it then. I don't know where to go from here." Unless I could get the ghost talking coherently through the static on the old telephone, my investigation had hit a wall.

"You could try the homeless guy," the husband said from the recliner.

I turned and stared at him. "What? Who?"

"Back by the boat launch," he said. "There's an old vet who hangs out there sometimes looking for handouts from people who come here to fish. I think he lives in his car. Comes and goes with the seasons. I don't know if he's there now or not, but it wouldn't hurt to check. He might have seen something."

The commercial ended and the man clicked the

sound back on. The noisy football game roared back to life, drowning out any further conversation.

Tamara and I followed the wife back to the front foyer. "Thanks so much for your help," I said. "I guess we'll go check out the boat launch and see if anyone's there."

The woman gave us a warm smile. "Sorry we couldn't be more help," she said. "I hope you find what you're looking for."

Back in the PT Cruiser, we turned around and headed back down the lane the way we had come. It didn't take long to reach the deserted boat launch. I parked the car and we got out, scanning the area for signs of life. All around us, the forest lay in deep shadow. The silence was ominous.

Suddenly, Tamara touched my arm. "We're not alone." She pointed with her chin to a brushy area on the far side of the parking lot.

Please, not a bear.

I looked, and saw a blue bandana above a scruffy face peering at us over a jumble of fallen logs and huckleberry bushes. I'm not good at estimating ages, but I put him at around sixty. The face was thin and angular with a grizzled beard and etched leather skin that looked as though it hadn't seen soap in some time.

Could this be the witness we were looking for? Tamara stood silently beside me; I knew she was thinking the same thing.

"Hey, there," I called out. "Can we talk to you for a minute?"

The figure ducked and vanished into the woods.

Tamara tapped my arm and pointed toward an

area of brush I hadn't noticed before. Barely visible among the trees, hidden behind a hedge of undergrowth, sat an old camper van painted in browns and greens to camouflage it from casual view.

"Living out here in that van, I'll bet," she said.

I called out again. "We just want to ask you if you saw something that happened here a couple of weeks ago. We're not police."

Beside me, Tamara stifled a snort.

"We just want to talk to you," I yelled toward the forest where the man had disappeared. "A guy fell out of his canoe and drowned. We're trying to find out what really happened. Did you see anything?"

As I pondered what to do next, he slowly emerged from hiding. He wore an old military camo jacket, faded jeans, and scuffed army boots. Gray unkempt hair was held back with a tattered blue bandana. He was gaunt but wiry, and while he didn't act threatening, I was relieved when he remained on his side of the parking turnout and made no move to approach us.

"Hello," I said. "My name's Brenna. This is Tamara. Can we talk to you for a minute?"

Overhead, a crow squawked loudly in the branches of a tall maple tree. More crows joined in, and as if on a signal, they burst onto the air and soared like a flight of wraiths high over the lake.

The scrawny man eyed me suspiciously and nodded. "Name's Griff." His voice was gravelly, as though from too many cigarettes over a lifetime. "You wanna know about the guy who drowned.

What's it to ya?'"

"His daughter's a friend of mine. I wanted to see the place for myself, and try to find out what really happened."

"Hunh." He scratched his chin under the scraggly beard. "Too bad about poor ol' Ed."

Surprised, I asked, "Did you know him?"

"Kinda." He shrugged. "I been here awhile. Got to know him and some of th' other regulars. Most of 'em are pretty genr'ous. They sometimes gimme a fish for my supper, or a coupla bucks." He looked at me hopefully.

"It's hard for me to believe he tipped his canoe over and drowned," I said, "experienced as he was." *Now who's fishing?*

"Huh-uh," Griff said, giving his head an emphatic shake. "That canoe didn't tip over. I think th' other guy shoved him out of it."

"Other guy?" I exchanged a hasty glance with Tamara. "Do you know who he was?"

"Nope, never saw him before. Ed usually came alone. Th' other guy came in his own car, brought his own rod. Ed seemed to know him."

"Can you describe him?" I asked.

Griff shrugged. "Naw. He was bundled up. It was cold that morning. But I'd say he was older, sort of stocky."

"Hair color?"

He shook his head. "He had a hat on, so I can't say for sure."

The description didn't fit lanky Arthur Bailey— unless he'd worn a thick, heavy coat. Couldn't rule him out just yet. I needed to get the appraisal back on that stamp collection. For now, my money was still on Kayla's crotchety old Uncle Simon. He was older and heavy set.

"What makes you think the canoe didn't tip over?" Tamara put in.

"I don't think it, I *know* it," Griff said. "I didn't actually see what happened—they both got in Ed's canoe and went around that bend there, behind those trees—but th' other guy was bone dry when he paddled that canoe back here by hisself. He didn't see me watching from the woods, but I seen him come back here and hop out, pretty as you please. Then he muscled that boat over and shoved it back into the water to make it *look* like it'd tipped over."

"Did you call the police?" I asked.

He shook his head. "I ain't gotta phone. Besides, a group of hikers showed up not long after. They saw the overturned canoe and called it in."

"Did you see what happened to the other guy?" I could feel myself getting excited. At last, I had a clue.

"Jumped in his car and took off," Griff said. "He was long gone by the time the cops showed up."

"Did you give them a statement?" I asked. "Did you tell them what you saw?"

How could they have ruled Ed Glassner's death a simple accident after this man's eye witness account? Why had there been no investigation? This was clearly a murder.

Griff frowned. "I don't talk to fuzz. I try to stay outta their radar. This is public land and I ain't hurtin' nobody, but the last thing I need is cops comin' around hasslin' me."

"But you might be the only witness to this murder," I exclaimed. "You have to tell someone."

"Tellin' you, ain't I?" His voice was a raspy growl.

"But..."

He shook his head firmly. "Look, I'm sorry about Ed, and I'm sorry for his daughter, but I ain't talking to the cops. We don't exactly get along. And if you send 'em back here to harass me, I'll just take off. It's time I was headin' south anyhow. It's gettin' too cold and fishing season's over."

Tamara stepped in then. "Can you describe the guy's car? Did you see his license plate?"

He chewed his lip as he thought about it. "Silver sedan, maybe gray. One of them foreign jobs, I think. Didn't pay much attention. Didn't see the license plate."

Great. How many silver-colored foreign model cars were on the road in Washington State? Thousands? But at least we knew more now than we had this morning.

"Well, thanks, Griff," I said. "Anything else you can think of?"

He gave a shrug. "I'd say check his phone—Ed was takin' lots of pictures—but I 'spect it went into the drink when he did."

Undoubtedly. And even if the phone had been stowed safely in his coat pocket, it would have been thoroughly soaked by the time his body was pulled from the lake. It was probably too late to recover any pictures that might have been taken that day. Still, it wouldn't hurt to ask Kayla about it.

It was past lunchtime, and the clouds were moving in again. The sky looked ominous.

"Time to go," I said to Tamara, and we headed for the car. Once safely inside, I dug into my purse and extracted a twenty dollar bill. As I rolled the car forward, I paused and lowered the window, extending the money. "Thanks for all your help, Griff. Take care."

I watched in the rearview mirror as he examined the bill. I had no doubt he'd be gone before I could ever persuade anyone to come out here and get his statement.

Chapter Fourteen

Before starting the hour-long drive back to Shoreline, we stopped for lunch in Carnation. A small, one-stoplight town, there weren't a lot of choices, but we settled on a pleasant café across from the public library. We got a table by the window and ordered soup and sandwiches.

"Well, now what?" Tamara asked, swirling the ice in her glass.

"I don't know. I'd love to just turn the whole thing over to the police and be done with it, but all I have is hearsay from a sketchy homeless guy and the word of a ghost." I gave a short chuckle and shrugged. "Not a lot to go on."

"Do you really think it's the uncle?"

"Sure sounds like it," I said. "But I don't know how to go about proving it without enlisting Kayla's help, and I'm sure she'd be devastated. She might even accuse me of slandering her uncle. I certainly can't tell her about the séance or the haunted telephone. She'd think I was crazy for sure."

Suddenly my cell phone let loose with a strident *cock-a-doodle-doo* causing a waitress walking past to nearly drop her tray.

Tamara laughed as heads turned.

"I've got to change that," I murmured for the hundredth time as I checked the text. "Gage and his sister just got home from visiting their parents in Florida. He wants to see me tonight."

"Of course he does," Tamara said with a sly smile.

"I just don't know if I'm up to it," I said. "I'm really exhausted. It's been a stressful last few days—Thanksgiving with my parents, the reception for Kayla's father, then the séance."

Tamara nodded and yawned. "I hear you."

"I was really hoping to go to bed early tonight. I've got work in the morning."

"Aren't you forgetting your date with 'tall, blond, and gorgeous?' Does Gage know about Troy?"

I gave my mouth a twist. "Yes, he knows about him. He knows Troy is my boss's son and that he helped me get my job, but he's never met him."

"You going to tell him you went out to dinner with Troy last night?"

I shrugged, feeling an uncomfortable flush rising in my cheeks. "Probably not."

I shouldn't feel guilty. No promises had been made. I could go out with whomever I pleased. Yet

I knew there was something between Gage and me, something unspoken. Maybe going out with Troy was my unconscious way of proving to myself that I wasn't ready for a commitment, though deep down I knew that excuse was beginning to crumble.

I texted back a quick note letting Gage know I'd be home in a couple of hours, but I was tired and needed time to recover from the long weekend. I wanted to see him, but I didn't feel like going out.

The waitress arrived with our lunch and we tabled the discussion. The smell of the hot tomato bisque set my mouth to watering. Until this moment, I hadn't realized how hungry I was.

Then a thought occurred to me. I looked at Tamara. "Next Saturday is the craft fair."

"Oh, goodie," she said, wrinkling her nose. "You get to sit all day in the school gym peddling your homemade rugs. Can't think of a more exciting way to spend the day."

"You're just jealous 'cause you don't know how to make one," I quipped back.

She gave a huffing laugh. "Not."

"You should come. There'll be lots of cool Christmas stuff for sale. Bill would love to show you his bird houses." I cracked an impish smile. "And you know you'd look cute a gingham apron."

That elicited a full-on guffaw. Tamara didn't cook, nor did her eighth floor downtown apartment give her any place to put a bird house.

"Yeah, yeah," I said. "You're not into handicrafts." I tapped a finger to my lips. "But I have an idea. You know who might like to come?"

My friend's brows rose curiously.

"Kayla and her aunt," I said.

Tamara narrowed her eyes. "What are you thinking?"

"I'm thinking it might be a good opportunity to talk to the aunt, maybe feel her out, see what she has to say."

"What?" Tamara took a quick glance around, then leaned forward and lowered her voice. "You think she knows her husband killed Kayla's father? That's pretty heavy."

I shook my head. "No, I'm sure she doesn't know anything about the murder, but if I can somehow get her to tell me that her husband was out of the house all that day, it would just help confirm him as the prime suspect."

I took a large bite of my sandwich and chewed absently as I considered how best to broach the subject with Kayla's Aunt Lilly.

Tamara sat pondering for a moment, then said abruptly, "I just had a thought. Imagine you fell or were pushed out of a canoe. You wouldn't just hang out there in the water waiting to drown. Your instinct would be to turn around and grab the edge of the canoe, right?"

"Right. You'd grab on and try to pull yourself back in."

"But if the other guy in the boat was trying to kill you..."

I nodded, catching on. "He'd probably smack you with an oar to make you let go."

"Maybe even hit you in the head hard enough to knock you out," Tamara continued.

"Or hit you in the head *first* while you were in

the canoe, and *then* shove you in the water." I could feel my pulse quicken. "Which would make it look like the canoe had tipped over and hit you in the process." The scenario made sense, and explained why Glassner hadn't swum to shore.

"Do you know if he was struck on the head?" Tamara asked.

"All I've heard is that he drowned."

"Can you get a copy of the coroner's report and find out?"

I shook my head. "Probably not. I'd have to get Kayla's signed permission. But there may be another way to find out. In the case of a simple accident where there's no inquest, the media often gets access to information through police blotters. I may be able to track down the reporter who wrote the article about the 'accidental drowning' in the local paper. They may know more about it than what was written."

"Good idea," Tamara said. "But now it's getting late. I think we should get going before Curtis calls out the National Guard."

When we got back to the house, Tamara wasted no time in collecting her things.

"It's been interesting," she said. "Let me know how things turn out."

I waved as she drove off, then turned to go inside. That's when I noticed Gage sprinting from his sister's house next door.

So much for my quiet evening at home.

But I couldn't help smiling. I really was glad to see him. The old telephone was still on the floor in the back seat of my car, but I decided to leave it there. To retrieve it now would undoubtedly invite questions.

"Hey, Brenna," he said. "What have you been up to?"

"What? You expected me to sit around the house all day pining for you?"

He grinned. "Something like that."

"No way." I laughed. "I'm a busy lady. I have places to go, people to see. I took my city friend for a drive in the country. We haven't had much time to hang out together lately."

Gage nodded and lifted an eyebrow slightly. "Sounds like fun."

His tone was skeptical. He had an annoying way of seeing through me.

"Look," he said, "I know you don't feel like going out tonight, and I get that—it's been an exhausting week—but how about coming over for a quiet evening at home, just the two of us? Maureen's going to Nick's for dinner and I'm sure she'll be there for a while. I thought maybe we could order a pizza and watch a movie or something. It won't be a late night. We've both got work tomorrow."

What could I say? "Okay, give me a few minutes to change."

———

"So, how was Tampa?" I asked.

We were settled on the couch before a crackling fire in Maureen's living room enjoying a glass of wine. A large pizza box rested on the coffee table in front of us. Gage had chosen an old movie from

Maureen's collection of DVDs, but we opted to talk first.

"Warm, humid. The opposite of Seattle in November," he said.

"I meant, how are your parents? How was Thanksgiving?"

He gave a shrug. "Surprisingly cordial. Like I told you, lots of tears and hugs. We had some good talks, cleared the air, got some closure."

"Gage, that's wonderful." The rift in the Moreland family had been so painful for so long that any kind of positive interaction was a step toward healing.

"I mean, we're still not the cheeriest family in the world," he said, "all things considered, but things seem to be moving in the right direction. They're even talking about maybe coming out for a visit next year."

I reached out and gave his hand a squeeze. "I'm so glad it all worked out."

That's when he noticed.

A faint line appeared between his brows as he gave me a searching look. "You took your ring off."

I straightened and looked at my hands, then gave a little shrug. "Two years—it felt like the right time."

He set down his wine glass and moved closer. "I'm glad," he whispered. Then he gathered me into his arms and pressed a warm kiss to my lips. I leaned into him, my hands reaching around his waist as I pulled him against me and inhaled the faint masculine scent of his cologne. My pulse quickened as long dormant feelings began to stir.

Finally, I drew back, catching my breath. *Slow down—it's been a long time. No need to rush.*

"Pizza's getting cold," I murmured.

He laughed and sat back, willing to let me set the pace.

"Can't let the pizza get cold," he said, eyes twinkling. He flipped open the box and held it up so I could pull out a slice. "Now, what about you? How was your week? Did you have a good time with your family?"

"Yeah, it was fun seeing them and getting caught up. Even spent an afternoon in Seattle at the waterfront."

"How'd it go with Bill Prescott?"

I gave a clipped little laugh. "As you said, surprisingly cordial, everyone on their best behavior. Even my mom played nice, so bottom line, it was a good visit."

"Glad to hear it," Gage said. "And no more supernatural encounters?"

"Uhhh," I kneaded my chin and turned away, studying the pizza on the table. He was making light of it, but what I had experienced this weekend was no joke. "Not exactly."

He gave an audible groan. "Don't tell me your ghost is still calling."

My lips tightened. "It's not *my* ghost."

"Or is it something else now? A haunted toaster? A flickering lightbulb?"

I glared at him, resisting the urge to throw my pizza slice at him. "It's not funny."

Grinning, he threw his hands up to ward off my anger. "No, of course not. These kinds of things happen to everybody."

I stood up in a huff. "Look, if you can't take this seriously, I'm leaving. I will *not* be told I'm crazy—especially by you." I could feel my heart hardening with every condescending word he said. A moment ago I had thought I could give in, put the past behind, and fall in love again. Now I wasn't so sure.

His face softened. He reached out and took my hand. "I'm sorry. Come on, Brenna, you know I don't think you're crazy. Sit down and tell me what happened."

I continued to stand. Then stiffly, I began: "My friend Tamara and I went out to the lake this morning where Kayla's father died."

"Ahh, that's what you were doing. What made you go out there?"

"I figured if I was going to help this ghost get justice, I needed to go to the scene of the crime and look for clues."

"What?" He looked bewildered. "What crime? What clues? I thought you said it was an accident. He fell out of his canoe and drowned."

"That's what everyone *thought*. Kayla said her father went out there alone and somehow fell out of his canoe. The police ruled it an accident, but I found a witness at the lake who saw him with another man."

"That doesn't prove anything," Gage said dubiously.

I ignored him and went on. "I think the other man hit him over the head with the paddle and knocked him out, then pushed him out of the canoe and left him to drown in the freezing water."

"Is that what the witness said?" His dark eyes took on a serious expression. "I think it's time you let the police handle it."

"No, the witness didn't actually see what happened. But I know Kayla's father was murdered."

"*How* do you know?"

"The ghost said so." I crossed my arms, daring him to contradict me.

"The ghost in the phone? I thought you said you couldn't make out what he said."

I took a deep breath. If Gage was skeptical now, how would he react to what came next? "Remember the old woman I told you about that I've become guardian for?"

He nodded. "The one with raccoons in the attic?" A faint smile betrayed itself on his lips.

"Yes. Well, it turns out she's a medium. She can communicate with spirits."

"What? Brenna..." He sputtered and made a face. "Next you're going to tell me you had a séance."

His tone was incredulous and I could tell he was fighting the urge to roll his eyes. *So much for keeping an open mind.* I clamped my mouth into a hard line. "Just forget it, okay? It was a mistake telling you. I thought of all the people in the world, you'd understand, but obviously I was wrong. To you this is nothing but a big joke, and I refuse to stand here and be made fun of."

I grabbed my purse and coat off the armchair where I'd tossed them, and headed for the door.

This was not how I'd expected the evening to go, but I was not going to stay there and be teased and ridiculed by the one person I had thought I could count on.

Gage came after me, his voice full of contrition. "I'm sorry, Brenna, *really*. I *do* take this seriously. That's the problem, don't you see? I worry about you getting in over your head. If there *was* a murder, then there's also a murderer, and that could mean real danger. You should stay out of it."

I glowered at him. "I can take care of myself."

"Remember last time?" he said. "You could have been killed."

"Well, thank you for that vote of confidence. Now, I'm tired. I'm going home. I've got a million things to do this week and I need a good night's sleep." I stomped to the door and yanked it open, leaving Gage standing behind me with his mouth open. Served him right.

Chapter Fifteen

I left home the next morning at eight thirty and headed straight to Norma Hansen's house. The exterminators were due at nine and I wanted to keep the lady company during the unaccustomed noise and disturbance at her home.

I was still fuming at Gage's ridicule and lack of sympathy for the unhappy ghost. If I didn't solve the man's murder his spirit would never have peace and would never leave me alone. I had thought Gage understood this.

When I arrived, a panel truck was parked in the driveway and two persons in hazmat suits were preparing for the job, propping a ladder in the garage at the attic access and arranging their equipment within easy reach. They explained that they would haul off the soiled insulation in heavy plastic bags, then sanitize the attic by thoroughly saturating it with an enzyme-based cleaner. After that, it would just be a matter of adding new insulation.

Norma met me at the front door. She greeted me in her usual genteel manner and offered to make tea.

"Have you had any further contact with the spirit in the telephone since the séance?" she asked eagerly.

"No," I said. "He's been pretty quiet."

I didn't tell her the haunted phone was still stashed in the same grocery bag on the back seat floor of my car. I hadn't had an opportunity to bring it inside yet. Besides, it was a relief not to have to worry about it ringing in the house at inopportune moments.

As we sipped tea at the kitchen table, I told her about my visit to the lake with Tamara and our encounter with Griff.

"He saw another man go out in the canoe with Kayla's father," I said, "and come back alone, but he didn't actually see what happened. I think the other man pushed Kayla's father out of the canoe and hit him over the head with the paddle to knock him out. Otherwise, he would have swum to shore. Kayla told me her father was a good swimmer. Problem is, we don't know who the other man was." I decided to keep my suspicion about Kayla's uncle to myself. Without proof, it was nothing more than conjecture.

The old woman pursed her lips thoughtfully. "Have you tried using the telephone to ask the ghost for answers?" She picked up her pretty rose pattern teapot and refilled my cup, then moved the sugar bowl closer.

What a relief to talk to someone who takes me seriously.

I shook my head. "I've tried talking to the ghost, but it's frustrating. It's like a one-way call. I talk and he either doesn't respond or I can't understand him through the heavy static."

"We could try the Spirit Board again," Norma said, looking at me with eyes as keen and bright as a woman's half her age.

I shuddered and gave a sharp laugh. "No, I'll leave that as a last resort. I'm not sure my nerves could stand another séance. I'm going to try a more conventional route first. I actually have a couple of potential suspects in mind."

"Do you have a plan?" she asked.

I shrugged. "Ask questions. Try to find clues."

She looked at me with concern, the wrinkles in her brow deepening. "Be careful, dear. There's a murderer out there, and he's not going to like you snooping around."

I gave her a reassuring smile. "Don't worry—I'll be very careful. But let's talk about something else. Didn't you tell me you came from Michigan? Were you born there? What's it like?"

I regretted mixing the old woman up in this whole sordid affair. I had the uncomfortable feeling that drawing her into this web of hauntings and murder didn't exactly align with my oath as her guardian. Yet she obviously was not troubled by the existence of ghosts, and her help had been invaluable.   In fact, she had seemed almost invigorated by the séance and the opportunity to show off her knowledge of arcane phenomena.

Just before noon the exterminators let us know they were wrapping up. The insulation contractors would arrive in a couple of days to blow in a new layer of loose-fill fiberglass. I thanked them and reminded them to send the final invoice to my office. Whatever wasn't covered by Norma's home-owner's insurance would be reimbursed from her ample funds.

Norma invited me to stay for lunch but I begged off.   Before going back to the office I wanted to make a quick detour to Kayla's coffee shop.   I wanted to personally invite her to the craft fair next Saturday and hopefully persuade her to bring her aunt along. If I could take Aunt Lilly aside and get her talking, maybe she would reveal where her husband had been on the day of the so-called accident.   Maybe she would even let slip whether she believed him angry enough to murder his brother-in-law. I felt terrible about it, but how else could I get to the truth?

Kayla's husband was behind the counter when I arrived.

"Hi, James," I said. "Is Kayla here?"

"Oh, hi, Brenna. No, she took the day off to get some work done at her dad's house. She contacted one of those estate sale outfits and they want to start organizing things for a sale, but there are things of her dad's she wants to go through first."

"Makes sense," I said. "I just wanted to invite her to our holiday craft sale this Saturday.   I thought it might be fun and a way to help take her mind off all this estate business for a few hours."

"Yeah, she'd probably like that," he said. "She's always been into that crafty stuff."

"Maybe I'll run by there on my way back to the office. I'm on my lunch hour."

James pointed to the front window of the shop. "Did you see? We put up one of your flyers. Connie brought it over this morning."

I turned around and looked. "That's great, thanks. I missed it when I came in, I was so focused on talking to Kayla." I hesitated a moment, then continued in a more serious vein. "James, could I ask you something?"

"Sure. Go for it." He leaned on the counter, giving me his attention.

I took a breath, then dove in. "I was thinking of asking Kayla if she'd like to invite her Aunt Lilly to come with her to the craft fair. I met her at the reception and she seemed real nice, but it was pretty obvious there were some bad feelings going on with her husband. I don't want to stir up any trouble."

James snorted. "Yeah, that Uncle Simon's a real piece of work. He never liked Kayla's father— didn't think he was good enough to marry his sister."

"I know it's none of my business," I said, "but Kayla told me he blamed her father for her mother's death. How is that possible if she died of cancer? What could her father have done?"

James shrugged and gave his mouth a twist. "It all had to do with medical insurance. Ed was self-employed. Twelve years ago, he and his partner were running the nursery on a shoestring. They didn't have money in the budget for insurance, so when Mary was diagnosed they put off treatment trying to save money. Mary herself refused to go to the hospital, afraid of bankrupting them. I don't think they realized how serious it was till it was too late. Uncle Simon accused Ed of being too cheap to get Mary the medical help she needed."

"Oh, that's terrible," I said.

"Yeah, and Ed felt bad enough without Simon badmouthing him about it all the time."

Now what? Should I pursue this angle, or would I just come off sounding nosy and unfeeling? The conversation was turning awkward. I was saved when a man and woman came in behind me and began peering at the baked goods on the shelves under the glass display.

"Why don't you give me one of those scones there," I said hastily, "and I'll get out of your hair. I should get moving if I'm going to have time to run by the house and see Kayla. Thanks, James."

When I arrived at her father's house, Kayla greeted me with a wide smile and pulled me inside.

"Brenna," she exclaimed, "I'm so glad to see you. I've been going through Dad's office trying to get all his papers organized."

I laughed. "Nobody said it would be easy."

I followed her as she led the way to the basement office.

"Dad apparently did a lot of the financials for the business at home," she said. "I'm finding all sorts of purchase orders, inventories, billings, and whatnot. The estate liquidators want to come in and start prepping for the sale, but I've been holding them off till I finish."

"Shouldn't you just turn all the papers over to your dad's partner and let him deal with it?"

"Probably," Kayla said. "I've got a whole stack here. I've been cleaning out the filing cabinet."

Suddenly, I remembered what the voice in the haunted phone had said: *find the letter.*

"What about correspondence?" I asked. "Did you find any letters? Anything important? Maybe something your dad was working on that he didn't get finished?"

She looked at me curiously. "Like what?"

I shrugged. "I don't know. I just thought maybe, since you were going through his papers, you might have found letters." I felt myself flailing. "You know—loose ends, things to be dealt with."

"Oh, no, nothing like that," she said. "But I did discover something else."

I raised my eyebrows.

"Look at this." She pulled a wide, thin book off the top of the desk and handed it to me. "It's Dad's high school yearbook. I found it on the bookshelf behind the desk. And look what was stuck inside."

I laid the book open on the desk and spread out the thin sheet of paper that had been folded and placed inside like a bookmark. "It's the contract for the roof replacement," I said, looking up. "Why would he keep it in his high school yearbook?"

"Look at the name of the company," Kayla said.

I glanced again at the contract and read aloud: "Gleason Roofing."

"Check the fine print," Kayla urged. "The owner's name is Tom Gleason. He and my dad went to school together. The contract was marking the page. See? Their pictures are right next to each other—Glassner and Gleason."

I studied the rows of smiling teenage faces, taking in the decades-old hairstyles and clothing fashions. Recalling the photograph of Kayla's father I'd seen at the memorial, I had no trouble picking out his younger self in the yearbook. He appeared fresh-faced and eager, with the same expressive eyes that had unnerved me the first time I saw them. Like any typical eighteen-year-old about to graduate, he looked ready to take on the world. Next to him in alphabetical order was a photo of a handsome boy with freckles and light, curly hair. Beneath the pictures were printed their names and school accomplishments.

"Read what Tom Gleason wrote in the margin," Kayla said.

I looked again. In the margin next to the pictures, written in black ink were the words: *Watch your back. I haven't forgotten last summer – Tom.*

I met Kayla's eyes. "Interesting."

"What do you think it means?" she asked. "Sounds kind of threatening."

I licked my lips thoughtfully. "I don't know. Remember, it was a long time ago."

"Do you think they had some kind of fight in high school and they've had it in for each other ever since? Do you think Tom Gleason's trying to get even for something, and that's why he screwed up the new roof on Dad's house and won't come back and fix it?" Her voice became shrill and she rubbed her hands over her face, obviously distraught.

Or did he knock him on the head and push him into the freezing lake to drown? Is it possible this was the letter the ghost wanted me to find? I was dubious. Technically, this wasn't a letter.

I shook my head. "Let's not jump to any conclusions. I'll take the contract like we planned, and I'll call Mr. Gleason from the office. If necessary, I can always invoke Mr. Cavendish as your attorney."

"Would you do that?" Kayla asked. "That would be great. You understand all that legal mumbo jumbo way better than I do."

Yeah, nine years in the profession had made me fluent in mumbo jumbo.

I folded the roofing contract and put it in my purse.

"Now," I said, "I really should get going. Lunch hour's over."

"Oh, of course," Kayla said. "I shouldn't have kept you so long."

"That's okay. But listen, the reason I came by was to personally invite you to the craft fair my neighborhood is putting on this Saturday at the Shoreline elementary school. I thought it might be a fun diversion for you. There'll be lots of cool holiday items for sale, including my own fabulous handmade rag rugs." I laughed, hoping to buoy up her spirits.

"Oh yes, Connie told me all about it. I'd love to come."

"And I was wondering if you'd like to invite your Aunt Lilly. She seemed real nice when I met her, and I thought she looked like she could use a day out of the house."

Kayla smiled and gave a nod. "You know, I think she'd like that. It was nice of you to think of her. I'll be sure to ask her."

Well, that was that. Now I had to be patient. Hopefully, Kayla would convince her aunt to come and I'd be able to wangle some information.

Back at the office, I plowed diligently into the pile of legal briefs left on my desk by Mr. Cavendish that morning. At three o'clock, he left for the courthouse and I allowed myself a short break. I filled my coffee cup, then searched the internet for the article in the local paper about Ed Glassner's drowning. The article was brief and contained only cursory information, no mention of the medical examiner's findings or any head injuries associated with the accident.

I called the phone number listed for the newspaper and asked for the reporter named in the byline. After a moment, a gruff male voice came on the line.

"Wilson."

"Mr. Wilson," I said, "my name is Brenna Wickham, and I'm calling about the article you wrote a couple of weeks ago about the drowning death of a local man, Ed Glassner. Do you remember?"

"Vaguely. What about it?"

"His daughter is a good friend of mine and she's totally distraught. Her father was an excellent swimmer and she just can't understand how he could have fallen out of his canoe and drowned. There must have been more to it. Did the canoe hit a log or something and tip over?"

"Has your friend seen the coroner's report?"

"I don't think so. That requires so much paperwork and she's too upset. I'm sure you can understand. I was just hoping you might remember and be able to shed some light on it, maybe give her some closure."

"Look," he said, "I don't remember the specifics and I've got to run pretty soon, so how about you give me your email address and I'll send you my notes and a copy of the full article as I wrote it. Maybe you'll find what you're looking for there." He gave an exasperated grunt. "The editors shortened it for publication to save space for some ads they wanted to run."

"That would be great," I said. "Thank you so much."

I gave him my personal email and hung up the phone. Across the room, I caught Rhonda giving me a quizzical look. Sharing an office with Mr. Torres's assistant made keeping secrets difficult, but I wasn't a rookie when it came to working in a small office with other women. I merely gave her a smile and went back to work, ignoring her as I buried my nose once more in the pile of papers on my desk.

At five o'clock, Rhonda gathered up her things and headed for the door.

"See you tomorrow," she said as she passed my desk on her way out the door.

I gave her a quick "bye," and as soon as she was gone, immediately brought up my personal email to check for the reporter's notes. Sure enough, there they were as promised.

A quick scan confirmed my suspicions. The medical examiner had found that Ed Glassner had sustained a blow to the head. The upside down canoe had been found floating in the lake near where his body was found. Since the man had purportedly been alone at the time, it was concluded that the boat had accidently overturned and struck him on the head as it went over, causing him to lose consciousness in the water and subsequently drown.

It was speculated that Mr. Glassner had attempted to stand up in the boat while reeling in a fish. This was a well known cause of tipover accidents. A fishing rod had been found floating nearby. The cold temperatures and hypothermia had also been factors in the unfortunate man's demise.

There you have it, I thought, *the perfect murder.* A swift blow to the head to incapacitate the victim and the freezing water does the rest. Then it's just a matter of turning the canoe over and pushing it back into the lake. If not for the dead man's ghost prompting me to investigate, I never would have gone out to the lake and discovered Griff, the recalcitrant witness.

But what to do now? Go to the police? They would demand evidence—which I didn't have.

Absorbed in these thoughts, I was startled by a sudden noise behind me.

Chapter Sixteen

"Hello, gorgeous," came a familiar voice. "What are you reading so intently?"

"Troy," I said, spinning my chair around to face him. "How did you know I was here?"

"Seriously?" He looked amused. "How many purple PT Cruisers do you think there are in this town, let alone on this street?"

I laughed. "Right. I guess there is that. But this isn't your usual route home, is it?"

"It's not that far out of the way, and I thought I'd take a chance that you might be here, see if you'd like to go grab some dinner." His smile was very persuasive.

Why not? Maybe it was time to give Troy a fresh look.

"Sure," I said, mirroring his smile. "Just let me

close this down."

I turned and reached to shut off the computer, then stopped. Troy had known Kayla and her father for a long time. Maybe I should confide in him, get his take on my suspicions. I didn't have to tell him about the haunted telephone or the séance, but there was no reason I couldn't tell him about my encounter with Griff and the notes sent to me by the newspaper reporter.

Instead of closing down the computer, I took a deep breath and turned around once more to face him.

"I need to tell you something," I said. "I've been doing a bit of sleuthing."

Troy's eyebrows rose, accentuating his blue eyes. "Sleuthing?" He peered around me to catch a glimpse at my computer screen. "Is that—?"

"The article about Ed Glassner's drowning accident," I said. "The more I look into it, the more I think it wasn't an accident."

"What?" He looked dumbstruck.

I stood up and moved aside, motioning him to take the seat. "Here—this is the full article written by the reporter. He said it was abridged for publication and some of the details were left out. I asked him to send it to me along with his notes. Read through it all, then tell me what you think."

He gave me a dubious look, but dutifully settled in front of the screen and absorbed himself in the text. I leaned against the desk and waited.

After a few minutes, he turned around and narrowed his eyes, giving me the sort of intense stare I imagined he used in court when sizing up a jury or challenging a witness during one of his criminal trials.

"So, what part of this do you find suspicious?" he asked.

I shook my head.   "The article itself isn't suspicious.   It simply helps confirm a theory I have."

Confusion furrowed Troy's handsome face. "You'd better start at the beginning."

Obviously I couldn't start with the ghost, so instead I began: "It started with Kayla. She kept saying how she couldn't believe her father would just fall out of his canoe and drown. He'd been going to the lake for the past twelve years and never so much as got his feet wet. Her words. She told me her father was an excellent swimmer and she couldn't understand why he didn't just swim to shore. So I decided to go out to that lake and have a look around for myself. I kept hearing Kayla in the back of my mind saying 'it doesn't make sense,' but the police didn't bother with an investigation. They just assumed he was alone and it was an accident."

"I thought the canoe tipped over."

"That's what everyone thought."

Troy frowned. "This reporter says in his notes that the medical examiner found a gash on the top of Ed's head. He attributed it to his being struck by the boat when it tipped over on him. He was knocked unconscious and subsequently drowned. It makes perfect sense."

"Right, but what else might cause a gash like that?" I said. "How about being bashed on the head by someone swinging a heavy canoe paddle?"

"*What?* You believe he was *murdered* because there was a gash on his head? Brenna, it won't stand up in court. Ed's death was a terrible tragedy, but bottom line, it was an accident."

I steeled myself. If he started calling me crazy or telling me I should mind my own business, it would be game over. I got enough needling from Gage. I didn't need it from Troy too.

"The witness says otherwise."

"Witness?" Troy said. "I thought there weren't any witnesses."

"He's sort of a drifter," I said. "I met him when I went out there. He lives in a van in the woods by the lake. Calls himself Griff. He looks like a grizzled old veteran. He told me he saw Kayla's father and another guy go out in the canoe that day, and only the other guy came back."

Troy's eyes narrowed. "How do you know it was Kayla's father he saw?"

"He called him Ed. He said he knows a lot of the regular guys who go out there to fish. They sometimes give him handouts. Besides, when I asked about the man who'd drowned, he knew immediately who I was talking about."

"Okay. Then how do you know it wasn't this Griff who killed him?"

I hesitated, not having a good answer. Finally, I shook my head. "I *don't* know for sure. I just don't think he did. Call it intuition. He had no motive, plus I got the feeling that the last thing he'd want to do would be to give the police a reason to come nosing around, hassling him."

He leaned back in the chair, elbows on the armrests, fingers clasped in front of his chest. "Okay," he said, "I'm with you so far."

I went on. "He said Ed and the other guy went out together in the canoe so they must have known each other. Griff didn't actually see what happened, but he said the other guy came back alone, turned the canoe over, and shoved it back into the lake. Then he drove away in a silver-colored foreign model sedan."

"So you think this other guy hit Ed over the head and pushed him out of the canoe?"

"Sounds like it."

Troy quirked his lips. "I don't suppose Griff gave you a description of the guy?"

"Just that he was a stocky older man."

"Could be almost anyone."

I nodded and leaned back against my desk. "At least you haven't dismissed the whole thing out of hand. I was half afraid you'd tell me I'm crazy."

His eyes twinkled behind the lenses of his tortoiseshell glasses. "I don't think you're crazy, Brenna. Possibly endowed with an overactive imaginative, but not crazy. In fact, I'm intrigued. I can't believe you drove all the way out to the lake on a hunch."

I shrugged. "It wasn't that far and I wanted to check it out. I hoped I might find something the police overlooked."

"You missed your calling, Sherlock. I don't know whether to be impressed or concerned. Have you told the police about any of this?"

"I thought about it, but Griff made it pretty

clear he wouldn't talk to the 'fuzz.' I had a hard enough time getting him to talk to me. Besides, he said he planned to leave right away to go south for the winter." I gave a little shrug. "Without a witness or any evidence, I'm not sure the police would even listen to me."

"Probably not." Troy looked thoughtful. "So now what?"

I ran my tongue over my bottom lip. Troy had been friends with Kayla and her family for a long time. What would he think of my accusing her uncle? So far he'd been pretty receptive. I decided to go for it. "Well, I am considering a possible suspect. Remember Kayla's Uncle Simon, how he acted at the memorial reception?"

"Yeah," his brows creased. "Wait—surely, you don't think..."

"James told me that Uncle Simon blamed Ed for Kayla's mother's death. Simon thought Ed was too cheap to pay for medical insurance, and then couldn't afford the cancer treatment she needed. I'm not saying it was premeditated, but maybe in the heat of an argument..."

"I don't know, Brenna. I find that really hard to believe. I mean, the guy may be a hothead, but to commit murder..." His expression left little doubt he thought the notion far-fetched.

"Think about it. It had to be someone Ed knew well enough to take fishing with him."

"So, you're saying you think Simon clubbed Ed with a canoe paddle then pushed him into the lake to drown?"

"The paddle," I exclaimed suddenly, fighting the

urge to smack myself in the head. That paddle could be a significant piece of evidence. "It probably has the killer's fingerprints on it, maybe DNA. I wonder what happened to it?"

"The killer probably still has it," Troy said.

"Griff didn't mention the paddle, and I didn't think to ask about it."

"It's probably still floating somewhere in the lake, forgotten," Troy said. "Maybe we need to take another run out there. How does this Saturday sound? The weather's supposed to be nice, and we could pack a picnic."

I looked at him askance. "I hope you're not just humoring me to get me alone out at the lake."

"Not at all," he said. He stood and took my hands. "But I like the idea."

Pulling me close, he leaned in for a kiss. His lips were soft and warm, and I felt my knees going weak. *God, he's sexy*, I thought. Tall, blond, and gorgeous barely covered it.

Before things could go any further, I stepped back and placed a hand firmly against his chest. "Slow down, tiger," I said. "Let's not rush into anything."

Troy sighed and ran a hand through his thick blond hair. He smoothed his jacket and gave a soft laugh. "Just friends," he said. "I know."

I smiled. "At least until we get to know each other better."

He mirrored my smile. "Okay, we'll take it slow. I'm willing to wait—" he leaned toward me again and whispered in my ear "—because I think you're worth it." Then he straightened and said, "But we could still have a picnic at the lake. No strings attached."

I shook my head regretfully. "Unfortunately, I'm busy this Saturday. I'm helping put on a craft fair with my cousin and a few people in my neighborhood. If you still want to go eat, I'll tell you all about it."

His soft laugh sounded resigned. "Absolutely. You like Thai? There's a great place just around the corner."

I shut down my computer and gathered my things, then sent a quick text to Connie telling her I'd be late, and not to wait dinner for me. The light was still on downstairs in Mr. Randall's office, but Shannon, the receptionist, had left so I locked the door behind us as we exited.

We walked to the nearby Thai restaurant, a brightly lit, casual dining space with tall green potted palms in the corners and colorful travel posters on the walls. Over crispy honeyed duck I told Troy all about my efforts to learn the old fashioned art of rug braiding, and how the idea of a craft fair had started out as a kind of therapy for my agoraphobic neighbor.

His thin Nordic face crinkled in all the right places as he smiled. "You're amazing, you know that?"

I laughed and made an embarrassed gesture. "I've invited Kayla. I thought she could use the distraction. She's up to her elbows sorting through her father's stuff."

"Do you know when the estate sale will be?" he asked.

"No, but I imagine they'll want to do it before Christmas."

His expression took on a more serious aspect. "Are you planning to tell Kayla about your suspicions?"

"No, at least not yet, but I've asked her to bring her aunt along to the craft fair. I'm hoping to get her aunt talking, see if she says anything about Simon being gone the day of the accident. She probably has no idea he went out to the lake to meet Ed, but—"

He frowned. "If she *did* know and didn't say anything, that would make her an accessory."

"I know, but I don't think she did. I just want her to say that he wasn't home that day and where he said he was. Then I might be able to check it out and debunk his alibi."

"Brenna," Troy said in his stern lawyer voice, "you've got to tread lightly here. If you're wrong and you start a rumor, you could find yourself in the middle of a nasty defamation lawsuit."

I knew he was right. "Don't worry, I haven't said a word about my suspicions to anyone else." *Except Tamara, but who's she going to tell? She doesn't know any of these people.*

He frowned. "But if you're right—"

Then Kayla's uncle is a murderer. "I'll be careful," I said.

I decided not to mention the negligent roofer. Matters were complicated enough already without throwing that into the mix as well. Besides, it was probably nothing. The comment in the yearbook could have meant anything. They had been teenagers, seniors in high school. Thinking back to my own high school days and remembering the boys I had known, I figured it most likely had had something to do with either sports or girls. To assume a feud had persisted all these years and culminated in murder seemed like a real long shot.

After we'd eaten, Troy walked me to my car and stood by while I dug into my purse for my keys. As I opened the car door, the telephone in the back seat began to ring, loud and dissonant. I stepped back with an involuntary gasp.

"What's that?" Troy asked. "Did you leave your phone in your car? No, wait. You had it in the office when you texted your cousin. You have another phone?"

I gave a quick, nervous laugh, trying to dislodge the icy fingers that were wrapping themselves around my insides. "Yeah, it's an old phone. Just ignore it. I keep meaning to get rid of it."

Before he could ask any more questions, I jumped into the car and jammed the key into the ignition. Mouthing a thank-you through the window, I gave a quick wave and started the engine. Behind me on the floor, the phone kept up its incessant ringing. It was well after dark and a winter chill was in the air. I stepped on the gas; I just wanted to get home. By the time I got there, the ringing had stopped.

———

The next morning when I got to the office, I barely had a chance to take off my coat when Kayla called. She sounded frantic.

"Dad's laptop is missing," she cried. "I've turned the house upside down and I can't find it. Besides work, he used it for everything—email, appointments, pictures."

"Could it be at the nursery? He probably took it with him to work."

"No," she said. "I called Ward—Dad's partner— and asked him to look for it. He says he searched all over the store and the grounds, and he can't find it." She gave a strangled sob. "It had years' worth of pictures on it that I can never get back. I think whoever broke into the house a week ago stole it. As far as I can tell it's the only thing missing."

"Who would want your dad's laptop?" I asked. Then immediately I knew: *the murderer*. If Kayla's father had taken pictures of himself and his companion at the lake that day, those pictures would be extremely incriminating. And if his cell phone and laptop were synced together then it followed that the murderer would want the laptop in order to destroy the evidence.

"I don't know," Kayla wailed in dismay. "It doesn't make sense. What good would it do them? I'm sure it was password protected."

"What about your dad's phone?"

"It was never found," she moaned. "I'm sure it's at the bottom of the lake."

As I feared. "Well, be sure to report the theft to the police," I said. "There's always a chance it'll turn up. If some kid stole it, he might try to pawn it."

I didn't want to get her hopes up just yet, but I

thought that if her father's phone and laptop were synced through a cloud account, there might still be a way to recover the data.

At three o'clock I took a break and fished the roofing contract out of my purse. I called the number printed on the heading and got a cheery woman on the line. I asked to speak to Mr. Gleason.

"May I tell him what this is regarding?" asked the woman.

In my most professional voice, I said, "I'm calling regarding the roof that was installed for Mr. Ed Glassner in August. Mr. Gleason has been informed that the roof leaks and yet has been blatantly remiss in making the repairs. I'm sure he is not eager for a law suit, so I would like to talk to him and see how we can get this resolved quickly and amicably."

There was a brief hesitation, then, "Just a moment."

After what I imagined was a quick conversation and a flurry of paperwork, a man came on the line. "This is Tom Gleason. How can I help you?"

"Good afternoon, Mr. Gleason," I said. "My name is Brenna Wickham. I work for Attorney Ross Cavendish, and I'm calling on behalf of Kayla Donnelly, the daughter of Ed Glassner for whom you installed a new roof back in August. As I believe you know, the roof leaks and needs to be repaired as soon as possible."

"Yeah, I know. I talked to Ed a couple of weeks ago and I thought we had it all worked out. I've had employee issues and supply chain problems. I told him he was first on the list and I'd get to it just as soon as I could. He said he understood, said he'd put a tarp over it in the meantime. What's he doing calling an attorney?"

Was it possible he didn't know?

"Mr. Gleason," I said, "are you aware that Ed Glassner died recently?"

"*What? No.*" The man sounded genuinely shocked. "How? What happened? Was he sick?"

"He died in an accident. It was reported in the local news. I thought you would have heard."

"No, I had no idea."

"His daughter is handling his estate now," I said. "She'll be wanting to sell the house, so you can see why she's anxious to have the roof fixed."

"Yeah, sure. Like I said, I'll get on it as soon as I can." His voice dropped, sounding shaken. "I can't believe he's dead. Gosh, we knew each other since grade school."

"Mr. Gleason, I have to tell you his daughter showed me her father's high school senior yearbook."

"Huh." He gave a short, humorless laugh. "He still had that?"

"Yes, and she was wondering about something you wrote in it. Something like, '*Watch your back— I haven't forgotten about last summer.*' Do you remember that? Can you explain what it means?"

Another harsh laugh. "Hell, no. It was forty years ago. Look, I'm sorry to hear about Ed, I really am. But the truth is we'd kind of gotten out of touch. I hadn't even talked to the guy in ten years, not till he called last summer about getting his roof replaced. Tell his daughter I'll be out to fix the roof by the first of next week. That's the best I can do, okay? Thanks for calling." With that, he hung up.

I stared for a moment at the phone. That was abrupt. Still, while he might not be the friendliest guy in the world, I didn't get the sense there was anything corrupt about him. He was just a business owner dealing with the same stresses and hardships as everyone else. With nothing more to go on than a vague feeling of annoyance, I had no real reason to add him to my list of suspects. Besides, I was convinced the murderer was Kayla's Uncle Simon.

Chapter Seventeen

I gave Kayla a quick call and filled her in on my conversation with the roofer. I told her everything he'd said, and that he'd promised to be at the house early next week to make the repairs. I suggested she have James call and arrange to be there when the work was being done.

She laughed. "I guess this means I'll have to take down the negative review I just posted."

"Yeah," I said, "this may not be the best time to get him upset with you."

On Saturday morning the gymnasium at the grade school was abuzz with activity as preparations got underway for the holiday craft fair. The floor had been configured like a capital E, with each vendor allotted a six-by-six-foot space either along the wall or down the center. Connie and I arrived at seven to unlock the doors, and people soon began arriving to set up their tables and arrange their displays. The sale would officially start at nine o'clock.

Connie and I staked out two spaces along the wall to the left of the door. I draped my hand-braided oval rugs over a wooden clothes rack I'd purchased at the thrift store. I thought spreading them out this way drew the eye and exhibited the colors better than laying the rugs flat on a table. To my left, Connie erected two card tables side by side and covered them with a Christmas themed cloth. On them she put the eight Yule logs she had decorated with holly, pine cones, and ribbon, as well as a plate filled with individually wrapped iced gingerbread cookies.

Looking around, I saw my neighbor Nancy Chumley setting out an array of candles, and near her Bill Prescott was arranging two tables full of wooden toys, jewelry boxes, and birdhouses. He saw me and gave a wave, his mouth spread in his usual hearty grin. Other neighbors around the room were laying out wide assortments of beautiful homemade crafts, like knitted scarves, aprons and oven mitts, beaded jewelry, dream catchers, and wind chimes.

Across from me in the center of the room, Nick Donato was preparing a table for his two young daughters, Gina and Carly. They were planning to sell Christmas ornaments they had made out of baked clay painted with bright acrylics and strung with green and red ribbons. I had seen a sample a few weeks ago when they had brought some to share at a neighborhood meeting we'd had when the fair was just in the planning stages. That had also been when Nick and Maureen Moreland had met and begun their romance.

I hurried over to say hello and give the girls some words of encouragement. They were busy dangling the colorful ornaments on a gnarled, widespread tree branch attached to a solid base.

"Hi, girls," I said. "What a clever way to hang your ornaments. Did your dad make it?"

They both looked up with eager smiles and nodded, their cheeks rosy with excitement.

"It looks beautiful with all your pretty decorations on it," I said. "I think you're going to sell lots of these."

A voice behind me called my name and I turned to greet Maureen who had just come in, her arms laden with quilts and throws she had made. I hurried to help her with one of the larger bundles.

"It's wonderful to see you," I said. "I just know this whole craft fair is going to be a huge success."

"Thanks to you," she said. "I don't know how to thank you for all the work you've done."

Beside her, Gage was busy unfolding the legs of a portable work table. Nick jumped to help him and in no time Maureen was arranging her hand stitched creations on the smooth white surface.

"Hi, Gage," I said, smiling awkwardly. I was prepared to let bygones be bygones. We had been friends for far too long to let one stupid argument wreck our relationship. He'd been kidding around, and I'd been tired and stressed. Not a great combination. In truth, I'd missed him.

He gave me a look. "So, does this mean I'm out of the doghouse?"

I pretended to consider, tapping my fingertips lightly against my chin. "I guess I'm willing to give you another chance"—my smile was teasing—"donkey face." I fell back on the childhood nickname I'd tagged him with over twenty-five years ago. It was a long-standing joke between us, and a tacit term of affection.

He snorted, then broke into a grin. "How magnanimous of you."

"How long are you planning to hang around?" I asked. "I can't leave, but I brought a sack lunch I'd be happy to share if you're still here at noon."

"Tempting," he said. "I'll think about it, but right now I've got to run out to the car and get something for Maureen. We brought one of those collapsible wooden clothes racks like yours to hang the quilts on. I'll be right back."

I watched him go, then began to make my way around the room, greeting the vendors and asking if they needed anything. As one of the organizers, I wanted to be sure everyone was happy and properly taken care of. Many of the sellers were neighbors I knew, but several I had never met. I answered questions, gave directions to the bathrooms, and secured extension cords for a couple of tables with lighted displays.

At nine o'clock, shoppers started to arrive. Nancy Chumley had made a large, brightly-painted sandwich board sign which she had set on the sidewalk in front of the school. Numerous other signs had been placed strategically around town with directions to the sale.

I hurried back to my position beside Connie's table, pleased as the crowd of curious customers grew, moving from table to table browsing the homemade crafts. It was fun watching my neighbors' successes as they made sales, but before long I was caught up in the excitement of showing off my own creations. The compliments I received were gratifying and I knew my grandmother would be proud.

An hour passed, then two, and I noticed that Gage was still here helping his sister. I smiled. He really seemed to be getting into it. I watched as he helped Maureen unfold one of the larger quilts so they could hold it up between them and allow an admirer to get a better look. It was beautiful, a kaleidoscope of colors, and I wasn't a bit surprised when the customer nodded and dug into her purse. I gave Gage a thumbs up as he refolded the quilt and slid it into a large shopping bag.

It was no surprise that Connie's gingerbread cookies were a huge success. Her Yule logs also garnered lots of interest, and so far, she had sold two. I had a lot of lookers at my rag rugs as well, and was thrilled when I made my first sale.

"Hello, Brenna," said a quiet voice. Surprised, I turned to find Norma Hansen with a small group of similarly aged women, all smiling and looking around.

"Norma," I exclaimed. "What are you doing here?"

"The senior center brought us on the bus. They thought this would make a nice outing. I didn't know you were going to be here, but I'm glad I ran into you. I have something to tell you."

I gave her a crooked smile. "Not more raccoons, I hope."

She laughed, a soft titter. "No, everything's quiet. But I wanted you to be the first to know— I'm moving to Denver right after the holidays. My nephew thinks I should be closer to family."

I gave her a concerned look. "Is that what you want?" I'd become quite fond of the elderly woman and didn't want her to feel pressured into anything, even by well-meaning family members.

She nodded. "Yes, he says he's found a lovely seniors' apartment near their house where they'll do all my cooking and cleaning for me. He's sent me pictures and it looks like a lovely place with lots of trees and flowers. This way, I'll be able to see him and his children more than just once every few years." She smiled wistfully. "Carl and I never had any children, so since my brother died my nephew is the only family I have left—and you know I'm not getting any younger."

I took her hands. "Well, if you're happy, I'm happy. But you'll have to be sure and write to me."

She leaned forward confidentially and whispered. "Have you discovered anything new"— she looked around to see who might be listening— "about that other thing?"

"No," I said, "but I'm working on it."

"Come on," said one of the other ladies. "I want to go look at those wooden birdhouses. Aren't they pretty? I want to get one for my granddaughter for Christmas." The little cluster of women in their colorful hats and shawls, chattering and milling about excitedly, reminded me in an amusing way of a flock of chickens.

Norma gave me a little wave good-bye and the whole group moved as one toward Bill Prescott's table. I felt a small pang as I watched her go. Her lively spirit had been an unexpected pleasure.

As the morning progressed, Connie and I chatted to pass the time. We were oblivious to the goings-on around us until I was suddenly startled by a voice close to my ear. "Hello, gorgeous."

I grinned and whirled around. "Gage..."

"Gage?" Troy said, a puzzled look on his face.

Oops. I grimaced. "Sorry. I thought you were someone else."

He tilted an eyebrow. "Obviously."

Connie chose that moment to stick her nose in. "Hi, Troy. Nice to see you. Didn't know you were coming to the craft sale."

"I was in the neighborhood, thought I'd check in and see what you ladies were doing for lunch."

This was the first time I'd seen Troy in jeans and a sweatshirt. I had to admit he pulled off the rugged casual look with finesse.

"We brought sack lunches," I said. "We can't really leave in the middle of the sale."

My eyes darted across the crowded space to Maureen's table. Gage was openly watching us. My guts twisted. I had been naïve, thinking I could date both men and keep them simply as friends.

Connie jumped in again. "Hey, I can watch your stuff if you want to go to lunch." She laughed. "It's only two rugs. I think I can handle it."

She had always favored Troy.

I took a breath and let it out again. "No, I'm going to stay here and eat my sandwich. I've already asked Gage to join us." I met Troy's eye. "You're welcome to pull up a chair too, if you'd like."

A crease furrowed Troy's perfectly tanned brow as he frowned. "Who is this Gage person, anyway?"

"He's a friend," I said. "I've known him most of my life."

"His family lived next door to our grandmother," Connie interjected, "where we live now. His sister Maureen still lives there. They're just friends."

"Talking about me?" Gage had approached unnoticed. He was slightly shorter than Troy, but broader across the chest and shoulders. His dark hair and square jaw lent him an imposing look.

"Gage," I said quickly, "I'd like you to meet Troy Cavendish. I told you about him. We met when I worked at the flower shop with Connie. He helped me get the job at his father's law office."

Gage turned to face Troy, sizing him up.

"Troy," I continued, "this is Gage Moreland. We've known each other since we were kids."

"Nice to meet you," Troy said. "You here selling something?"

"No, I'm here helping my sister."

Troy smiled and put a possessive arm around my shoulders. "I just came by to take my favorite rug maker out to lunch."

I pulled away, annoyed. "I told you—"

"That's okay," Gage said abruptly. "I just came over to tell you I'm off to pick up something for Maureen, then I'm outta here. I'll see you later."

"Gage..." I felt bad. I didn't want him leaving like this.

He pivoted to go, then suddenly turned around again and looked at me with mischief in his eyes. He tipped his head toward Troy. "Does he know about the phone?"

"What phone?" asked Connie and Troy simultaneously.

As Gage disappeared out the door, I thought, *That's it, first chance I get, I'm going to kill him.*

I unclenched my teeth and put on an innocent face, turning first to Connie. "You know—you saw it. It's that old rotary dial desk phone." I looked at Troy. "Kayla gave it to me. It used to be her father's."

He nodded. "Go on."

I laughed. "It's quirky, that's all. It's not hooked up, but sometimes it rings. If it was electric, I'd say it had a short." I shrugged and threw my palms upward, indicating bemusement and hoping to put an end to his questions.

Connie interrupted. "If you guys are going to go out and eat, you should probably get going. I predict it'll get even busier in here after lunch."

Troy arched his eyebrows, inviting me with a look.

I gave in. Turning to Connie, I said, "Keep an eye out for Kayla. She said she'd come by with her aunt and I don't want to miss them."

"We won't be long," Troy said.

———

I suggested a small family restaurant half a mile from the school. Judging by Troy's expression, it was not the sort of highbrow establishment he would have chosen, but seeing my face, he quickly backpedaled and graciously agreed.

In truth, I liked the simple fare—traditional comfort food—and the understated décor. It was the sort of place my grandmother had often taken me for lunch as a child. We slipped into one of the vinyl cushioned booths and were promptly waited on by a smiling, middle-aged waitress. I ordered a salad and Troy got a hamburger with the works. The food arrived promptly and we talked while we ate.

"So, tell me about Gage," Troy said. "Should I be jealous?"

"I already told you. He's an old friend. We've known each other a long time, and dated once or twice, but nothing serious, okay? I told you I'm not ready to make any commitments."

I made an impatient gesture. I did not want to talk about Gage, nor was I interested in becoming embroiled in any juvenile jealousies. I would date who I wanted and not be pressured into any promises.

He must have gotten the message because he changed the subject. "What about this phone? That's what I heard in your car the other day, isn't it? There's got to be more to it than you're letting on. Your friend Gage wouldn't have mentioned it otherwise."

Chapter Eighteen

I was furious with Gage. He had wanted to get me flustered. He knew very well I couldn't talk about the old phone without sounding crazy. Troy was a lawyer, a pragmatist, a dealer in facts and evidence. I had a feeling there was no way he'd believe the telephone was inhabited by the spirit of Kayla's father. I would have to feel him out carefully and see how open-minded he was.

"He was just being cute." I said, brushing a crumb off the table. "He has this theory the phone might be haunted, possessed by a ghost."

"Of course it is." Troy roared with laughter. "Obviously, the guy's an idiot."

I felt unexpectedly affronted by the offhand criticism. Gage had his shortcomings, but he was not an idiot.

Troy grinned, then eyed me sideways. "You're not going to tell me you believe in ghosts, are you?"

"I don't know," I said, giving a shrug. "It *is* weird how the phone just rings by itself. You could sure build a case for its being haunted." *There's reasonable doubt, isn't there?*

He laughed again. "Other than the fact that there's no such thing as ghosts. Come on, Brenna, you're an intelligent woman."

I felt my cheeks flush. *Guess not.*

He shook his head in a manner that brooked no dispute. "There's *always* a logical explanation."

Maybe it was jostled. I knew this argument by heart.

"It probably just got bumped," he said, "rattling the chimes somehow, making it sound like it's ringing."

How many times have I heard this?

I grabbed my glass of ice water and took a long pull to keep from making a snide remark.

"Yeah," I said finally, "I figure it's something like that. I asked my father about it and he said those old phones contain a pair of mechanical brass bells that ring whenever they're jostled."

Of course, if Troy were being truthful he'd have to admit the phone had not been touched, let alone bumped when it had been sitting on the floor of my parked car. But I wasn't going to press it. I had my answer.

"Or someone's tampered with it," he continued, "maybe installed some sort of electronic switch inside as a joke."

I nodded and gave my shoulders a dismissive

bounce. "Maybe. But it doesn't matter. It's a spiffy antique and very retro. I just like the way it looks. I'm going to put it on my bookshelf at home. Now, I think we'd better get back. I don't want to miss Kayla."

His tone turned serious. "You still planning to ask about her uncle's whereabouts on the day of the drowning?"

I blew out a breath. "I'm going to try."

"I'll follow your lead," Troy said. "Maybe I can help turn the conversation."

The parking lot at the school was packed, indicating a large afternoon turnout as Connie had predicted. I couldn't help but be thrilled at the success of the sale.

Troy parked his car and we turned to head inside when he suddenly touched my arm and said, "Wait a minute—I almost forgot. I have Kayla's stamp collection. I got it back from the appraiser yesterday."

He opened the trunk of his sporty Nissan, grabbed a plastic bag and handed it to me. "You can give this back to Kayla. According to the appraiser, it's a nice amateur collection, but it has no real value."

Strike this as a motive, I thought, not really surprised. I'd seen all kinds of collections in my years working on estate settlements, but I'd only seen one or two that had any real value. Most people collected things for fun or nostalgia, but rarely had the means to procure truly rare, sought-after pieces. It did leave me wondering though why the neighbor Arthur Bailey wanted it so much. But it was Kayla's decision. Now that we had the appraiser's report back, and I was confident she wasn't giving away thousands of dollars' worth of rare stamps, she could do whatever she wanted with it.

We found Connie at her table brimming with excitement. She had sold two more of her Yule logs, most of the gingerbread cookies, and another of my rugs, leaving only one left—the one I had dubbed the autumn rug, done in blacks, oranges, and reds. If it didn't sell, I planned to keep it for myself. I thought it would look perfect on the front porch at Halloween surrounded by pumpkins and corn stalks.

I left Troy with Connie while I took a few minutes to circle the room and check in with some of the other vendors. Everyone seemed pleased with the success of the sale, and most said they'd be happy to do it again next year.

Bill Prescott was just finishing up a transaction as I approached. He greeted me with a buoyant smile. "Hey, Brenna, how's it going?"

"I was just going to ask you that," I said. A glance at his table told me he had sold quite a few of his handmade toys. "Looks like you're doing all right."

Maybe it was the red shirt and holiday tie with tiny blinking lights he'd chosen to wear, or perhaps the fuzzy red Santa hat on his head, but with his neat gray beard and beefy frame, he could easily have passed as some version of the jolly old elf.

He grinned. "People do love good ol' fashioned wooden toys at Christmas. I could have sold a hundred more of those little slide whistles. And the birdhouses are nearly gone."

Just then, Nancy Chumley came bustling over, her mouth going at full speed as usual. "Brenna, isn't it wonderful? We've had a marvelous turnout. Everyone's talking about how pleased they are. I heard that Marge Stillman has sold out of Christmas aprons, and Nick's girls hardly have any of those ornaments left. I heard them giggling a little while ago. They're so cute. I know Maureen's happy."

She paused just long enough to take a quick breath, then continued in a rush. "I, myself, have sold nearly all the candles I made. Next year I'll have to see if I can get Bill to make me some fancy candle holders." She looked up at him with a coquettish grin, her fleshy cheeks crimson with excitement. "Oh, and I'm thinking of expanding into mosaic stepping stones. Have you seen those? I saw a tutorial online where you make them with concrete and little colored marbles."

"That sounds awesome, Nancy," I said. "I can't wait to see them." Fearful of being drawn into a long discussion on the merit of stepping stones, I edged away and pointed back toward her table where a middle-aged couple had paused to look over the remaining candles. "I think you have some customers."

I gave Bill a quick "see you later." He responded with a wink and a two-finger salute. Then I moved off quickly and continued my circuit of the room.

As I was admiring an intricate beaded bracelet

at a nearby table, I heard a familiar voice and turned to find Kayla and her aunt behind me.

"Kayla," I exclaimed, "you made it." I gave my friend a hug.

"And you remember my Aunt Lilly?" Kayla said, drawing the older woman closer.

"Yes, of course." I turned to face her. "So glad you could come."

"Thank you," she said, then glanced at the adjacent table strewn with brightly colored jewelry. Her dowdy face crinkled in a cheery smile. "I may even find something to buy."

"Have you had a chance to look around?"

She's such a nice lady, I thought regretfully. *And here I am trying to expose her husband as a murderer.*

"Not yet," Kayla said. "We just got here. Where's your table?"

I pointed. "Troy's over there talking to Connie. Come and say hello."

I led the way, and soon Kayla was making introductions.

Aunt Lilly smiled at Troy. "I met you at the memorial for Kayla's father, didn't I?"

He nodded. "I hadn't seen him in awhile, but I always thought of him as a great guy. I was so sorry to hear about the accident."

I exchanged a quick glance with Troy. Was there a way to use this as an opening?

But Kayla interjected and the moment was lost. "Troy and I dated back in high school. He and Dad got to be good friends. They bonded over football."

"It was nice of you to come," Aunt Lilly said, her

expression sweet and genuine.

Kayla continued her introductions. "And this is Connie Kestler, Brenna's cousin. She owns the florist shop next to the bakery. She donated the flowers."

Aunt Lilly took Connie's hand in both of hers. "They were lovely," she gushed. "Thank you so much." She turned her attention to the festive Yule logs on the table. "Did you make these? My, you have such an artistic flair."

Broaching the subject of Ed Glassner's drowning was going to be harder than I thought.

Then Lilly herself gave me the opening I needed. She was studying the rug I had on display, admiring the difficult braidwork when she looked up and said, "This is beautiful. Everything here is just amazing. What a lot of work you've all put into this. I'm so glad I came." She laughed. "Kayla said she thought I would enjoy getting out of the house for a few hours, and she was right. Ever since Simon's surgery, he's just been a bear to live with."

She waved an embarrassed hand in the air. "I know I should be more sympathetic—he can't help himself. He's still recovering." She looked at Kayla. "That's why he was such a grouch at the memorial. I hope you can forgive him, Sweetheart. He wasn't himself."

"It's all right, Aunt Lilly," Kayla murmured. "I understand. The last few weeks have been hard for everyone."

"I'm so sorry," I said to Lilly. "When did he have surgery?"

"It's been almost three weeks to the day," she said. A tear moistened her cheek as she reached out to take her niece's hand. Their eyes met in mutual sympathy. "Worst day of our lives."

Kayla took over, speaking softly. "It was the same day as the accident. Dad left to go fishing at the same time Uncle Simon was having a serious appendicitis attack."

"He woke that morning in terrible pain," Lilly explained. "I had to call an ambulance. At the hospital they took him straight in for emergency surgery. It was two days before we heard about Ed's accident."

"Oh, how awful," Connie said, verbalizing for all of us.

Kayla pulled her aunt into an embrace. I looked at Troy. He had to be thinking the same thing I was: *that's about as airtight an alibi as you're ever going to get.* Uncle Simon may have had issues with Ed Glassner, but he didn't murder him.

Which left me back at square one. My lips tightened. I had to fight to keep the letdown from showing on my face.

Troy lifted his eyebrows ever so slightly, his expression quizzical: *Now what?*

As far as he knew, my whole murder theory was based on the dubious account of some homeless guy living in the woods by the lake. A guy who lived off handouts, refused to talk to police, and had in fact probably absconded by now. The clues I had gleaned—the blow to the head and the fact that Kayla's father had been a good swimmer—were circumstantial at best and easily explained.

I couldn't tell Troy about the séance or the voice in the haunted telephone. I couldn't explain that I seemed to have a natural propensity for connecting with restless spirits seeking help.

Instead, I forced a smile and said, "Troy, there's really no need for you to hang around here all afternoon. It was great to see you, and thank you so much for lunch, but I can't leave till the end of the sale, and then there will be a lot of cleanup to do. After that, I just want to go home and collapse in front of the TV."

He ran a hand through his hair and nodded. "Sure, I guess I should get going. I'll talk to you later. Good luck with your sale. Nice to see you again, Kayla." He gave me a peck on the cheek, then turned and strode toward the door, disappearing in the crowd. I watched him go with muddled feelings.

Kayla cleared her throat and looked at her aunt. "Why don't we go look at some of the other tables."

Lilly nodded and they started to move away.

That's when I remembered. "Kayla, wait. I have your dad's stamp collection. Troy picked it up at the appraiser's yesterday." I grabbed the bag from under my chair where I had stashed it. "The appraiser said it's a nice collection, but unfortunately has no value."

Kayla laughed. "Too bad. And here I thought we'd uncovered a hidden treasure. I was all ready to sell and retire to the Caribbean."

"Sorry." I gave her an apologetic smile.

"Oh, well," she said. "I guess I'll go ahead and give it to Mr. Bailey."

"Any idea why he wants it?"

She shrugged. "No, but I'll probably see him tomorrow. I'll ask him."

"You're going over to your dad's house again?"

"Yeah, I'm still going through Dad's stuff. The estate liquidators will be there too. They're trying to get things organized for a sale."

"I don't have anything going on tomorrow," I said. "Why don't I come over and help you?"

"Are you sure? It's kind of a dirty job. You wouldn't believe all the junk my dad kept."

I smiled to myself as I thought of Norma Hansen and the piles of paper she had stacked all over her house. Then it occurred to me that this might give me the opportunity I needed to search Ed Glassner's basement office. The ghost's pressing demand that I "find the letter" was always lurking in the back of my mind. I just hoped I would recognize this letter when I saw it. If only I had more to go on.

The rest of the day proceeded smoothly with an almost constant parade of buyers and curious looky-loos wandering among the tables admiring the various crafts. During occasional lulls, the sellers themselves would move among the tables and visit with each other, chatting and comparing notes.

Before leaving, Kayla and Aunt Lilly returned to our table to show off the things they'd bought, including several of the Christmas tree ornaments Nick's girls had made. I glanced in the little girls' direction and smiled as Carly and Gina giggled and danced around while their father packed up the display tree which appeared nearly empty. There was still an hour left till the official end of the sale, but I knew that eight- and ten-year-olds could only endure so much sitting still.

When my last rug eventually sold I took the opportunity to spend some time with Maureen.

"Brenna," she said, "this has been a simply wonderful day. I am so grateful you talked me into doing this. I've had so much fun showing off my quilts and talking to people. I never could have done this a year ago." Her cheeks had a healthy glow and her wavy hair glistened with auburn highlights. The difference between her looks now compared to three months ago was astonishing.

"So, how'd it go?" Gage's voice interrupted. "Ready to pack it in?"

"Where did you come from?" I asked, spinning to meet him.

"Maureen said to come and get her at five o'clock," he said. "It's five o'clock."

"The sale was great," Maureen said with feeling. "I sold two big quilts, plus two baby quilts and three lap throws. Better than I expected."

"And I sold all three of the braided rugs I made, which I never could have done without your help." I gave her a grateful smile then gazed around. "All in all, I think it went pretty well. Everyone seems happy."

Gage's eye roved the gym's interior. "Is Thor still lurking around somewhere?"

My mouth closed in an exasperated frown. "No, Troy left right after lunch."

I noticed people starting to put things away.

"I'd better shut the doors and go help Connie."

"Brenna, just one more thing," Gage said as I made to leave.

I looked at him expectantly.

"Don't forget our date next week.   I have something special planned."

"What?" My brows furrowed. "What date?"

"Your birthday, remember?"   He gave me a rakish smile. "You didn't think I'd forget, did you?"

I laughed and rolled my eyes. "No, but I did."

Chapter Nineteen

When I arrived at her father's split-level the next morning, Kayla greeted me at the door and ushered me eagerly inside. In the kitchen, two employees of the liquidation sales company were already hard at work removing dishes, glasses, and cookware from the cupboards. Each item was being carefully cleaned and arranged on the countertops or dining room table for perusal by potential buyers during the upcoming sale.

In the living room were boxes of carefully sorted books and magazines. The once cluttered bookshelves now held an array of carefully displayed knickknacks, vases, ashtrays, and picture frames. All the furniture, including the television, end tables, and several lamps had been polished and fixed with price tags. Under the window lay a pile of assorted throw pillows.

In one corner, a vinyl album was spinning on an old record player. I recognized the tune. It was a World War II love song that my grandmother had often sung to me, "Don't Sit Under The Apple Tree." It brought back an unexpected pleasant memory.

I barely had a chance to remove my coat before there came a rap at the front door.

"Want to bet that's Mr. Bailey?" Kayla said, giving a short laugh. She grabbed the stamp collection off the kitchen table and I followed her back down the stairs to the door.

Sure enough, Arthur Bailey stood on the porch wearing the same shabby corduroy coat, but this time he wasn't alone. His right hand rested on the shoulder of a dark-haired boy who appeared to be about nine years old, and bore a striking resemblance to the older man.

"Good morning, Ms. Donnelly," Mr. Bailey said. "I'd like you to meet my grandson, Tyler. He's here visiting for a few days."

Surprised, Kayla smiled and addressed the boy. "Hello, Tyler. Nice to meet you."

He didn't look up but kept his face averted, eyes moving left and right.

"He's not good at communicating," Mr. Bailey explained. "He has autism, but he's a great kid and he's smart." He gave the boy's shoulders a quick squeeze. "Aren't you buddy?"

A shy smile spread over the young face as he nodded, still keeping his gaze directed at the floor.

Suddenly, it made sense. Stepping forward, I

said, "This is why you want the stamp collection, isn't it? For Tyler?"

Arthur Bailey nodded and looked from me to Kayla. "The doctor said it would be good for him to have a hobby, something he could do to keep busy. He seems to like collecting stamps, the different colors and pictures, and I thought if you didn't need your dad's collection any more..."

"Absolutely," Kayla exclaimed. "Why didn't you say so earlier?" She held the album out to Tyler. "I'd love for you to have this. You can add your own stamps and make it into a really awesome collection."

The boy took the book and began eagerly flipping through the pages. "Polar bear," he said, pointing to a stamp. "Giraffe."

Kayla bent and looked at the page of stamps. "*Wow*—I had no idea there were so many animal stamps. "Look, there's a tiger."

"Thank you," Mr. Bailey said. "I really appreciate it, and I know Tyler'll get a big kick out of it. Your dad showed me the collection once and told me how much he enjoyed finding all the different stamps. I think he'd be happy knowing it's going to a good home." He smiled affectionately at his grandson who was deeply engrossed in studying all the diverse stamps.

Kayla smiled. "I think you're right—and I hope you and Tyler get lots of enjoyment out of it.

He looked at Tyler. "Hey, buddy, can you thank the nice lady for giving you her awesome stamp collection?"

Without making eye contact, the boy graciously said, "Thank you."

"You're welcome," Kayla said. "Now, I'd better get back to work. We're trying to get ready to have a sale, and I've still got tons of stuff to sort through."

"Sure thing," Mr. Bailey said. He took his grandson's hand and led him down the steps and back toward the house next door.

Kayla watched them go, then turned to me with tears brimming in her eyes. "Kind of makes you feel all warm and fuzzy, doesn't it?"

I smiled. "It does—and I'm sure you're right. Your dad would be happy."

We went back inside and I followed Kayla to the basement rec room.

"I've gone through most of the stuff in here," she said. "What a job. I found boxes of slides and old photos going clear back to my grandparents. I don't know what I'm going to do with them, but I can't throw them away."

"You might be able to get the slides converted to disk," I suggested. "My mom did that to some of my grandparents' old slides."

She nodded. "That's a good idea."

Glancing around the room, I could see that some order had been achieved since I'd last been here. Things had been sorted, cleaned, and labeled: holiday decorations, tools, boots and outdoor gear, canning jars, an old vacuum cleaner, and myriad odds and ends. The sorts of random things one collected living in the same house for over thirty years.

"Find anything interesting?" I asked. "Or valuable? How about a letter signed by a famous celebrity? Or a map to a secret treasure?"

The mysterious letter was uppermost in my mind. The ghost was insistent that I find it, that it was important, but how on earth was I supposed to do that?

Kayla laughed. "I wish."

"You never know," I said with a shrug. "You always hear about people finding lost antiques and collectibles stashed away in attics and basements. I recently read about some guy who found a letter signed by George Washington locked in a trunk at his grandmother's house."

This was a complete fabrication of course, but I was at a loss. Somehow I had to get her thinking about finding letters.

Her expression sobered. "Actually, I *am* sitting on a treasure of sorts, and I've decided to take advantage of it."

My eyebrows rose. "Really?" Had she found something after all?

She nodded. "My share of the nursery and garden shop. I've decided to sell."

The sound of voices came to us from upstairs, reminding us that there were other people busy in the house.

"Let's go into Dad's office where we can talk privately," Kayla said.

She led the way through to the adjoining room and shut the door. Even with the light on, the dark wood paneling made the room feel dreary and closed in. Shapeless curtains hung over windows beaded with condensation. The smell of dust and mildew permeated the air.

I was surprised to see the once fastidious desktop covered with boxes and heaps of papers. The filing cabinet drawers stood open and nearly empty, and a paper shredder in the corner looked stuffed to capacity.

"You've been busy," I said.

"I don't let anyone else work in here," Kayla said. "I'm trying to get all Dad's papers organized, sorting out what's personal and what belongs to the business."

I gave her a searching look. "You said you've decided to sell?"

She took a deep breath. "I know you said I should get an appraisal, but I've been so busy, and it's almost the holidays, and we have so many expenses at the bakery..." Her gaze dropped to the floor in a look of surrender.

I nodded. "I get it, Kayla. Believe me, I've been there too."

She looked up again and met my eye. "The thing is, Ward Thurmond has tripled his offer. He says he'll give me three hundred thousand dollars cash. *Three hundred thousand*, Brenna. That's twice what we make at the bakery in a year."

"Still," I persisted, "without an appraisal..."

She shook her head. "James and I have talked it over and we've made a decision. For that kind of money Ward can have it. I thought I'd be more sentimental about the place, but I can't afford to be. Don't you see? This will totally take care of Ruby's college fund, as well as cover any unforeseen expenses we may have at the bakery. Besides, he says the place is in dire need of some capital improvements. The roof needs replacing, some of the plumbing needs fixing, and the parking lot is full of potholes. As a partner, I'd be liable for half the expenses."

"But there's no hurry, is there? It can wait till after the holidays, after things settle down."

"Doesn't matter," she said. "It won't change anything. I've already told Ward I'd take it. He's going to go ahead and draw up the papers."

Her look was defiant and I knew there was no point trying to talk her out of it. And maybe I shouldn't. It was a lot of money.

I gave her a reassuring smile. "I'm happy for you. I know it'll be a huge relief to get out from under the responsibility of owning two businesses. And you're right. It *is* a lot of money." I looked around at the boxes and piles of paper. "So, moving on, what are we doing in here today? How can I help you?"

She blew out her cheeks and rubbed her hands vigorously together. "Okay, I've got a box full of papers here that just needs shredding. And those books over there need to go upstairs and be put with the rest for sale." She pointed to a short bookcase I hadn't noticed before tucked against the wall behind the desk. "They mostly deal with business and horticulture. The sellers have some kind of sorting system for different types of books. If you want to start carrying them upstairs, I'll empty the shredder."

"Sounds like a plan." I went behind the desk

and started pulling books off the shelf two at a
time, placing them in stacks on top of the desk. As
Kayla said, most of the books dealt with the
nursery business: Washington native plants, fruit
trees, grafting, pruning, methods of fertilizing. *Not
your classic reads,* I thought with a wry smile. Talk
about a yawnfest, but someone out there would
probably be happy to have them.

After a few minutes, my nose began to tickle
from the stirred up dust and I stopped to dig a
tissue out of my purse before I started sneezing.

Suddenly, we were interrupted by the sound of
the doorbell. From behind the closed door in the
depths of the basement, it sounded muffled and far
away.

We looked at each other. "Mr. Bailey again?"
Kayla asked, eyebrows raised. She began wiping
her hands off on her jeans.

"Maybe someone else coming to help with prep
for the sale," I ventured.

A moment later, there came a soft rapping on
the office door. "Ms. Donnelly? There's someone
here to see you."

Kayla opened the door and was met by one of
the women who had been working upstairs.

"Do you know who it is?" Kayla asked curiously.

The woman shook her head and shrugged. "A
man. He's waiting on the porch."

I followed Kayla upstairs to the entryway. She
opened the front door and was faced with a stocky
middle-aged man with a ruddy face and receding
curly hair. He wore a brown bomber jacket, jeans,
and work boots.

"Hi," Kayla said. "I'm Kayla Donnelly. Can I help you?"

He nodded. "You're Ed Glassner's daughter? I'm Tom Gleason. I wanted to come by and pay my respects. I knew your dad years ago and always thought of him as a friend. I was really sad to hear he had died."

"Um, thank you," Kayla said, taken by surprise.

I was standing next her, so she hastened to introduce me. "This is my friend, Brenna Wickham. I think you talked to her on the phone."

He turned to me with a cool expression. "From the attorney's office."

I nodded, feeling awkward.

"Look, about that," he went on rapidly, speaking to Kayla, "I wanted to apologize again for the delay in getting your roof repaired. I'll spare you the details, but lately I've had some internal company matters to deal with, employee problems, supply chain issues, a real headache. I explained all this to your dad before he died and he said he understood. But I'm ready to move forward now."

"That's fine," Kayla said, waving her hand in a careless gesture. "All I care about is getting the roof fixed as soon as possible before the heavy rains set in. I'll probably be selling the house in the spring."

He nodded. "I think you said there was a stain on the ceiling inside. Mind if I take a look?"

"Not at all," Kayla said. She opened the door wide and invited us to follow her up to the living room. The two women from the estate sale enterprise watched us curiously for a moment then retreated into the kitchen.

Gleason stood facing the fireplace, studying the brown stain that had spread from the edge of the brick outward in a circle the size of a dinner plate across the white ceiling. He scowled and made a scurrilous comment under his breath.

"They didn't get the flashing installed correctly at the base of the chimney," he muttered. "That's what I get for hiring my nitwit nephew and his numbskull friend. I was told they were experienced, but obviously their skill was exaggerated." He turned to Kayla. "I'll be taking care of the repairs myself."

"What about the stain?" Kayla asked.

Gleason rubbed his chin thoughtfully. "I'd just hit it with a bit of white spray paint. That'll cover it so you won't even see it. I can do that for you, too, if you want. Whoever you sell the house to will probably just scrape off the old popcorn ceiling anyway."

I knew he was right. That sprayed-on popcorn texture had been all the rage back in the 70s, but now it was the first thing to go in a modern renovation.

Kayla nodded. "Okay, sounds simple enough. I think I can manage that myself. Thank you, Mr. Gleason. Just let me know what day you plan to be out here so my husband or I can be here."

I assumed that was the end of it and expected him to go. Instead he hesitated and shuffled his feet awkwardly. Then he licked his lips and said to Kayla, "Um, your friend here told me you'd found your dad's old high school annual. I was wondering if you'd mind if I had a look at it. I don't know what happened to mine, probably got thrown away years ago."

Kayla looked at me and I shrugged. Maybe we'd learn something.

"Sure," she said. "Hold on while I run downstairs and get it."

Two minutes later, he was flipping through the pages, occasionally stopping to comment nostalgically about some person or event captured in the forty year old yearbook. He stopped on the page of senior pictures where he and Ed Glassner smiled in teenage perpetuity. Tilting the book slightly to get a better angle, he read aloud the scrawled words he had written: "Watch your back. I haven't forgotten last summer."

His face knotted as he concentrated, apparently trying to remember what the words signified.

"Sounds kind of threatening, doesn't it?" Kayla said finally. "I have to admit, after reading that I kind of wondered if maybe the problems with the roof had been intentional as a way of getting back at my dad for something."

"Oh, god, no." He shook his head emphatically. "I remember now. It was a *joke*. A bunch of us had gone up to this lake—somebody's uncle's cabin, I think. We were all horsing around, standing out on the end of the dock, when Ed came up behind me and pushed me off into the water with all my clothes on. I didn't think it was funny at the time—I wasn't much of a swimmer—but he thought it was hilarious. I didn't have anything else to change into so I spent the rest of the weekend in damp clothes. I kept telling him to watch out 'cause I was going to get even. It was sort of an in-joke between us. But I never meant anything by it."

"That's ironic," I said, looking at him askance, "considering Ed Glassner died by drowning."

Next to me, Kayla gave a muffled little sob.

"*What?*" The roofer said. "Oh, my god. I swear I didn't know."

"Apparently, his canoe tipped over while he was fishing on a small lake not far from here."   I decided to bait him to see if he would incriminate himself.   With Uncle Simon eliminated as a suspect, this man had moved by default to the top of my list. "Given what you wrote there..."

I let my voice trail off, saying no more, but implying that I had my suspicions. In my head I could hear Gage's voice telling me to be careful, and Troy's cautioning me to tread lightly.

"What?"   His tone was agitated.   "You're not saying you think I had something to do with it, are you?"

I shrugged.

"For god's sake," he roared, "it was forty years ago. It was a joke, we were friends. I would *never*..." With an indignant huff, he turned and marched back toward the front door, his heavy boots clomping on the stairs. Just before exiting, he paused and hollered back at us. "I'll call you before I come back to do the roof." A moment later, the door shut with a firm bang.

I hurried to the living room window to watch as he pulled away. His car was some kind of small gray sedan. I couldn't tell the make for sure at this distance; I'd never been much good at identifying cars anyway. But I thought it could easily have fit into Griff's description of the other man's car at the lake that day.

When I turned around, I found Kayla staring at me in confusion.

"What was that all about?" she asked. "You practically accused him..."

I put up a cautionary hand, glancing around for the other two women working in the house.

In a low voice, I said, "Let's go downstairs where we can talk." I had hoped somehow to avoid this, but I knew now it was time I told Kayla about my suspicions and what my sleuthing had uncovered. I would leave out the part about the ghost.

Once more in the privacy of the basement office, I turned to my friend and took a deep breath, bracing myself. "Kayla, I really hate to tell you this, but I think your father might have been murdered."

"What? *No!*" She stared at me in disbelief. "Because of what Mr. Gleason said? I don't believe it. They were kids. Like he said, it was just a stupid prank, not something you'd kill over. The police said it was an accident. The canoe tipped and Dad fell out and drowned."

My lips pressed together in a grim line. "I know this is hard to hear, but think about it. You're the one who said it didn't make sense. You told me he'd been going out to the lake for years. And you said he was an excellent swimmer. I kept asking myself if he was such a good swimmer, why didn't he just climb back into the canoe or swim to shore?"

Her eyes got big and her mouth worked, but no words came out.

I continued. "So I finally drove out to the lake myself to have a look around, and I met a guy who said he saw your dad that day with another man who went out with him in the canoe. But only the other man came back and he was perfectly dry. I think he made sure your dad couldn't get back into the canoe or swim to shore. I think he might have hit your dad over the head with the canoe paddle and knocked him out, and that's why he drowned. In fact, the witness said he saw this other man on the beach turn the canoe upside down manually and shove it back into the lake. That made it *look* like your dad had accidently tipped it over."

Kayla's eyes went wide. "Why didn't you tell me this before?" Her voice rose to a high pitch. "Who was this guy you talked to? How did he know my dad? Did he tell you who the other man was?"

"He was a homeless guy, a drifter, living in a camper in the woods by the lake. He said he knew your dad and a few of the other men who go out there to fish because they sometimes give him handouts. He didn't know who the man was with your father but he described him as stocky and older, probably around your dad's age. Apparently someone he knew."

"And you think it was Tom Gleason?" Kayla asked, sounding uncertain. "Dad's old friend from high school? Did this witness tell the police what he saw?"

I shook my head. "He refuses to talk to the police."

"Well, a fat lot of help that is." Kayla's shoulders slumped. "What are we supposed to do now? We don't know if any of this is true, and we certainly don't have any proof."

I pressed my palms together against my lips as I thought. "He did make one suggestion," I said. "He saw your dad taking lots of pictures with his phone and he thinks your dad probably got pictures of the guy who was with him. He said we should look at the pictures."

"But Dad's phone was lost in the lake."

I nodded. "I think the murderer made sure of that."

Kayla pressed her hands to her face. "Oh, my god."

I gave her a serious look. "I also think he's the one who stole your dad's laptop. He wanted to make sure you wouldn't find any incriminating photos."

"So there goes our only proof," Kayla said in dismay.

"Let's not give up just yet," I said. "I've been thinking. You said your dad kept pictures on his laptop—pictures he took with his cell phone, right?"

"Yeah," she said slowly, not following.

"Which has to mean that his phone and laptop were synced. Therefore, he must have had an online photo sharing account. Do you know which service he used?"

Kayla shook her head. "I'm afraid I'm not very techy."

"Did your dad have a computer at work?"

"In the office at the nursery," she said. "Do you think...?"

I nodded. "Did he ever access his pictures from his office computer?"

"Of course," she cried, getting excited. "Why didn't I think of that? He always loved showing his pictures to anyone who would look. I remember Ward complained once that Dad was boring everyone in the shop with his pictures of our vacation to the Oregon Coast a few years ago." Her voice caught. "He was so proud of the pictures he took. Vacations at the beach, James and me at the bakery, Ruby when she was a baby. He use to show them off to everyone."

This is just what I'd hoped. "Then there's a good chance he had a shortcut to the website on his desktop. If so, we should be able to get the pictures from there."

She clasped her hands together and gave a little bounce. "Yes, of course! Now that you mention it, I remember that he *did* have an icon on his desktop. He showed it to me once."

"Do you know the password?"

She frowned, scrunching her face as she concentrated. "I know he used the same password for everything. He told it to me once—but I can't think of it." She knocked her forehead with the heel of her hand. "It was something I should remember."

"Would he have written it down somewhere?"

She chewed her lip, thinking. "He told me it was on the wall in the office at the nursery. He

said it was right where he could see it every day so
he'd never forget it. We've got to go and search."

"Do you want to go tonight?" I asked. "I've got
all evening." *The sooner the better.*

She glanced at the time on her phone. "It's
getting late. Ruby's at a neighbor's. I should go
pick her up and get dinner started at home. How
about if I meet you at the coffee shop later, say
eight o'clock? That way the nursery will be closed
and everyone should have gone home."

"Perfect. Can you get into the nursery after
hours?"

She smiled and pulled open the top drawer of
the desk, producing a set of keys. Jangling them in
the air between us, she said, "I found Dad's keys
when I was cleaning the desk this morning."

She looked up and addressed the empty air.
"Thanks, Dad."

I gave her a questioning look. Was she talking
to her father? Was she more of a believer than I'd
given her credit for?

She gave a shy little laugh. "I like to think his
spirit is watching out for me. Like helping me find
the keys." She gazed around the room. "I know it
sounds crazy, but sometimes I can feel his
presence, like he's right here in the room with us."

Did I dare tell her about the voice in her father's
old telephone?

Chapter Twenty

The sign in the window of the coffee shop said closed when I arrived at eight o'clock. Kayla let me in and we went into the back room where she had set up a couple of chairs and a small café table laid out with coffee and chocolate croissants. It was very cozy there among the ovens and storage cabinets.

"You're going to make me fat," I said with a laugh as I reached for a pastry.

She shrugged and gave a skittish little giggle. "Chocolate always helps when I'm nervous."

I nodded. This had to be terribly hard for her. I almost regretted telling her that her father had been murdered. But I had felt certain she'd want to know and would want to get justice for him. The pictures he'd taken might be the only lead we had.

Those pictures were critical evidence, and I knew Kayla was probably the only person who could get them off her father's computer at the nursery.

And then there was the ghost. It definitely wanted something and was not going to leave me alone until I found it. The letter. If only I knew what it was. Apparently the ghost had steered Kayla to finding the keys to the nursery office. It made sense that her father would have kept important correspondence at his place of business. I should have looked there earlier, but how would I have explained what I was doing?

"By the way," Kayla said, interrupting my thoughts, "Ward called this evening. He's anxious to move forward with the sale. I think he wants to get it done before the end of the year."

I wasn't an accountant, but I supposed there might be tax benefits.

Kayla continued. "I told him my attorney advised me to wait and get an appraisal first."

"I thought you'd already made up your mind to go ahead without the appraisal."

She shrugged. "I don't know. I've just been thinking about it."

"What did he say?"

She rubbed absently at a spot on the table. "He sounded almost hurt, like I was saying I didn't trust him. He said he thought he was doing me a kindness by offering to buy me out. Like he's doing one last favor for Dad by helping provide for me and Ruby's future."

"Wow," I said. "He really laid it on thick."

She nodded. "He said he thought I'd prefer the

three hundred thousand cash to having to mess with all the hassle of dealing with the business." She let out a sigh. "And I have to tell you, he's not wrong."

I shrugged. "I still think, from a business point of view, an appraisal's a good idea, but I'm not going to tell you what to do. It's your decision."

"He said we should get together and talk about it. He wants me to bring my husband—like I'm just a hysterical female and James will be more reasonable."

"Typical," I said with a snort. "Did you tell him we were going up to the nursery tonight?"

She shook her head. "I didn't want to have to explain. There's no point getting him involved until we know something. He and Dad were best friends for over thirty years. I'm sure he'll be devastated when he finds out what happened. I told James where we were going, but only that we were hoping to retrieve Dad's pictures off his computer. Nothing else."

"Well, we should be going," I said. "I'll drive. There's something in my car I want to take."

———

The parking lot at the garden supply store was dark and empty. Street lamps and ambient light from adjacent businesses provided the only illumination. An icy winter mist cast a shroud over the streets and hung like a pall in the shadows.

Kayla instructed me to park at the end of the lot near the corner of the garden store. Off to our left loomed an enormous greenhouse. Through foggy glass panes I could just make out the shadows of small evergreens and rangy shrubs. Christmas trees, holly, and poinsettias at this time of year, I guessed.

We went around the back of the building and entered through a door marked employees only. A sickly yellow bulb above the door lit a dim circle over the threshold. In my arms I carried the grocery sack I'd kept hidden in my car for a week. When Kayla questioned me about it, I said I'd explain inside.

A bleak hallway led straight ahead to the retail space where the earthy smells of soil and vegetation combined with those of chemicals and fertilizer. At this hour it was deserted and swathed in shadows. Our footsteps echoed on the linoleum floor sending shivers up my back.

After a few steps, Kayla pushed through a door into a large private office and switched on a light. Gazing around, I got the overwhelming sense that this was a masculine space. The air was thick with the acrid stench of stale cigarettes. Outdoor pictures of lakes and mountain lodges with hunting and fishing scenes adorned the walls.

Two steel desks sitting ninety degrees to each other filled the center of the room. Each was equipped with a desktop computer and monitor. Filing cabinets and bookshelves took up more space, and a table against the back wall held a copy machine and printer. There was also a coffee maker, a waste basket, an umbrella stand, and a coat tree—all accoutrements of a busy workplace.

One desk sat under the window, facing the door. A wire basket sat precariously on the left-hand corner overflowing with a messy accumulation of papers. A tall glass vase filled with wilted yellow chrysanthemums occupied the other corner. There was also a stapler and a dirty ash tray, as well as a half-full cup of cold coffee next to a rumpled copy of a hunting magazine. A gray sweater hung haphazardly over the back of the chair behind the desk, and a pair of muddy boots lay discarded on the floor nearby.

Ward Thurmond's desk, I concluded, feeling slightly repulsed.

By contrast, the other desk had a distinctly deserted quality. It had been cleared of all personal items and now seemed to be used merely as a catch-all for miscellaneous mail and catalogs.

"They shared the office," Kayla said unnecessarily.

While she turned slowly, absorbing the atmosphere of this place that had meant so much to her father, I pulled the old rotary dial telephone out of the bag and set it atop her father's big metal desk.

Kayla looked at it curiously. "Why did you bring that?"

I gave her a sober look. "Because of something you said."

Her brows arched slightly, questioning.

Here goes nothing.

"You told me you sometimes feel your father's presence, like he's watching over you. Like when you found your dad's keys? Remember?"

She nodded.

"Well, I think you're right. I believe your father is still with us, watching us, helping us. I brought the telephone because it was something that belonged to him—something he used for many years." I shrugged. "Call it a vessel or a talisman. I thought it might help to bring his spirit closer."

Kayla ran a caressing finger over the smooth plastic surface of the telephone. She gave the dial a spin, smiling as it ratcheted back around to where it had started.

"I have memories of playing with this when I very small," she said. "Sometimes I would sit on Daddy's desk and pretend I was making important phone calls. He had an old manual typewriter too. Remember those? He'd put a piece of paper in it and it would keep me occupied for hours. You never see those anymore except in antique stores."

She looked up with a determined expression. "I'm glad you brought this. I think you're right. My dad's spirit is very close. I can feel it. And if you're right that Tom Gleason killed him out of spite to get even for some stupid prank, then I won't rest until we've got the proof we need to bring him down."

I looked at the computer on the desk that had once been Ed Glassner's. "If we can find your dad's password and access the pictures he took at the lake, then hopefully we'll be able to see who he was with that day. It won't exactly be proof of murder, but it'll sure give the police a solid place to start an investigation."

Kayla's eyes roved the wood paneling in the

office. "He told me it was on the wall."

We both began to search, starting on opposite sides of the room, scouring every inch of the wall. I looked at dozens of random notes pinned to a bulletin board, while Kayla examined pencil marks scratched onto the surface of the dark wood. We looked behind a calendar tacked to the wall, and then scrutinized a large poster illustrating native deciduous trees.

I also took the opportunity to snoop in Ed Glassner's desk, pulling open the drawers and rifling through the scanty contents, hoping to uncover the mysterious letter. Kayla seemed satisfied that I was simply looking for any scrap of paper that might have a password scribbled on it. Unfortunately, it appeared the desk had been emptied of everything important. Where was I supposed to look now?

After twenty minutes of fruitless searching, Kayla gave a huge sigh and dropped into her father's old chair, resting her elbows on the desk, chin in hands, gazing mournfully at the wall opposite.

"I don't get it," she groaned. "He said he'd never forget the password because he looked at it every day. I got the impression it was written somewhere obvious."

She slapped the desktop in frustration. "He told it to me once and I ought to remember. I thought just being here would jog my memory."

I sighed and pushed my hair back, glancing around. "Well, you're sitting at your dad's desk, in your dad's chair. Imagine you're him. Look up.

What do you see? Unless Ward rearranged the furniture...?"

She shook her head. "No, it's the same as always." Raising her head, she focused on the opposite wall. Suddenly, she gasped and sat bolt upright. "Oh, my god, *that's it!* I know what the password is!" She began to laugh. "I'm such an idiot."

I arched my brows. "Care to share?"

"The name of the lodge." She pointed to a framed picture on the wall opposite the desk. It was a black and white tintype of an idyllic mountain resort nestled among tall fir trees with jagged peaks in the background. Above the front entrance hung a carved wooden sign declaring the name of the place: Timber Haven.

"It's in Idaho," Kayla said. "We went there once when I was a kid. Dad bought that picture as a souvenir. He loved the place, always said he wanted to go back there. That's the password— TimberHaven—all one word, capital T, capital H."

"Sure hope Ward didn't wipe your dad's computer," I said, suddenly realizing a potential glitch in the plan. Unless he planned to hire another person to work in the office, he probably didn't need two computers.

"I doubt it," Kayla said. "For one thing, there's got to be business stuff on here he wouldn't want to lose, and for another, I don't think he'd even know how. Ward's not very computer savvy."

I stood behind Kayla as she reached to turn on the computer. A moment later, the screen on the monitor lit up, displaying a scenic background covered with myriads of small icons in various shapes and colors, shortcuts to numerous programs and accounts.

Looking over her shoulder at the dozens of icons covering the screen, I quipped, "Great. Now, which one goes to the pictures?"

If Kayla could identify an icon that corresponded to the online photo sharing website, and indeed she had the correct log-in password, then we should be moments from finally accessing the incriminating pictures taken by her father at the lake on the day of the "accident."

She leaned forward, studying the tiny symbols: circles, squares, birds, books, butterflies, folders, squiggles, boxes, and more. She made a couple of wrong guesses, and groaned in frustration.

"Would it be a camera?" I asked, imagining a miniature graphic of a 35mm camera.

"No, nothing so obvious. Dad liked to be creative. Wait, I think this is it."

She moved the cursor over the image of a small pine tree. "Ha!" she declared. "Timber Haven, get it?" She clicked on the icon and was rewarded with the correct website and a box inviting her to log in with a user name and password. Fortunately, her father had saved his user name so all that was required was the password.

Using TimberHaven, it took only seconds to gain access to the pictures on Ed Glassner's cloud account. Kayla murmured happily as a slideshow started, randomly shuffling photos taken by her father. For the moment, she was content to immerse herself in nostalgia as pictures of family vacations, birthday parties, baby Ruby, and scenic lake pictures alternated at five second intervals.

Suddenly, the mood was broken when, without warning, several reference books devoted to horticulture fell from the shelf behind the desk, hitting the floor with a resounding thud.

Startled, Kayla turned at the sound.

"Sorry," I said, cringing apologetically. "I must have bumped the bookcase."

I hastened to pick up the books, but no sooner had I placed them on the desk than the top book slid off and landed with a plop at my feet. For a moment, I just stared. *Had it fallen or had it been pushed?* I glanced around, not sure exactly what I expected to see.

Finally, I reached down and picked it up. A paperback titled "Easy Investment Tips for Beginners," it seemed anomalous considering the rest. That's when I realized there was something stuck between the pages. Apparently, Kayla's father had a quirky habit of stashing important papers inside books. I opened it and pulled out a folded sheet of stationery.

My heart quickened. Was this *it?* Was this the elusive letter? I took a deep breath. *Relax, it may be nothing.* Biting my lips, I unfolded the paper and began to read.

It was a business letter from a real estate broker in Seattle addressed to "Mr. Edward Glassner and Mr. Ward Thurmond, GreenGro Nursery and Garden Supply." They represented an apartment development company that had built numerous rental properties in the Pacific Northwest. They were interested in acquiring the land on which the nursery and garden supply store were located for the purpose of redevelopment.

When I got to the second paragraph I stopped and looked at Kayla. She was engrossed in looking at pictures on her father's computer.

"Kayla," I said, "take a look at this. It was stuffed inside one of your father's books."

She glanced up curiously and plucked the sheet of stationery from my fingers. As she read, her eyes widened.

"Oh, my god," she stammered as her hand flew to cover her mouth. "Did you read this?"

I nodded. "They're offering fifteen million dollars for the nursery property."

All the color had drained from Kayla's face. "Dad never said a word about this."

"He must have had his reasons," I said. "Maybe he didn't want to say anything till it was a done deal. Sometimes negotiations, environmental studies, and any number of restrictions can drag these things out for a long time."

"What if we'd never found the letter?" Kayla murmured.

My eyes traveled involuntarily to the old black rotary telephone sitting on the desk. *What indeed?*

Then Kayla clenched her lips in an angry frown, blood rising in her cheeks. "Ward offered me three hundred thousand to hand over my share. Can you believe it?" Her fists clenched and her face turned crimson with fury. "Three hundred thousand measly dollars. So he can keep the *millions* all for himself. And I told him I'd take it."

"Let's not get ahead of ourselves," I said. "You haven't signed anything, right? You still own half the property and Ward Thurmond can't sell it or do anything with it without your say-so. I think the first thing we should do is call this company and see if this is a real offer, and what, if anything, has been done about it."

"That's right," Kayla said, dollar signs gleaming in her eyes. "Let's call them right now."

"Hold on. It's Sunday night, remember? Tomorrow's soon enough. If you like, I can call them for you from my office."

She readily agreed and I stuffed the letter into my purse. But as I did, an insidious misgiving intruded on my thoughts. To some, fifteen million dollars might be considered more than enough motive for murder.

Suddenly, I felt uneasy being here. I glanced around the office. All was quiet. The parking lot outside the window was dark and deserted. The store had been closed for hours and the employees had all gone home. I took a deep breath and forced myself to relax.

Chapter Twenty-One

"It's getting late," I said to Kayla. "We should be going soon. Now that you know where the pictures are stored online you can look at them at home. For now, let's just see if we can find the pictures your dad took the day he died. With any luck, we'll get a clear image of that roofer, Tom Gleason. If you click at the top where it says 'date,' it will put them in the order they were taken. The last pictures should be on top."

As expected, the three most recent photos were taken at the lake, dated the day Ed Glassner died. One was an artfully composed picture of a Great Blue Heron balanced on a log poised to strike at something in the water. After that was a photo of the canoe sitting at the edge of the lake with a man standing nearby bundled in a heavy coat. His head was turned and he wore a thick woolen hat pulled low over his ears.

Just then, a light briefly flared at the window— headlights in the parking lot. Then a car door slammed.

"Someone's outside," Kayla whispered. She rose and hurried to the window to peer through the blinds. Lumbering footsteps could be heard approaching the back entrance, and a moment later the door to the office swung open.

"Ward," Kayla gasped, rigid with fear as though she'd been caught stealing.

"I was driving by and saw the lights on," Ward Thurmond said, eyeing us suspiciously. His rugged face bore an unnerving resemblance to an angry grizzly bear. "What are you ladies doing in here?"

Kayla roused, mustering her anger. "We found the letter from the developer. Why didn't you tell me about the offer to buy the property? You wanted to keep it all for yourself, didn't you? *Fifteen million?* And you thought you could sucker me into settling for a few meager thousand."

The color rose in Ward's face. Despite the chill in the air, the man's face glistened with sweat.

"I was doing you a favor," he growled. "Just think what you could have done with three hundred thousand dollars. And you wouldn't have had to deal with this place at all. It's a dump, the business is failing. But your father refused to sell. That stubborn old goat. He kept insisting we could turn it around, renovate, make it bigger and better." He waved a hand in a derisive gesture. "He was a fool."

"He was your friend," Kayla said.

While they argued, I continued to stand behind the desk facing the computer. I bent to get a better look, clicking on the last photo to enlarge it. As expected, the picture clearly showed Ed Glassner holding the phone out at arm's length, capturing an image of himself in the canoe with a man sitting behind him. The rippled surface of the lake provided a picturesque backdrop. The man behind Kayla's father scowled reluctantly at the camera, obviously not happy at having his picture taken.

Stifling a gasp, I leaned forward and clicked on "share," typing in the first email address that came to me. I was determined this evidence should not be lost. I looked over at Kayla still standing by the window glaring at Ward.

"Kayla," I interjected, "don't say any more. You're upset. We need to go. Your husband will be looking for you. You told him we'd only be here for a little while, remember?"

Suddenly, Ward narrowed his eyes at me. "What are you doing back there?" he demanded.

Heart pounding, I hit "send" just as the burly man strode around the desk shoving me roughly out of the way so he could get a better look at the picture displayed on the screen.

"That's not the roofer," Kayla cried, coming closer to stare. Her mouth dropped open and her fingers went to her lips as realization dawned. "That's *you*—in the canoe the day my father died."

Before I could warn her to keep quiet, Kayla turned on Ward with everything she had. "Oh, my god, it was *you!* You killed my father!" Her face was flushed blood-red, her voice a high-pitched shriek. "He was your best friend. Your partner for over thirty years." She gave a little sob. "How could you?"

Great. Now he's not only dangerous, he's on the defensive.

I took her by the arm and pulled her around to the other side of the desk out of reach. If this guy was a killer, we needed to get out of there.

"This doesn't prove anything," Ward grumbled.

"It proves you were there with him in the canoe the day he died," Kayla spat angrily.

"So what?" He snapped. "I went out in the canoe with him. Big deal. That doesn't mean I killed him."

"Did you know there was a witness who saw you there?" Kayla persisted.

"Kayla," I hissed, "that's enough, let's go." I glanced toward the door, gauging the number of steps it would take to reach it and yank it open.

Kayla refused to be shushed. "If you're so innocent," she shouted, "why didn't you tell the police you'd been there? Why hide it?"

Unexpectedly, Ward sidestepped to his own desk and yanked open the top drawer. He pulled out a small handgun and leveled it in our direction. "We started keeping this here after we were robbed a year ago," he said menacingly. "And yes, it is loaded."

Kayla began to tremble, her hands clenched at her sides as she suddenly realized the danger we were in.

"What happened to the canoe paddle?" I asked,

figuring at this point there was nothing to lose. Things couldn't get much worse. "Do you still have it or is it floating somewhere in the lake? Will it have blood on it, and your fingerprints?"

Ward narrowed his eyes. "It'll never be found."

Then he looked at each of us, taking our measure. The timbre of his voice shifted, becoming mocking and disdainful. "Now the question is what to do with you? I suppose offering you money to keep quiet is out of the question."

Kayla gave a little sob. Her face went ashen. I took note of the heavy glass vase sitting on the corner of the desk. If necessary, it might be wielded as a weapon.

With his free hand, Ward grabbed the bunch of wilted flowers from the vase and tossed them on the floor, leaving about three inches of murky water in the bottom of the container. He waved the gun at us. "I want you to drop your cell phones in here."

We both hesitated.

Inwardly, I groaned. *My whole life is on my phone.*

"Don't be stupid," he said, pointing the gun at Kayla's middle. "Do it now."

Of course, he's probably going to shoot us anyway.

Then without warning, an earsplitting metallic jangle rent the air. I had forgotten about the old rotary telephone sitting in the middle of Ed Glassner's desk where I had placed it.

Now it reverberated against the metal desktop with a jarring sound loud enough to make us all jump and reel back.

"What the hell," cried Ward, thrown off balance. He glared at the antique phone like it had materialized there out of empty space.

This was my chance. While his attention was diverted, I grabbed for the glass vase and threw it at his face as hard as I could.

"Run!" I yelled at Kayla.

I spun around and yanked open the office door, pushing my friend ahead of me.

I heard Ward Thurmond gasp and stumble back against the wall. Glass shattered and the pistol roared sending a bullet zinging over my head to lodge in the ceiling. Quickly, I followed Kayla into the hallway and we raced for the exit.

The outer door opened easily and we dashed outside into the cold, heavy darkness of the December night. I could hear Ward pounding after us, breathing hard. He was close and he still had a gun. Frantically, I groped for the car keys stashed in my coat pocket.

This is going to be close.

The car was parked just around the corner of the building. We were in an alleyway of sorts, submerged in dark shadows behind the garden store. A tall fence running along the edge of the property concealed it from nearby businesses. In front of the fence were stored stacks of wooden pallets and bags of compost and fertilizer, as well as pots, wheel barrows, and garden implements—all effectively blocking the scene from public view. Combining this with traffic noise from the nearby highway and Ward stood a good chance of killing us without drawing any attention.

As I ran, I hazarded a glance over my shoulder. The angry man emerged from the building into the halo of dim light from the bulb over the door. His lips parted in a wicked grin. He halted to level the gun.

This is it, I thought. Beside me, Kayla sobbed.

I waited for the shot, but it didn't come. Instead, I heard Ward make a guttural protest, invoking the name of his late partner. This was followed by a creak and a scrape as a towering heap of wooden pallets toppled over. Ward barely had a chance to cry out before he was knocked against the wall and buried under the heavy structures. The gun was knocked from his hand. It skittered across the pavement and came to rest against a terracotta planter sitting by the fence.

"Call 911," I yelled at Kayla as I ran to retrieve the gun.

My only experience with guns was the two times my dad had taken me to the firing range in Phoenix when I was fifteen. He had thought every kid should be taught gun safety, or at least how to hold one without freaking out.

Fortunately, I'd seen enough cop shows on TV to know better than to grab it with my bare hands and obliterate the incriminating fingerprints on the weapon. Instead, I pulled a tissue from my pocket and gingerly wrapped it around the barrel, picking it up with the same cautious consideration I would give a poisonous snake.

Keeping my fingers well away from the trigger, I turned to find Kayla standing frozen where I'd left her. She was staring at the space where the pallets had been stacked against the fence. Ten paces beyond, the dim yellow light over the back door threw eerie shadows into the darkness. At first, I saw nothing. Then gradually a shape emerged surrounded by a faint ethereal glow: a man, tall and thin, with dark hair and a pencil mustache. He smiled and tipped his head to each of us. Then blowing a modest kiss to Kayla, he slowly vanished and the night closed in once more.

"Daddy," she murmured.

The stack of pallets shifted slightly and a deep moan came from underneath. I didn't know how badly Ward Thurmond was hurt or whether he could extricate himself from the jumble of wood, but I wasn't going to stand around waiting to find out.

Kayla still appeared to be in shock, staring with wide eyes into the darkness, her mouth open. I pulled her with me around the corner of the building to the parking lot. I noted with interest that a compact silver-colored sedan was parked next to mine. We got into my car and locked the doors.

Laying the gun carefully on the dashboard, I pulled out my cell phone and dialed 911 for the police. I told the dispatcher where we were and explained that my friend and I had been threatened by a man with a gun, but we'd gotten away when we'd managed to knock a stack of pallets over on him.

I told her I thought he was injured but alive. She said the police were on their way, and advised us to stay well clear of the offender. She didn't have to tell me twice.

Within minutes, I heard sirens approach and got out of the car to flag them down. Soon the nursery parking lot was lit up with flashing red and blue lights. I hastened to the first police officer, blurting out that we had been held at gunpoint by the man who had murdered my friend's father.

I spent the next ten minutes explaining what had happened, showing him the gun, and the avalanche of pallets that had "by lucky accident" fallen over onto the man chasing us.

The officer asked us a few questions, then we were instructed to keep back as efforts were made to lift the pallets and free Ward Thurmond from beneath the pile. He struggled as his injuries were treated, ranting about seeing a ghost. The EMTs chalked this up to his fall. Apparently he had cracked his head against the masonry wall of the building sustaining a nasty contusion and possible concussion.

As we stood aside watching, Kayla turned to me finally and asked, "Did you see him?"

I didn't have to ask what she meant. I looked her full in the face and nodded. "He was protecting you."

"And the old phone," she said, "he made it ring, didn't he? So we could escape."

Again, I nodded.

She let out a heavy sigh and turned to face the darkness, deep in her own thoughts.

I knew there would be further police interviews

followed by an in-depth investigation, but for now I was just grateful to have the ordeal behind me. The murder had been solved and the ghost could rest in peace. I would never have to hear that old telephone ring again.

As if reading my thoughts, Kayla turned to me again and said, "Brenna? I've been thinking about my dad's old telephone. I'm glad you brought it. I don't know how to explain it, but I feel like his spirit was somehow connected to it, like he was able to be here with us through the phone."

If only you knew.

I smiled. "Yes, I think so too."

"I know I gave it to you," Kayla said, "but I think I'd like to have it back, if you don't mind. I think I'd like to keep it."

"Absolutely," I said. "You should definitely keep it. Once the police have finished their investigation, you can get it back and take it home."

And I'll be happy if I never see it again.

Headlights and the sound of tires on the pavement announced the arrival of another car. A door slammed and I was surprised to hear a familiar voice call my name. I turned to greet Gage with a warm smile, grateful for his presence.

"Brenna, are you all right?" He ran up and seized my hands. His brows were drawn tightly together in a worried frown.

"What are you doing here?" I asked.

"I got the picture you emailed. When I saw where it came from, I put two and two together and knew it had to be you. No one else would have sent that picture to my personal email. And since there was no caption and no explanation, I figured you'd sent it in a hurry. I was worried about you."

He glanced around at the flashing lights of the emergency vehicles. The police had Ward Thurmond in custody. He was being taken away by aid car.

Gage turned to me with a wry smile. "Looks like you were right."

I snorted and gave him a mocking look. "Of course I was right. I don't know why you insist on doubting me."

He grinned and put an arm around my shoulder, giving it a squeeze.

Kayla looked at us curiously.

Of course, I thought to myself, she doesn't know Gage. She probably thinks I'm with Troy. And why wouldn't she? But I know now it's Gage I want to be with.

It was Gage my subconscious had turned to when I'd sensed danger, the one I had emailed the picture to. I had known he'd understand the implications of the picture, and would know what to do with it.

I put an arm around his waist and returned the squeeze.

"Kayla," I said, "this is Gage Moreland." I turned my eyes up to his. "My very good friend."

He held me in his gaze and murmured, "Don't forget Saturday. I have your whole birthday planned."

Chapter Twenty-two

Reports of the incident traveled fast, making the local news by the next day. Tamara called, eager to hear every detail. She was especially intrigued by the intervention of the ghost. "Maybe you should get one of those Ouija boards," she exclaimed. "You could start your own ghost whispering business. Think of all the murders you could solve."

"Not funny," I said, scowling into the phone. "Solving murders is dangerous, remember? Even with a supernatural sidekick." My friend had a tendency to get carried away. I was going to have to shut this down immediately. "Don't forget, I'm a rational, levelheaded, no-nonsense legal assistant in an office full of lawyers."

"Yeah, yeah, yeah," she interrupted. "By *day*. But after work and on weekends... Ooh, I'll bet we could get special t-shirts made up."

I rolled my eyes. "Will you knock it off!"

She laughed aloud. "Have you talked to Norma? She would love to hear how you solved this ghost's murder."

"I know. I'm planning to go see her tomorrow on my lunch hour. By the way, I don't think I told you, she's moving to Denver after the holidays to be near her family."

"Oh no, I'll miss her," Tamara said. "She's an amazing woman. Eccentric, but in a good way."

"Absolutely," I said. "But I'm sure it's for the best. Her nephew cares about her. She's eighty-six years old and she deserves to be with people who love her."

"Of course," Tamara said. "By the way, happy birthday! Who are you celebrating with? Troy or Gage?"

"Gage."

"Good," she said, sounding satisfied. "I always knew he was the one."

———————

Connie was aghast that Kayla and I had been so near death. She knew nothing about any ghost, but she saw all the news reports about the murder of Ed Glassner at the hands of his business partner and the subsequent attempted murder of his daughter and "a friend" at the nursery. She insisted I fill her in on every detail, then wasted no time in gossiping the word around the neighborhood. I was soon inundated by questions and commiserations from all my acquaintances, including nearly every person who had participated in the holiday craft fair. Maureen Moreland, Nancy Chumley, and Bill Prescott all rushed over to see that I was all right. Nancy brought a tuna casserole because, in her words, that's what neighbors do for each other. It was nice of them, and I appreciated the concern, but it did get to be a little much after awhile.

Kayla called me Tuesday morning to report that she'd talked to Tom Gleason, the roofer. He'd been very sympathetic and they'd worked it all out. He would be at the house on Wednesday to make the repairs.

At noon, as promised, I went to visit Norma Hansen. The elderly woman was delighted as usual to see me. Eagerly, she led me to the kitchen where she had set out tea and finger sandwiches on the cozy table by the window.

"Tell me everything," she said in her soft, reedy voice. "Did you see the ghost?"

"I did—just for a moment, and so did Kayla. He saved our lives, then blew her a kiss. It was very touching."

She clasped her hands. "Oh, I'm so glad it all worked out."

I reached over and put my hand on her arm. "You know we couldn't have done it without your help."

She smiled, her eyes shining merrily in her crinkled face. "I was glad to help." Then abruptly she stood up. "Come with me. I have something for you."

Curiously, I followed her to her bedroom. Several large cardboard boxes on the floor indicated that she had begun packing for her upcoming move. She stepped around these and moved to the bed, motioning me closer. There on the green damask coverlet lay the strange wooden board with its painted rows of letters and numbers.

Rational, educated, levelheaded, I sternly reminded myself. *Not superstitious.*

"I'd like you to have this, Brenna," Norma said.

"No," I said, taking a step backward, "I couldn't."

"You don't have to use it, dear, if it makes you uncomfortable. Just let it be a keepsake, something to remember me by." She looked at me with her kind, grandmotherly eyes. "I don't have anyone else to give it to. My nephew's family isn't interested in this sort of thing, and I've fallen out of touch with my husband's relatives. I doubt they would want it anyway. But you have a special gift, an empathy for the spirit world. Even if you never use it, it will make me happy just knowing the Spirit Board is in your care."

I swallowed, took a deep breath, and smiled. "I'd be honored, Norma. Thank you." *It's going right into the back of my closet.*

———

Not surprisingly, Troy showed up at my office at the end of the day insisting I have dinner with him. I agreed on the condition we walk to the nearby Thai restaurant where we'd eaten before. I claimed

I was dying for another taste of their delicious crispy honeyed duck, which was true, but I also didn't want this turning into a late night date at some intimate candle-lit restaurant.

"Looks like your hunches were all correct," Troy said once we were seated. "I've talked to Kayla. She still seems to be in shock."

I nodded. "It's hard to believe her father was murdered by his own partner. She told me they'd been friends for over thirty years."

"It was the money," Troy said sagely. "It's amazing what people will do for a few million dollars."

"Yes," I said, "and this morning I called the real estate broker and confirmed that the offer to buy the property is still good. In the future, Kayla will be included in all negotiations."

"And now," Troy said, "with a civil suit and a good lawyer, she could wind up with the whole thing. Once the property is sold, Kayla and James will be set for life."

"I'm sure she'd happily trade it for her father's life."

"Maybe," he said with an arch smile. "It *is* a lot of money."

Surely he didn't mean that the way it sounded. Perhaps he was implying that he would make the perfect lawyer for the civil suit. A successful judgment in a wrongful death case against Ward Thurmond could easily result in the man having to relinquish his share of the business in favor of Kayla. I wondered dourly what percentage of the judgment the attorney would receive. A hefty chunk, no doubt.

Before I could say anything, he continued. "I'm a little worried about Kayla. I know she's suffered a terrible shock, but I'm afraid she's losing her sanity. Did you know she's claiming to have seen her father's ghost?"

I was jolted back to the conversation. "What?" I tried to look concerned.

"Yeah," he laughed. "She swears it was his ghost who saved the day by ringing the phone and knocking the pallets over on Thurmond so the two of you could get away. Have you ever heard anything so crazy?"

Well, actually...

"If she's not careful," he continued, "she's liable to wind up in a mental hospital. She's always been a little flighty."

"Oh, I don't think it's that bad," I said. "As you said, she's had a shock. I'm sure she didn't mean an *actual* ghost, but the metaphorical spirit of her father watching over her. Lots of people think that way, it's not unusual." I waved a hand as though brushing it off as immaterial.

"I suppose," he said, nodding thoughtfully. "And as for the phone ringing and the pallets falling, there has to be a logical explanation, right? Of course, a telephone ringing in the office after hours is no big mystery, and the pallets might have been stacked off balance to begin with. They fell when you bumped into them as you ran by."

I forced a laugh. "There you go—a logical explanation. Just give Kayla a little time to recover and she'll be fine."

The food came and I ate quickly, eager to be gone. Troy was sounding a bit self-righteous, and it was putting me off.

"By the way," Troy said in an oddly stilted voice, "Kayla told me that you and Gage got kind of cozy at the crime scene."

I glanced up and detected the green glint in his eyes. *Oh boy, here it is, the real reason he wanted to see me tonight. Well, let's get this over with.*

He continued. "She said you sent the incriminating picture of her father and Thurmond in the canoe to Gage. Were you hoping he'd come running to your rescue? I live closer to the nursery, you know. Why didn't you send the picture to me?"

"I don't know," I said. "I thought of him first." I picked distractedly at the rice on my plate.

He gave me a searching look. "I had sort of hoped we had something going. Now I'm not so sure."

I sighed and put down my fork. "After my husband died two years ago I didn't think I'd ever want to be with anyone else ever again. I thought loves like that only came around once in a lifetime. But then I moved in with my cousin and ran into Gage again after twenty-five years. We'd been friends as children. In fact, I had a crush on him when I was nine years old." I took a deep breath and let it out again, then continued. "When he came back into my life, I tried to push him away. I told him—and tried to convince myself I meant it— that I didn't want a new relationship. It's the same thing I told you. I just wanted to be friends. Just good friends. I wasn't looking for anything more."

"But now that's changed," Troy said matter-of-factly.

I nodded. "Yes."

He adjusted his glasses and folded his napkin, placing it next to his plate. "I understand, and it's okay. I'll survive." He smiled. "Gage seems like a nice guy. I wish you both the best of luck."

"Thank you," I said, relieved. "And Troy? I hope you and I can remain friends."

He gave a little chuckle, his eyes twinkling amicably behind his glasses. "Of course. You work for my father, so I imagine we'll still see a lot of each other."

I laughed and the evening ended on a good-natured note.

———————

Gage picked me up at four o'clock on Saturday. He wouldn't tell me where we were going, but he did warn me to dress warmly and expect to spend time outdoors. The weather was fair but cold, which was normal for this time of year. He got on the freeway and turned south toward Seattle, but after a few minutes, to my delight, we took the 50th Street exit and headed for the zoo.

"WildLights!" I exclaimed. "I've always wanted to go!"

Every year the Seattle zoo puts on a winter festival with brightly colored light displays: glistening dragons, sparkling giraffes, glowing pandas, and more.

We spent an hour holding hands, wandering

through the twinkling decorations. Finally, Gage steered us to a quiet picnic table in a grassy area away from the crowd. He pulled off the backpack he'd been carrying and withdrew a flowered table cloth followed by several small plastic food containers and two bottles of water.

"How does a picnic dinner sound?" he asked. "Chicken sandwiches, potato salad, chocolate chip cookies. Nothing but the best for my girl."

My face broke into a spontaneous grin. *My girl.* I liked the sound of that.

Lastly, he lit a candle in a glass jar and set it in the middle of the table. "Happy birthday, Brenna."

"Candlelight dinner," I murmured approvingly. "How romantic."

"And not a ghost in sight," he added with an impish smile.

"Amen to that."

He handed me a sandwich, then asked, "So, what happens now? Are the police investigating? Will you have to testify?"

I shook my head. "It's all over. I talked to the detective on the case yesterday. He said Ward Thurmond was pretty rattled and talking nonsense." I gave a short, wry laugh. "He confessed to everything. Seems he had an 'Ebenezer Scrooge' moment."

"Let me guess," Gage said. "He saw the ghost of partners past."

I snorted. "I imagine his lawyer will be looking at an insanity plea. But the detective told me that not only do they have the photo, they also found the canoe paddle in the back of Thurmond's garage.

They're testing it now, but I'd say its mere existence is pretty damning."

He shook his head and chuckled. "I guess you were right again."

I gave a modest shrug. "Of course."

"So, what happened to the haunted telephone? I'm assuming since you solved the case the ghost has moved on."

"Don't know," I said. "Don't *want* to know. I never want to see or hear that stupid phone again. Kayla took it back. She's all sentimental about it now."

Suddenly, the mood was shattered by a loud, obnoxious sound emanating from the depths of my coat pocket.

Gage stared. "What was *that?*"

"Like it?" I asked, pulling the cell phone from my pocket. Tamara, right on cue. "That's my new text alert. It's a donkey. I changed it in your honor, in light of our new...understanding. Now, whenever I get a text I'll think of you."

"A donkey," he said, a slow smile spreading over his face. He gave me a tender look. "That may be the most romantic thing anyone's ever done for me."

He blew out the candle and in the glittering light of a nearby giant emerald dragon, he took me in his arms and kissed me.

END

I hope you enjoyed reading book two in the
Brenna Wickham Haunted Mystery series.

If you liked Families and Felons please be sure to
take a minute and leave a review on Amazon

Thank you.

**Watch for the next book by Kathleen J. Easley,
A stand-alone paranormal story of love, mystery,
and suspense:**

UNDER THE APPLE TREE

<u>An excerpt:</u>

I swung the flashlight up, edging closer. The light seemed dimmer now. The batteries were going. In a pinch, it would do as a makeshift weapon. I thought of my brother asleep in the library on the other side of the house. Would he hear me if I screamed?

Heart convulsing, I aimed the failing beam at the piano where a shadowy figure bent over the keyboard. To my astonishment, the light revealed a wizened old woman, thin and frail. Her white hair fell in limp strands about her shoulders.

Softly she began to sing the lyrics to the music. I recognized it from a record my grandmother used to play. It was a lively old song, popular in the 1940s. But the old woman slowed it to a melancholy tempo, murmuring the words, changing what should have been an upbeat ditty into a heart wrenching ballad: *"Don't sit under the apple tree with anyone else but me..."*

As I watched transfixed, her voice faded. She stopped playing and slowly rose. A shaft of moonlight shone through the curtains just enough to illuminate a rectangular patch on the old carpet. The elderly woman drifted into the light, her pale features radiant in the faerie glow, her diaphanous gown floating just above the floor.

I couldn't move, couldn't speak. I just stood and stared at the ghostly apparition. Profoundly old, her withered skin hung loose and sallow on a frame of brittle bone. Her craggy face was etched with pain.

My breath did a sharp intake as she seemed to notice me for the first time. She stretched out her hand and took a tiny step toward me.

Before my eyes, she began to change. For a moment, her face appeared both old and young at the same time—firm, youthful skin superimposed over great age, like two transparencies laid upon one another. Then the wrinkled visage vanished completely to be replaced by that of a lovely young maid with long dark curls. Only the doleful expression in her eyes remained the same. A glistening tear trickled down her cheek.

A true denizen of the Pacific Northwest, Kathleen Easley loves deep blue water, tall green trees, and The Seattle Seahawks. She can often be found with her husband on their boat cruising the San Juan Islands of Washington State. She is the author of the *Brenna Wickham Haunted Mystery* series. Set in Seattle, these are contemporary murder mysteries with a paranormal twist and a hint of romantic suspense. Kathleen is a member of the Puget Sound Chapter of Sisters in Crime.

News about upcoming books can be found at www.kathleenjeasley.com

Made in United States
Troutdale, OR
11/05/2024

24460276R00188